Praise for *Never Fear*

"Frost wraps his narrative in an atmosphere so thick with foreboding that its disorienting events take on a surreal quality . . . eerie storytelling."
—*The New York Times Book Review*

"With enough plot lines for several crime novels, Scott Frost provides a page-turner in *Never Fear* . . . [Frost] keeps the audience in suspense . . . fast-paced plotting makes it hard to put the book down."
—*The Tampa Tribune*

"Scott Frost is a heck of a good storyteller . . . we will probably be hearing more about Alex Delillo . . . [She] has all the makings of a series character."
—The Associated Press

"Another pulse-pounding, complex thriller in the tradition of Peter Straub . . . Frost's combination of psychological depth, complex plotting, and an evocative, arid Los Angeles setting will have lovers of intellectual suspense counting the days until his next book."
—*Publishers Weekly* (starred review)

"*Never Fear* is to mystery novels about Los Angeles what *Chinatown* was to movies . . . Even when you know what happens at the end, you want to go back and start again."
—D. W. Buffa, author of *The Defense*

"Amazing . . . a great sequel to his knockout debut novel *Run the Risk* . . . It gets creepier as the tension mounts and the body count rises . . . Frost's expertise is brilliant; this is ideal for the compulsive page-turner who enjoys excellent writing and suspense." —*Lansing State Journal*

"Frost delivers a superlative scorcher with a cast of memorably eccentric characters (including a brilliant schizophrenic hell-bent on revenge) and a sinuous plot that crackles and pops. Fans of Robert Crais and Michael Connelly should check out this series." —*Booklist* (starred review)

"Frost makes good on the promise of *Run the Risk* as L.A. police detective Alex Delillo returns in a case as intricate as a diagrammed compound-complex sentence . . . Tight, tricky, and wickedly complicated, with sharp, swiftly drawn characters." —*Kirkus Reviews*

"Thrilling." —*The Birmingham Post*

"Vivid and riveting . . . Strong writing, an increasingly complex heroine, and an enthralling plot full of cops, both good and bad, highly recommend this for public and academic collections." —*Library Journal*

"A classic crime novel." —*Independent on Sunday* (London)

Praise for *Run the Risk*

"A riveting thriller, implacable in its intensity." —Catherine Coulter

"Alex Delillo is a single mother and L.A. homicide detective, and one of the best main characters you'll ever meet. This is an absolutely heart-stopping debut, the kind of book that owns you by the end of the first chapter. If this really is Scott Frost's first novel, then he's clearly a writer to watch." —Steve Hamilton, author of *Ice Run*

Titles by Scott Frost

RUN THE RISK
NEVER FEAR

never fear

SCOTT FROST

JOVE BOOKS, NEW YORK

THE BERKLEY PUBLISHING GROUP
Published by the Penguin Group
Penguin Group (USA) Inc.
375 Hudson Street, New York, New York 10014, USA
Penguin Group (Canada), 90 Eglinton Avenue East, Suite 700, Toronto, Ontario M4P 2Y3, Canada
(a division of Pearson Penguin Canada Inc.)
Penguin Books Ltd., 80 Strand, London WC2R 0RL, England
Penguin Group Ireland, 25 St. Stephen's Green, Dublin 2, Ireland (a division of Penguin Books Ltd.)
Penguin Group (Australia), 250 Camberwell Road, Camberwell, Victoria 3124, Australia
(a division of Pearson Australia Group Pty. Ltd.)
Penguin Books India Pvt. Ltd., 11 Community Centre, Panchsheel Park, New Delhi—110 017, India
Penguin Group (NZ), 67 Apollo Drive, Rosedale, North Shore 0632, New Zealand
(a division of Pearson New Zealand Ltd.)
Penguin Books (South Africa) (Pty.) Ltd., 24 Sturdee Avenue, Rosebank, Johannesburg 2196,
South Africa

Penguin Books Ltd., Registered Offices: 80 Strand, London WC2R 0RL, England

NEVER FEAR

A Jove Book / published by arrangement with the author

PRINTING HISTORY
G. P. Putnam's Sons hardcover edition / July 2006
Jove premium edition / June 2008

Copyright © 2006 by Scott Frost.
Cover design by Steven Ferlauto.
Text composition by ReadSmart® from Language Technologies, Inc.

ISBN: 978-0-515-14319-5

JOVE®
Jove Books are published by The Berkley Publishing Group,
a division of Penguin Group (USA) Inc.,
375 Hudson Street, New York, New York 10014.
JOVE is a registered trademark of Penguin Group (USA) Inc.
The "J" design is a trademark belonging to Penguin Group (USA) Inc.

PRINTED IN THE UNITED STATES OF AMERICA

10 9 8 7 6 5 4 3 2 1

For Valerie, Ginsy, and Warren

never fear

．　．　．

We all have secrets. In childhood they're innocent, tucked away in the imagination like a favorite toy hidden from a sibling under the bed. If you're lucky, that's the way they remain. I haven't met many lucky people.

My mother divorced my father when I was five. What I know of him comes mostly from reruns that appear late at night on Nickelodeon, replacing actual memories of my own. On an episode of *Gunsmoke* he was a hapless traveling salesman who was tarred and feathered by drunken cowboys for trying to sell them bicycles to replace their horses. On an episode of *Bonanza* he played an Indian who was shot to death for falling in love with a white woman. He was in one movie titled *War of the Colossal Beast*, a low-budget horror film about a giant Cyclops that terrorizes L.A. The beast stepped on Dad while attacking the Griffith Park Observatory. They're what I have instead of home movies.

He was in his late twenties when he got the roles. A journeyman actor whose Richard Widmark–like features and crisp, penetrating eyes even today seem to look right through me from the television screen. Shortly after the divorce he disappeared from our lives. Not one letter was ever sent. Not one phone call made. Not on birthdays, or Christmas, not ever. Two episodes of television, a Cyclops movie, and my presence are the only evidence of his existence.

I don't know what his secrets were. I don't remember the touch of his hand, or the smell of his aftershave.

I imagine for a brief moment he dreamed of becoming a star, but instead played a hapless salesman, an Indian, and a Cyclops victim. What I know for sure is what's left on the screen—a perfect smile, dark hair, and a voice that sounds just a little too high for his good looks. And I also know that without any proof to the contrary, I don't believe my father was one of the lucky people.

.　.　.

1

It was 6:30 A.M. when the dream woke me. I've had it for as long as I can remember. Or at least for as long as I can remember since I became a cop. There's a dead body in my bedroom closet going through all my clothes. I smell the ripening of decaying tissue. I hear the sliding of the hangers on the rail—the soft fall of fabric, as one outfit after another is dropped to the floor. A Maurice Sendak nightmare for the clothes-challenged homicide detective. If it were about anything more than that, I'd rather not know.

I pulled the sheet up around my chin and tried to settle back into the pillow. I knew from experience that there would be no more sleep, but with a little luck I could at least hold off thinking about what was ahead for another hour.

The heat of the day was already beginning to gather, slipping in through the open window. It has a sound all its own, or more accurately a quality of silence that is different from any other—and one that always seems to hold the potential for change.

The slap of a newspaper landing on the driveway interrupted the spell. A mourning dove's singsong and the soft rustling of wings outside my window marked the first rays of sunlight reaching over the San Gabriels. I took a long, deep breath and pulled the sheet over my head.

Five minutes passed, and another. I listened for a sound coming from my daughter's bedroom down the hall, as I have every morning since the killer Gabriel turned our house into his own private horror show. For weeks after we returned home Lacy greeted every dawn with a shriek of fear as the memory of what he did invaded her dreams. Months gradually turned shrieks to soft whimpers, the night sweat–soaked sheets gradually dried. A year later each day finally arrived with silence, if not promise.

I slipped out of bed and walked down the hallway to her open door. I've done it every day, even after the dreams had quieted. And now, three days after she left for college, I'm still doing it. Staring at her empty bed. "Small steps" is what the therapist called these routines. Each step taking you that much closer to the life we had before, as if normalcy were something that had just slipped through our fingers and could be retrieved like a misplaced set of car keys.

I hate therapists.

It was Lacy who ended the sessions with the shrink by saying to him, "You just don't have a fucking clue, because if you did, you would be embarrassed to listen to yourself. It's not your fault, you've just never had a bomb wired around your neck."

After she said it she looked at me and smiled. I knew right then that she was going to be all right. *You go girl. My girl.*

She's just across town at UCLA, but it may just as well be across the country for my ability to protect her. Not that being within arm's reach worked out so well before. She's registered under my maiden name of Manning. I had wanted her to use a completely fictitious name but she wouldn't have it. Gabriel had taken enough of her life and she wasn't going to let him take anything more. Using my maiden name was as far as she would go.

She'd had firearm training and self-defense, and both of us knew it would probably make no difference should Gabriel ever descend into our lives again. I lingered at the door for a moment, then the phone rang. The clock on Lacy's nightstand read 6:40. *Someone in Pasadena is dead.*

I sat down on Lacy's bed and picked up the phone. "Delillo."

"You were staring into Lacy's room, weren't you?" said my old partner Dave Traver. "You were standing at the door, staring into the room. That's why it took four rings for you to answer."

"No, I was sleeping."

"I bet you're sitting on her bed."

I started to stand, then sat back down. I thought I could hear Dave smile over the line.

"You can't help it, you're a mother."

"That would be Lieutenant Mother to you."

"You want to come over and look at the twins? You've never seen anything so perfect. I still can't figure out how I produced something so beautiful."

"You know the first night they go on a date you'll be hospitalized."

"They're never going on dates."

If Traver were as natural a detective as he was a parent, no crime would ever go unsolved.

"Where's the body?" I asked.

"An apartment near Caltech. ME believes it's natural causes."

"You want me to come and look?"

"No, I think he's right."

"So you called because . . ."

"Because you're alone for the first time in years, sitting in Lacy's room."

"I'm not alone, I have you."

The silence on the other end lasted a moment longer than is natural between us.

"What?" I asked.

"It's probably nothing, but you got a fax last night at the office—part of a fax, a cover sheet. It's on your desk."

"From?"

"That's the thing, it's the same last name that Lacy's registered under at school."

"Manning?"

"Yeah, first name John. It said one page to follow but it never came through."

"Where's it from?"

"Two-one-three area code."

"Downtown?"

"You know a John Manning?" Traver asked.

"No."

"You want me to look into it?"

"No, I will."

"You think it's something?"

He meant did I think it could be Gabriel.

"I don't know."

The truth was, even a year after our encounter I thought just about everything could be a result of Gabriel's work. I saw his face in passing cars on the freeway. I heard his voice in telemarketers trying to sell phone service.

I quickly hung up and called Lacy's cell as I had done a half dozen times when I thought she was at risk. On the third ring she answered.

"Did I wake you?"

"No, I was having a PTSD moment."

My heart jumped a beat.

"Are you—"

"I'm joking. I'm lying in bed listening to the radio. I have a class at nine. Are you being a cop, or is this an empty-nest thing?"

"I received a fax from someone using the name John Manning. It's probably nothing, but until I check it out I want you to be alert."

Lacy said nothing for a moment.

"How could Gabriel know I've changed my name?"

"He couldn't."

"Then why are you calling?"

"You know why. I'll figure this out; until then, you remember the drill?"

"Don't be alone, stay in public places."

Neither of us said a word for a beat. At some level words seemed useless when it came to what Gabriel had done to us.

"Like I said, it's probably nothing."

"Then who's John Manning?" Lacy said.

It was just before nine when I pulled into headquarters on Garfield. A Santa Ana wind was beginning to blow down out of the mountains—hot desert air, that can blow fifty miles an hour, rushing toward the Pacific. If the winds continued for twenty-four hours you could bet the car that crime would be up in Pasadena. If they blew for forty-eight hours, bet the house that a fire freak with a box of matches would start an inferno.

Detective Dylan Harrison was waiting for me at the entrance to the building with a cup of coffee. The crescent-shaped wound near the corner of his eye, from Gabriel's explosion in my kitchen, had healed into a thin raised line of pink skin. He held out the coffee and looked at me with those penetrating green eyes. Though as supervisor of Homicide I didn't have an official partner, if I decided to take a case, Harrison would be it. It was probably the only reason I hadn't made a fool of myself with him yet. Too many people are always looking for ways to see me fail. Falling in love with a subordinate would be like lighting a fuse to my own career. Being five years older than him didn't particularly help, either, at least in my own head, which of course is the most dangerous place.

"Traver call you?" Harrison asked.

I nodded as we headed into the building. "Have you tracked the number?"

"It came from a Western Union office in downtown L.A."

I stopped walking. "They would have video surveillance."

Harrison nodded. A wave of relief swept through me. There wasn't a single photograph of Gabriel in existence as far as we knew, and he wouldn't walk into an office where he knew a camera would be watching.

"It's not Gabriel," I said.

Harrison nodded. "I don't think Lacy's in any danger."

"So who's John Manning?"

Harrison looked at me for a moment, then looked away. "He's dead."

A gust of hot wind blew open the door to the lobby

and sent leaves and scraps of paper swirling across the floor.

"There's something else," I said.

Harrison nodded. "The coroner called. They'd like you to come and ID him."

"Why me? I don't know a John Manning."

"They said he's your brother."

2

The county coroner is housed in a nondescript white industrial building a few miles east of downtown L.A. Twelve million people, give or take, live in L.A. County, and a good percentage of them are eventually headed right here. I'd been to the coroner's dozens of times investigating murders, but never as a next of kin.

The choice of placing the building on a street named Mission Road never struck me as ironic until that morning. The Spanish peasants of the land-grant days would bring their dead to the missions to be blessed and then buried. The ceremonies performed here were slightly less spiritual. Outside of New York City, more bodies passed through this building than anywhere in the country. More than a few cops have referred to it as the death factory.

"You want me to come in?" Harrison asked.

I nodded and got out of the car.

"I was an only child," I said, looking at the

entrance. "I don't know who they have in there, but I want to know why he tried to send me something last night."

I showed my badge to the receptionist, who directed us to the suite of cubicles where the investigators did their work. The air smelled of a little too much cleanser, but other than that, nothing gave away what took place on the examining tables and in the toxicology labs at the far end of the building.

The coroner's investigator in charge of determining cause of death was waiting in the hallway when we stepped inside.

"Lieutenant, I'm Margaret Chow."

She was a small woman in her mid thirties with shoulder-length jet-black hair, dressed in black slacks and a white blouse. There was a wedding ring on her finger. She looked like she should be teaching sixth grade rather than sifting through the remains of L.A.'s dead.

"I'm sorry to—" she started to say.

"I don't have a brother, Ms. Chow."

She looked at me with a certain amount of doubt in her eyes. Denial of all sorts was something she dealt with on a daily basis. The fact that I was a cop didn't appear to register on her radar.

"I know these things are difficult."

"It's not difficult. I was an only child."

She nodded uneasily and glanced at Harrison as if to get a reading on my state of mind.

"I'm sorry, this is Detective Harrison. You talked on the phone."

"I don't know what to say, Lieutenant," Chow said. "The paperwork I found in his apartment left no doubt that you are his only known relative, at least in his mind."

"What was the cause of death?" I asked.

"Single gunshot to the head. Pending the autopsy, ballistics, and residue tests on his hands, it's being treated as a possible suicide. Detective Williams from the Northeast division is in charge of the investigation."

"I'd like to see the body."

"Should I move him into a viewing room?" she asked.

Assuming I wouldn't need privacy, I shook my head.

She nodded and started walking toward a door at the end of the hallway. The body vault was a large open refrigerated room with the deceased lying on gurneys. Most of the dead were wrapped in white sheets, a few of the more seriously decayed or damaged were wrapped in plastic. There appeared to be at least forty individuals awaiting the final disposition of their remains, and there were two more rooms just like this one. Even with refrigeration the air inside the vault was filled with the odor of death.

Chow walked down the center of the room checking the numbers taped to the sheets. When she found the one she was looking for she quickly double-checked it with the number on the toe tag. There is nothing private about dying. Bodies are probed until the last piece of information gives itself up. For the most part secrets aren't taken with someone at death. More often than not they're spread out for all to see.

"This is him," Chow said. "There's a wound on the right—"

"You can uncover him," I interrupted. If there was something I needed to find out from a body, I preferred to discover it myself.

Chow slipped on a pair of surgical gloves, then stepped to the other end of the gurney and unfolded the sheet that covered his head and shoulders. John Manning's skin had the look of old bone china that had faded and yellowed. I stepped forward and examined the small wound in his temple just in front of the ear— a little dark hole barely big enough for a pencil to fit in. A small amount of fatty tissue was evident in places around the wound. The skin surrounding it was discolored by the powder blast of a close contact wound. The black hair above it was matted with dark blood that hadn't completely dried yet.

"No exit wound?"

"No," Chow said. "The gun was a thirty-two. We haven't retrieved the slug, but I'm guessing it mushroomed enough to slow the trajectory down so it couldn't penetrate the other side of the skull."

I stared at the wound for another moment and then looked at his face for the first time. Death had relaxed the muscles. There wasn't a line anywhere on his face.

I tried to take a breath, but my lungs fought it. I knew him, but I had never seen him before.

It reminded me of the face that occasionally looked out from the television set at two in the morning. The Cyclops victim, the hapless salesman, and the Indian who kissed a white woman on *Bonanza*. My home movies. I was looking at a memory.

"Can you identify him?" Chow asked, though I didn't hear her.

As a cop I knew there was often nothing more unreliable than memory. What people remember is often more a reflection of desire than of fact. Was I seeing my father's face in his because that's what I wanted—a connection to a man who had vanished from my life when I was a child? I felt Harrison's hand on my back and I unconsciously leaned into it.

"What can you tell me about him?" I asked.

"He was thirty-one. Lived alone in Los Feliz in a one-bedroom apartment. He was a private investigator for a lawyer named Gavin. They were involved in a car accident yesterday afternoon that critically injured Gavin. Sometime shortly after midnight he took a pistol registered to Gavin from the office and later fired one shot."

"Where was he found?" I asked.

"Next to the river just south of Griffith Park. A park ranger found him by chance about three-thirty."

I tried to think like a cop, but working it like just any other investigation seemed a long way off.

"How did he get there?"

"Apparently he walked. He wasn't wearing shoes and his feet have a number of cuts in them."

I stepped to the other end of the gurney and lifted the sheet off his feet. Pieces of grit and sand were embedded in his skin. More than a dozen deep cuts, now filled with dried blood, marked his feet like lines on a map.

Harrison stepped next to me and quickly examined them.

"He must have run over broken glass," I said.

Harrison nodded. "Why would a person do that?"

I tried to imagine a reason for a person to continue to run in such condition.

"If he was suicidal, maybe he didn't feel it."

I let the other explanation go unsaid, but I could see in Harrison's eyes that he was thinking the same thing I was. There were two motivations that consistently rendered pain meaningless—love and fear.

"Do you know him?" Harrison asked.

I took a breath. "I've never seen him before, but it's not impossible that he could be my brother, or half brother."

"Would you like a moment alone?" Chow asked.

I shook my head. "Like I said, I've never met him before."

"What makes you think it's possible that he may be your brother?"

I stared at his face—the face of my father.

"Home movies," I said.

"But you know nothing about him?" Chow asked.

"I know for the first time in his life he tried to make contact with me last night."

Chow looked at me for a moment.

"How?" she asked.

"He sent a cover sheet of a fax to me, but the rest didn't follow."

"That doesn't sound inconsistent with someone contemplating suicide," she said. "Maybe it was a suicide note and he changed his mind."

"Maybe," I said. "Can you release his personal effects?"

"Everything but his clothes; we'll need them if this is determined not to be a suicide."

She started to say something, hesitated, then finished the thought.

"Will you be making arrangements for his remains?"

I nodded. "If he's my brother."

I looked at his face one more time, turned away as Chow slipped the sheet back over him.

Outside the coroner's office I called Lacy and left her a message saying everything was okay, that Gabriel wasn't back in our life. But that was all I told her. The contents of the manila envelope I held in my hands, and the secrets that stretched all the way back to my father, if indeed that's what it was, could wait. I looked beyond the concrete banks of the river at the towers of downtown.

"Where do you want to start?" Harrison asked.

"What was the name of that lawyer she said he worked for?"

"Gavin."

"Chow said he broke in there and stole the gun. We'll start there, work it forward. Chow didn't know about the fax, so I assume the detective in Northeast is unaware of it also."

"You okay?" Harrison asked.

The Santa Anas were gaining strength, blowing all the pollution toward the coast, where a brown layer of sky stretched across the horizon.

"Okay?" I shook my head. "If he is my brother, I would like to know who his mother was. How he knew about me. Did our father stick around for him, or run from it all like he did to me?"

I looked at Harrison. "I'd like to know if my father ever told him about me."

I looked at the envelope in my hands. "How are you at chasing windmills?"

"I've done my share," Harrison said.

I thought about his young wife, whose death was never solved, and regretted asking the question.

"Do you have a brother?" I asked.

"An older one."

"What's he like?"

Harrison smiled, or nearly smiled. "He's my brother . . . which I guess means he's a bit of a mystery to me."

I looked back toward the river. "How many miles

would you say it is from downtown upriver to Griffith Park?"

"Eight, maybe ten miles."

I looked north, where the river traveled past railroad yards and industrial complexes before running past the hills of Griffith Park.

"I want to know why John Manning walked or ran all that way without any shoes on, and then put a bullet in his head."

3

The lawyer Gavin had an office in the Ensor building at Seventh and Grand in downtown L.A. It was a stone building from the turn of the century that appeared to have resisted the gentrification that was making over the rest of the block.

We stepped off the elevator and found the office halfway down the hallway. A notice from LAPD forbidding entry was taped over the door. The dark wood of the door frame had been splintered around the lock.

"Why would he break into an office where he worked?" Harrison said. "Wouldn't he have a key?"

I opened the envelope containing Manning's effects and removed a key chain with half a dozen keys. A key with the number of the office stamped on it slipped into the lock and easily turned the dead bolt.

"He did," I said.

I looked around the corridor; at least half the nearby

offices were empty. The likelihood of anyone being around to hear the crack of the door was remote.

"Why do you break into an office you have a key for?" I said.

"To make it appear that someone else broke in," Harrison answered.

I pushed the door open and looked inside. It was a secretary's office, though from the dust on the desk it didn't appear to have seen much work lately. A pair of black hard-soled shoes sat on the desk. The door to Gavin's inner office had been broken just as the outer door had. I tested the same key and it opened the lock with a smooth, worn motion.

Gavin's office held the scent of decades of cigar smoke. I flipped on the light and we stepped inside. Papers were scattered across the floor, the desk drawers had been rifled. A computer hard drive lay smashed in a corner where it appeared to have been thrown. A heavy wooden chair lay on its side just beyond the swing plane of the door.

"What if John didn't break in?" I said.

Harrison studied the room for a moment. "Then I'd like to know if whoever did this was here before or after Manning, and I'd like to know what they were looking for."

I stepped over to the window and looked out. A fire escape dropped down to street level.

"What if they were here at the same time?" I said.

Harrison stepped over to the window and looked

down at the escape, then back out to the secretary's office.

"He removed his shoes so he wouldn't be heard on the marble floors."

"And it didn't work."

I played it out for a moment, imagining his movements as he frantically searched the room for whatever he was looking for.

"What would you do if you heard the crack of the outer door being forced?"

Harrison walked over to the wooden chair on its side by the door and righted it. "The top rail of the chair back is dented. It's possible he tried to brace the door."

I looked around the office. Pictures, most of them looking to be at least twenty years old, adorned the walls. Whatever brief fling Gavin had had with success appeared to have been long since past. There were half a dozen calendars from funeral homes and chiropractors tacked on the walls. From the papers spread across the floor it was clear Gavin was little more than an ambulance chaser. I looked at the door and tried to imagine John Manning hearing the sound of the door splintering, but it eluded me. What could possibly be in this room that could cost someone his life?

"The simplest solutions are always the best," I said. "John Manning, in a state of emotional distress, broke through two doors that he had a key to, then searched the office looking for the gun that he used to take his own life."

"So what was in the fax?" Harrison said.

The Western Union office where the fax originated was three blocks south of City Hall on Broadway between Second and Third. The corporate towers of downtown were a mile to the west. This was old downtown, the part of town that was as alien to most suburban residents of L.A. as the Lower East Side of New York was to residents of Scarsdale. A line of mostly middle-aged men who transited in and out of a residential hotel down the block snaked out the door onto the sidewalk. Harrison pulled the squad car to a stop across the street.

"Disability checks must have come in," Harrison said.

I looked at the men, most of whom had taken notice of the two cops parked across the street. A few who probably had outstanding warrants slipped out of line and quickly walked away.

"How far have we come from Gavin's office?"

Harrison checked the odometer.

"Almost two miles."

"So why would he pick this place? Why didn't he send the fax from the office or go home?"

"If he was suicidal, reason probably didn't have much to do with it."

"And if he wasn't suicidal?"

"Something couldn't wait."

"Or he ran out of time."

We walked across the street and into the office. The

smell of malt liquor and body odor from the line of men followed us inside. I stepped up to the bulletproof glass partition and showed my badge. The teller was Middle Eastern, probably Iranian. He had the imperious air of someone who held power over everyone who stepped up to his window.

"I'd like to see the manager."

He leaned in and looked at my badge, then at my face, and motioned with a nod of his head to a door to his right.

"Camera," Harrison said, motioning toward the ceiling behind the teller.

The heavy reinforced door buzzed and we stepped inside. The supervisor was in his early thirties, white, and looked like he never ate or slept. I introduced Harrison and myself.

"I'd like to see your surveillance tape from last night."

He looked at me for a moment as if the question surprised him.

"You guys have it already."

"What guys?"

"Cops. They took it last night."

"What cops—LAPD?"

"I don't know, that's what my night supervisor said when I got here this morning."

"What time did they take the tape?"

"All he said was the middle of the night."

"Did he tell you the name of the officer?"

"Nope."

"Uniform or plainclothes?"

He pulled a cigarette out of his desk drawer and flicked it into his mouth but didn't light it. "You know everything I know."

"Was he the only one working here last night?"

"You don't pay two people to stay up all night and do one person's work."

"Call him," I said.

"Now?"

"Now."

He reached behind him, pulled a clipboard off the wall, ran through the list of numbers until he found what he was looking for, and dialed the number.

"He's probably sleeping, or out eating breakfast."

It rang a dozen times, then he hung up.

"You want me to write down his number for you?"

I handed him one of my business cards. "And address."

He wrote the information down and handed it back.

"A fax was sent from here last night. Would you have a record of it?"

He shook his head and motioned to the fax machine on the counter.

"Just a cash register receipt, fifty cents a page for local calls, a dollar for long distance."

Harrison and I walked outside and stood on the sidewalk. I glanced at my watch. It was already nearly noon. Waves of heat were shimmering off the pavement. Neither of us made a move toward the squad, as if we both knew that by taking that next step a line would be crossed that there was no turning back from.

"A ranger found him around three-thirty," Harrison said. "It would have been at least another half hour before Homicide reached the scene; that's four o'clock."

The knot in my stomach began to tighten.

"Why would a cop confiscate a security tape before an investigation had even begun?" he added.

Neither of us needed to answer that one.

"So who took it? Another agency—ATF? FBI?"

"How would they have known about it?" I said.

"He was under surveillance."

"There's another possibility."

Harrison nodded. "It wasn't a cop at all."

We stepped onto the street and walked over to the squad. I started to open the door, but stopped and looked back at the yellow sign on the building across the street. PUBLIC FAX.

"He would have seen that sign last night; that's why he stopped here. He walked or ran nearly two miles in his socks, his feet were cut from glass, and he saw the sign and thought of me. Why? What could I do for him that no one else could? And it's not because I was the sister he never had, not at that time of night."

Harrison looked over at the sign for a moment, then turned to me. "You're a cop."

I nodded.

"Why would someone take a tape?" I said.

"They don't want their picture taken."

"And who doesn't want their picture taken?"

I felt myself crossing that line that there was no turning back from.

"Someone about to commit a crime," Harrison said.

4

A piece of crime-scene tape blowing in the Santa Anas hung from the chain-link gate that John Manning walked through before he died. The fence was off a side road that passed behind a small manufacturing plant. There were no streetlights, no houses. Across the river was a DWP power substation. The nearest traffic was a block to the south, where a bridge crossed the river. The sound of the 5 freeway on the other side of the manufacturing plant would have muffled the sound of a gunshot.

I pushed open the gate and stepped through. The wind carried the heavy odor of the bright green algae that bloomed in the river. Ten feet inside the fence I stopped where a dark stain discolored the soil on the trail leading to a bike path along the riverbank.

"Anything could happen here and no one would know it," Harrison said.

I looked at the stain for a moment and allowed myself to think briefly that it really was my brother or half brother who bled to death on this spot. I took a deep breath to try to slow things down, but filling my lungs with the stench of the river was not what I needed.

"You okay?" Harrison asked.

I nodded and walked back up the path and through the gate to get away from the smell. I took a breath, and another, and things began to settle. Harrison stepped up behind me but didn't say a word.

"I spent years wondering what secret life my father led. This wasn't what I expected," I said.

A tan Crown Victoria pulled onto the side street and parked behind our squad. Detective Williams of the Northeast division stepped out and walked toward us. He wore the crisp white shirt, pleated pants, and stylish tie that were the standard uniform of LAPD detectives. You always wanted to look good in case a murder got you a stand-up on the six o'clock news, or you met a producer at a crime scene who might option the screenplay you were writing on the weekends.

I had called him on our way here and he'd reluctantly agreed to meet us. Courtesy toward smaller agencies within the county was something LAPD doled out in very controlled bits and pieces. LAPD was the biggest dog on the block, and they liked reminding others of this as often as possible. If he believed that John Manning's death was a suicide, I knew from experience he wouldn't like the suggestion that the death was anything else.

"Lieutenant," he said, extending his hand.

I shook it and introduced Harrison.

"I understand he was your brother."

"It's possible he was my half brother, but I never met him. I'd appreciate any information you can share."

He glanced at Harrison.

"Is this a personal inquiry?" he said, as if firing a warning shot across our bow.

"Yes."

He motioned toward the gate. "You've looked at the scene."

I nodded.

"It appears he felt responsible for the car accident yesterday afternoon involving a lawyer named Gavin."

"Is there someone he expressed that to?" I said.

Williams looked at me suspiciously. "He shot himself. I think that's a pretty good indication that he didn't feel very good."

"Have you been able to talk to Gavin?" I asked.

"Gavin died around dawn."

Williams seemed pleased that I hadn't known that bit of information.

"What can you tell me about Manning's movements?" I asked.

"After leaving County USC he went to Gavin's, broke in, removed a thirty-two-caliber pistol belonging to Gavin, found his way here, and took his own life."

"You don't think it's odd that he didn't use the key he had to the office door?"

Williams looked off toward the horizon for a moment.

"I find the whole notion of putting a bullet in your own head odd, Lieutenant. If you've already made that decision, logic has long since stopped being a part of your thought process."

"Do you know where they were prior to the accident? What case they were working on?"

Williams glanced at his watch. "No."

"Last night he sent me a fax from a Western Union office downtown, but it never arrived. I'd like to know why."

That I knew something Williams didn't clearly annoyed him.

"Which office?" he asked.

"On Broadway between Second and Third."

"Sounds like whatever he was going to send you, he changed his mind."

"The supervisor at the Western Union office said that someone identifying themselves as a police officer confiscated the tape from their surveillance camera last night sometime after John sent the fax to me."

"It wasn't me," he said.

"That wasn't my suggestion. But I'd like to know what was on that tape."

"Did it occur to you, Lieutenant, that they may have been lying to you at the Western Union office?"

"Why?" I asked.

"Maybe they didn't want you to see something. Maybe they're skimming money from checks they were cashing. Maybe they're dealing. Maybe the supervisor forgot to turn the thing on and didn't want to get in trouble. You'd be amazed at what happens in the big city."

Harrison looked at me as if to say, *Be nice*.

"I'm not trying to step on your toes, Detective," I said.

Williams glanced at his watch again. "Good."

"Is there anything else you can tell me?"

"I'm sorry for your loss." He started to walk away.

"How the hell did you ever get into Homicide?" I said.

He turned and looked at me. "I didn't have to sleep with anyone, I'll tell you that."

"Do you have any idea who you're talking to?" Harrison said.

Williams looked at Harrison and smirked. "The boyfriend."

Harrison moved in one quick motion, taking Williams by the neck and dropping him onto the hood of his squad car.

"Apologize," Harrison said.

Williams smiled. "Fuck you."

I walked over, touched Harrison on the shoulder, and looked down at Williams. "Thanks for the information."

"Stay the hell out of my investigation," Williams said.

"From where I stand, Detective, I've seen no evidence of any investigation at all."

Harrison let Williams go.

"If he was your brother, he was a two-bit investigator working for an ambulance chaser," Williams said. "He put a gun to his head and pulled the trigger. There's nothing else to find. Don't waste your time, or mine." He opened the door to his squad and got in.

We walked back to our car without saying a word to each other until Williams began to pull away.

"Sorry. I shouldn't have done that," Harrison said.

I turned to watch Williams drive off.

"It's not the first time I've heard that," I said.

"It's the first time I've heard it," Harrison said.

I looked over to the gate John Manning walked through just before he died.

"Williams could be right," I said.

"I don't think so," Harrison said. "I'd know it if I was your boyfriend."

We looked at each other for a second longer than was permitted in professional relationships, then I walked back through the gate to the spot where the blood stained the soil.

"Maybe I'm chasing a ghost," I said.

"A ghost didn't send you that fax," Harrison said.

"I think I'll take a look at his apartment by myself. I'll drop you back in Pasadena."

"Sure," Harrison said. "I'll see if any other agencies had surveillance working on either Manning or the lawyer Gavin."

In the distance, the San Gabriels rose into the bleached sky above Pasadena. A gust of hot wind swept across the surface of the river, nearly knocking me off my feet. The air felt as if one misstruck match and all of Los Angeles would disappear in flames.

5

It was nearing dusk when I arrived at John Manning's apartment in Los Feliz. It was an old neighborhood with elegant Spanish houses bordering Hollywood and Griffith Park. Dried palm fronds as long as two-by-fours, blown down by the winds, littered the street. The building was a Moorish-looking structure from the thirties painted mustard yellow. I imagined the original builder must have thought the movie *Casablanca* was going to create a flood of tenants hoping Ingrid or Humphrey would drop by regularly for drinks.

I parked across the street but made no move to get out of the car. From the moment I learned that I might have had a brother I had wanted to make a phone call but resisted. I took out my cell and set it on my lap as I tried to imagine the conversation. None of the scenarios I came up with went particularly well.

I picked up the phone and punched in the number. "Hello."

"It's me, Mom."

I heard her take a breath as if steeling herself for the next few moments.

"I was thinking of calling you," she said.

It was the same way she began every conversation we had now, though I was always the one to actually make the call. A coyote wandering from the hills of Griffith Park trotted down the middle of the street right past my car.

"There's something I need to ask you," I said.

"Oh, I see, it's one of those calls."

"What calls—" I stopped myself before I let her pull me into an argument.

"I think you know—" she started to say.

"Is it possible that I had a half brother?" I said.

There was silence on the other end for a moment, then she cleared her throat.

"How can you ask me that?" she said.

"It's a simple question. Is it possible?"

"I suppose someone claimed they were your brother and told you that I knew about it," my mother said.

"He's dead," I said.

I heard her take a deep breath.

"It's a police matter?"

"Yes."

"Of course, God forbid you ever talk about living people," she said.

I let the comment pass without taking the bait. Another palm frond blew loose from a tree and hit the sidewalk next to the car with a loud slap.

"What was his name?" my mother asked.

"John."

I thought I heard her whisper the name to herself.

"Years ago a friend said she saw your father with a woman. . . . I pretended she was wrong."

"You did the right thing."

"What about . . . Did you see . . ." She let it go.

I wasn't certain until that moment that my mother was still in love with my father after all these years.

"I don't know anything about him," I said.

I managed to say good-bye without any more accusations flying between us, then walked over to the apartment building.

He was in apartment eight on the second floor. I let myself in and walked upstairs. The carpeting was a deep maroon. Wall sconces in the shape of Moorish arches lit the hallway. His was the first apartment at the top looking out over the street. The faint sound of opera drifted out from an apartment at the far end of the hall.

I slipped the key in, pushed open the door, and stepped inside. It took a moment for my eyes to adjust to the dim light. The living room was a good size, with an overstuffed couch and a couple of chairs. A dining area was to the left with the kitchen beyond that. A door to the right led to what I assumed was the bedroom. A small tiled fireplace dominated the far wall.

I took a deep breath and could smell the lingering scent of what had been his life. I stepped to the entrance to the kitchen and stopped. The scent of garlic and other spices I couldn't identify hung in the air.

John Manning had liked to cook. Well-seasoned pans hung on hooks on the wall. Fruit that would never be eaten sat in a bowl on the small kitchen table. Bananas, apples, and kiwis. My father had liked kiwis. They were always in the house until the day he left us, and then my mother never bought another.

I walked over to the mantel of the fireplace, where several framed photographs were displayed. There was a picture of Manning as a little boy in a Scout uniform, and a recent picture of him with a woman on the beach. I looked at the next photograph and felt my chest tighten. I had seen the picture before. An early head shot of my father when he was still living with my mother and me—the handsome young actor about to be stepped on by the Cyclops. The same picture sat on my parents' dresser in their bedroom until my mother removed it after he vanished.

I tried to take a breath but it was as if all the air in the room had settled to the floor. I rushed over to the window and pushed it open. The dry hot wind felt almost like water washing my face and I drew it in, breath after breath.

John Manning was my half brother; whatever doubt I had clung to was gone. He had been held and raised by the same father who had abandoned me. He lived twenty minutes from Pasadena, a secret hidden in plain sight. And on the day he died, nearly to the moment, he had tried to reach out to me.

I closed my eyes and saw his face on the gurney in the morgue, the muscles relaxed in death, the jawline slightly twisted from the impact of the bullet.

I walked back across the living room to the fireplace. The last picture on the mantel was of a pretty young woman with long blond hair. Her clothes, and the peace button on her turtleneck, dated it to the early seventies. She looked as if she could have been an actress. I assumed she was John's mother.

I started to reach for a light switch, but stopped when I saw the desk in the opposite corner of the room. All the drawers had been pulled out and the contents dumped onto the floor. A computer monitor sat on the desk, but the hard drive was missing. I took a step, then heard the creak of the door behind me.

"I have a gun. Don't move."

It was a woman's voice.

"I'm not moving," I said.

"Who are you?"

"I'm a police officer."

"I don't believe you. The police were already here," she said.

"I can prove it."

"I have a fucking gun," she said.

"I know you do. Let me show you my identification. It's on my belt; all I have to do is turn around."

"Turn slowly, and don't move your hands."

I slowly turned around. The woman was in her late twenties, early thirties with short black hair. I guessed she was the same woman in the photograph on the mantel. A small-caliber silver-plated revolver was pointed right at my face.

"Look at my badge," I said.

She glanced at it quickly but didn't lower the gun. Her hand, holding the weapon, began to tremble.

"Why are you back here?" she demanded.

"Would you please lower the gun?"

"Answer my question first."

"I'm John's half sister," I said, the words sounding as if a stranger had spoken them.

She looked at me for a moment, then lowered the pistol to her side.

"He once said he had a half sister."

"You're John's girlfriend?" I asked.

She nodded.

"What's your name?"

"Dana Courson," she answered.

"Why the gun, Dana?"

"Because I don't want to get killed, that's why."

She stepped forward out of the shadow of the doorway and I could see that she had been crying. She bent down and put the gun in a paper bag at her feet, then stood up and drew her arms around her chest.

"By who?" I asked.

"Whoever killed John."

"The investigating detective thinks it was suicide."

Courson shook her head.

"He didn't kill himself," she said angrily.

"How do you know?"

She started to say something, then her eyes appeared to mist over.

"Because we loved each other," she said.

"You were going to say something else."

She nodded.

"What?" I asked.

"He was afraid of guns. I tried to take him shooting; he wouldn't even touch mine. You can't tell me he would . . ." The words slipped away from her.

I stepped around the couch and sat down on the arm.

"How did you find out he died?" I asked.

"He called me last night from the hospital, said he'd been in an accident and that Gavin was hurt."

"You knew Gavin."

She looked at me in surprise.

"He's dead, too, isn't he?"

"Yes."

She took a deep breath and wiped away a tear from the corner of her eye.

"Did John say anything to you that was unusual?"

She looked at me for a moment and then nodded. "He said he had found something."

"He didn't say what it was?"

"No."

"Do you know what case they were working on?"

"Just the usual things, personal-injury stuff."

"How did he sound?"

"I thought he was just shaken by the accident, but that wasn't it."

"What was it?"

"He was scared. He told me not to come over here until I heard from him. But he never called so I came this morning. A woman from the coroner's office and a detective were here," Courson said.

"Detective Williams?" I asked.

She nodded.

"Did they take the computer and leave the desk like that?"

She shook her head. "Someone else did."

"Who?"

She took a breath. "He was here a couple of hours ago. I came back to get some of my things and he came walking out of the apartment with the computer. He looked at me and asked my name. I said it was Janice and I lived down the hall."

"Why did you do that?"

"He frightened me," she said.

"You don't think he was a cop?" I asked.

She shook her head. "My father was a cop. I grew up around them, and this guy was different."

"What was different about him?"

"The way he looked at me."

"How was that?"

She took a breath as if she needed to steady herself just thinking about it.

"Like I was nothing," Courson said.

"Could you ID him?"

She shook her head. "I just glanced at him for a second. He was older, beyond that I couldn't tell you. I didn't want him to see my face."

She picked up the brown paper bag at her feet,

walked over to the mantel, and took the picture of my brother and herself and put it in the bag.

"Can you tell me anything about his parents?" I said.

"His mother died of breast cancer when he was in college. I don't know about his father. John had lots of secrets when it came to family."

She looked at me. "But I guess you know about that?"

Courson looked at me for a moment as if she were trying to find a piece of John in me.

"I never knew him," I said.

"You should have. He was . . ." The rest drifted away from her.

"I have to go," she said.

"How do I get ahold of you?"

"I think I may go away for a while. You can leave me a message at the public defender's office downtown."

"You're a lawyer?"

"Paralegal."

I took out a card, wrote down my cell number on the back, and handed it to her.

"If you need to reach me for anything."

She looked at it for a moment. "You're not LAPD."

"Pasadena."

"This isn't your case. It's not even your jurisdiction," she said. "If LAPD thinks it's a suicide then that's the end of it. There's nothing you can do." She started toward the door.

"Dana," I said.

She stopped.

"John tried to fax something to me last night but it never arrived. I think it was whatever he had found."

"And he was killed because of it?" Courson said.

I nodded. "It's possible."

She glanced nervously at the door.

"I don't want to die, Lieutenant," Courson said, and then she turned and looked at me. "Do you?"

"I want to talk again. I want to know who he was," I said.

She looked at me for a moment in silence. "He was your brother. What more do you need to know than that?"

Dana looked back into the apartment as if to find one last memory to hold on to, then rushed out.

I listened to the fall of her footsteps as she ran down the stairs, and then I closed the door and looked around the room. If I was ever to know anything about my brother, the answers were here for me to sift through like an archaeologist. I could find out what he liked for breakfast, what music he listened to, what clothes he wore, what medicine he kept in his bathroom, what books he read. And none of it would matter because I would never hear the sound of his laughter, or know the look in his eyes when he smiled.

I walked over to the bedroom door, pushed it open, and turned on the light. Just inside the door the phone machine sat on top of a small bookcase. A blinking red number said there were three messages. I hit play.

"Johnny, it's me. Call me . . . John, where are you? Call me."

The calls were from a bad cell-phone connection, but I guessed it was Dana's voice. The last message was silent.

I hit the button to play my brother's recording.

"I'm not home. You know what to do at the sound of the beep."

I played it again and again, though I already knew the voice. I was hearing a memory speak out loud to me. The voice was just an octave higher than you would expect. It was the sound of my father saying good night to me for the last time before he disappeared from my life, and the hapless salesman on *Bonanza* trying to convince cowboys to trade in their horses for bicycles.

I went through the desk looking for a thread to connect the events of the last twenty-four hours—a meeting in a date book, a phone number on a Post-it— but there was nothing.

I stepped over to the window to get some fresh air. I could search the apartment for hours but I already knew what I needed to know. The one person who loved him didn't believe he would take his own life.

I walked back into the living room and took the photograph of my father off the mantel, slipped it into the inside pocket of my suit, and walked out. A siren was wailing somewhere in the distance. The wind carried the faint presence of smoke with it. Someone had lit the first match, and L.A. was beginning to burn.

6

The clerk from the Western Union office lived in a large ten-story apartment building a block off Vermont on the edge of Koreatown. It was a short drive from Los Feliz so I decided to check it out rather than wait until tomorrow.

It was a prewar building that in its day must have been elegant, but was now, like most of its inhabitants, just barely hanging on. The sun had been down an hour, but the street was still crowded with people of every age trying to escape from the heat indoors. I parked across the street and got out.

Mariachi music drifted out of one of the building's windows. Rap music boomed from a car down the block. A street vendor with the heavily lined face of a Mexican peasant was doing a brisk business selling flavored ices on the corner. As I walked across the street there wasn't an individual within a block radius who failed to take notice that a cop had just arrived.

If I was lucky, the clerk would be able to ID the man who confiscated the security tape. If I was right, that man would turn out to be the same individual who took the computer from my half brother's apartment.

An old Otis elevator with brass doors that were faded with grime and tarnish dominated the lobby. The floor was a diamond pattern of black-and-white marble tiles. Two young women holding small children sat on benches across from the elevator talking in Spanish. As I walked toward the elevator one of the women said, *"Peligro,"* and pointed toward the stairs.

I thanked her and started up the stairs to the seventh floor, where the clerk lived. The air inside the building felt as if it hadn't been circulated in years, and it carried the scent of the thousands of lives that had passed through the building. On the seventh-floor landing, a large window looked toward the east, where a thin orange line of flame glowing in the dark snaked across the Verdugo hills above Burbank.

A baby was crying somewhere, and the soft voice of a mother singing in Spanish drifted into the hallway. The clerk, Hector Lopez, lived in apartment 715 at the end of the hallway. I could hear a television inside when I stepped up. I knocked on the door, but no one responded. I knocked again.

"This is the police, Mr. Lopez."

A small dog began barking in the next apartment. A door across the hallway opened a crack and then quickly closed.

"Mr. Lopez, I have a few questions."

I started to knock again, then saw a thin stream of blood trickle out from under the door at my feet. I pulled my Glock and took hold of the door handle. It wasn't locked, and I flung it open and raised my weapon.

The only light in the room was the glow of the TV but it was enough to see the shape of a body lying faceup on the floor. I reached around the corner and flicked on the light switch but nothing came on. I took a step in and let my eyes adjust to the dark. The kitchen was beyond the living room and there was a door to the right and a door to the left, both closed. I took a step toward the body and saw that it wasn't Lopez.

The front of the crisp white shirt of Detective Williams was darkly stained with blood. His tie was flipped up across the middle of his face. A large open wound had cleanly cut his throat.

The small-speed holster on his belt was empty. I checked his hands and the floor around the body but the gun wasn't there. When I looked up I saw out of the corner of my eye that the door on the left was partly open. I started to turn and raise my weapon but I knew it was too late. I saw a rush of movement, and then felt the blow strike me in the ribs on my left side. The pain shot through my body like a jolt of electricity. My knees buckled and I collapsed onto the floor. I gasped for breath, but the air felt as if it were a fire spreading through my lungs. I tried to raise my gun but it was kicked out of my hand before I could.

"I didn't do this," said a voice with a Latino accent.

I tried to look up but even the simple movement of raising my head caused a wave of pain to shoot through my entire body. I looked down expecting to see blood blossoming on the fabric of my shirt but there wasn't any.

"I didn't do this," he said again, louder.

The walls of the room began to spin as I started falling into unconsciousness. I felt a hand groping inside my pocket and removing my ID.

"Delillo," my attacker said. "Do you understand, I didn't do this."

For an instant I saw his face as he tossed my ID onto my chest. He said something else, but I couldn't hear a single sound, and then the world slipped away from under me.

The sound of the TV brought me back. It was a Spanish station, a clown chasing two women in bikinis around a stage. Had a minute passed? A few seconds? I couldn't tell. I was on my back, just as I had been when I passed out. I took a breath and a jolt of pain shot through my chest and I nearly vomited. I felt myself beginning to slide back toward unconsciousness but I fought it off, repeating *No, no, no*, to myself in my head.

I took a shallower breath, just managing to get enough air before the pain sent me reeling. *Where am I? Put the pieces back together.* I hadn't been shot or stabbed. Something had hit me.

"Williams," I whispered.

He was lying several feet from me, the throat wound glistening in the light from the TV. I slowly rose to my knees and saw that I was sitting in a stream of blood. I could feel the moisture soaking through the fabric of my slacks. My heart began to race out of control. I tried to move away from it, to wipe it away from my legs, but with every exertion my head spun faster and faster back toward unconsciousness.

The sound of the door opening and the flood of light from the hallway snapped me back to the moment. The dark shadow of a figure in the doorway reached into the room and seemed to envelop me. I grabbed for my weapon, then remembered that it had been knocked from my hand. I was helpless. I stared at the shadow, waiting for it to close on me, waiting for another blow, but it didn't come.

As I started to turn toward the door, numbness began to spread the length of my arms and into my hands. I took a shallow breath, then another and another, then slowly turned to the door. A small child, a boy, maybe five years old, was staring at me.

"Police," I managed to say.

The child stared in wonder at me, and I felt myself beginning to drift again and tumble back toward the darkness.

"Police," I whispered. "Pol . . ."

7

It was nearly 2 A.M. when LAPD Robbery Homicide detectives released me from the scene. The first uniforms to arrive at the apartment put me in cuffs for several minutes, thinking I was Williams's killer. Even after the detectives had cleared me, the look of suspicion that I was somehow responsible for Williams's death accompanied every glance my way. In LAPD minds I was an amateur, a woman who had gotten one of their own killed.

The chief of Pasadena police, Ed Chavez, and Harrison were waiting for me as I stepped out of the paramedics' truck. EMT had done their best to wash Detective Williams's blood off me with saline, but it still clung to my pants and stained the skin on my legs. The bandage around my ribs where Hector Lopez had hit me with the baseball bat had softened the searing pain, but each breath was still accompanied by a dull, lingering ache.

Lacy's big Latino godfather, the tough ex-marine, took one look at me and began to fume.

"Goddamn LAPD," Chavez said.

I looked into his big brown eyes and shook my head. He had spent much of his career protecting me, even when I didn't need it. The thought that LAPD would have put me in cuffs for even a second was enough to ignite his fuse.

"I really need a bath," I said.

He softened, if just a little.

"They wouldn't even let me take a look at the scene," Chavez said.

The image of Williams's dark glistening wound and the severed pearl-white windpipe flashed in my mind.

"I could have done without seeing it," I said.

They each took an arm and began walking me to my car. There were more than two dozen LAPD units, a SWAT truck, crime-scene investigators, and a mobile command center surrounding the apartment building now. A secure perimeter had been set up in a two-block square. Most of the residents of the building were still out on the street awaiting questioning or because they were afraid to go back inside, thinking a madman was loose in the building.

We crossed the street and stopped at my car. The smell of smoke was stronger now. Tiny flakes of ash were drifting on the wind, covering windshields like a dusting of snow.

"What do I need to know that can't wait until tomorrow?" Chavez asked.

I took a careful breath, easing the air past my damaged ribs.

"He didn't do this," I said.

Chavez looked at me, not understanding.

"I think the wrong man has a target on his back right now," I said.

"Lopez?"

I nodded. "He told me he didn't do it."

"Right after he whacked you with a baseball bat," Chavez said. "Innocent people don't whack cops with baseball bats."

I glanced at Harrison and saw in his eyes that he understood.

"There was no reason for him to let you live if he killed Williams," Harrison said. "He had nothing to gain, not the way Williams died."

Chavez chewed on that for a second, then looked over toward the members of SWAT walking by dressed in tactical black and carrying Mac-10 machine guns.

"LAPD has a different opinion," he said. "We would be doing the same thing if we lost one of our own."

"That doesn't change the fact that Lopez isn't a killer," I said.

"So what is he?"

"He's the only person who can ID the man who took the surveillance tape," Harrison said.

I started to nod, then realized that might not be entirely accurate.

"There may be someone else. Dana Courson, my . . . Manning's girlfriend may have seen him."

"If so, she could be in danger," Harrison said.

"She said she sensed something was wrong and told

him she lived down the hall. He may not know who she is."

"He found Lopez," Harrison said.

"And he killed Williams by mistake."

Chavez looked at me for a moment. "You think the killer thought he was murdering Lopez?"

I nodded. "At least until it was already over, then it was too late."

"And Lopez walked in and found a dead cop on his floor," Chavez said.

"I'll need an address for a Dana Courson in the public defender's office. She's a paralegal," I said.

"I'll get it," Chavez said. He took a breath and looked up toward the ash falling out of the darkness. "I could ask what the hell is going on, but I don't like feeling foolish in front of two of my officers."

He leveled his big eyes on me. "Is it true Manning was your brother?"

I nodded. "Half brother."

"And you're sure it wasn't suicide?" Chavez asked.

I looked down at the blood staining my pants. "I am now."

Chavez thought about it for a beat.

"This is all about a fax?" he asked.

"That's the starting point," I said. "I don't know what it's about."

The chief looked across the street at the small army of LAPD personnel that had taken over much of the block.

"We have to make this look like it's entirely about your brother," Chavez said. "Any hint that we're interfering with the investigation of Williams's murder, LAPD is not going to be happy."

I nodded.

"I'll need to find out what Williams knew so far," I said.

"I'll see what I can do," Chavez answered. "And I'll find Dana Courson and have a squad watch her. I want a doctor to take a look at those ribs, and then Harrison will take you home."

He opened the passenger door, helped me gently into the seat, and wrapped my seat belt around me.

"Worrying about you is turning me into an old man," he said with a half smile.

"You were an old man even when you were young," I said.

He looked at me with his big eyes that seemed to take on more sadness with every day on the job.

"I'm sorry about your brother," Chavez said.

We looked at each other for a moment.

"I'm sorry I didn't know him," I answered.

I touched his cheek, and he closed the door and walked back toward the crime scene. I stared at the coroner's van for a moment.

"Williams apparently was a better cop than we realized," I said. "That could just as easily have been me in there."

Harrison let the silence swallow the thought for a moment and looked back across the street.

"It wasn't, though."

8

The X-rays showed cracks in the fourth and fifth ribs on my left side, but they remained in one piece and hadn't punctured a lung. The doctor rewrapped them, suggested as little movement as possible for several days, and gave me some pain meds to get me through the next twenty-four hours. He offered me hospital scrubs to replace my bloodstained slacks for the ride home, but I refused them. I didn't want it to be easy to distance myself from what had happened in the apartment. Williams deserved at least that much, and I wanted to remind myself that I was only alive because Lopez wasn't a killer.

The winds were blowing harder up in the hills above Pasadena, where I lived. We pulled onto Mariposa and drove up to the end of the block where my house sat on the edge of the San Gabriels. Smoke from the fires in the Verdugo hills was west of us. The air was clear here. The glow of the flames was just visible above the ridgeline in the distance.

Harrison pulled the car up to the top of the driveway and stopped. I reached for the buckle on the seat belt and a spasm of pain shot through my chest. It took a moment to catch my breath.

Harrison reached over and unbuckled the belt, then got out, walked around, and opened the door. He took my arm and gently helped me to my feet. I looked into his eyes for a moment and felt my breath come up short but it wasn't because of any pain, or at least not the kind a pill can dull.

"I think I'll need some help inside," I said. "I don't think I can get into the tub."

He reached up and carefully pushed several strands of hair off my face and smiled.

"You want me to call Traver?" Harrison said.

I shook my head.

"Don't worry about it," he said.

Harrison put his arm around me and walked me inside, placing me on a stool in the kitchen while he went into the bathroom and ran the water in the tub. A minute or two later he walked back out.

"I found bath oils. I put some in."

He took my hand and eased me off the stool, then slowly walked me down the hallway to the bathroom. The scent of eucalyptus oil drifted out of the water as he helped me into the bathroom and closed the door. A candle was burning at the foot of the tub, softly illuminating the room.

"I thought you might want to soak for a while," Harrison said.

I stared at the water for a moment, then reached for the first button on my shirt. Even the simple movement of raising my arm sent shock waves of pain through my chest.

"Let me do that," Harrison said, stepping around me. "I have done this before, you know."

I looked into his eyes.

"Not with me," I said.

He reached down and gently pulled my shirt out of my slacks, then undid the buttons until my shirt fell open. He slipped it off my shoulders, then carefully folded it and walked around behind me, placing it on the vanity.

"I'll rewrap the bandage after the bath," he said, and began to unravel the bandage around my ribs.

"Does that hurt?" he asked as he eased the last wrap of the bandage off.

I tried to say something but could only manage to shake my head. He placed his hand softly on my back between my shoulders.

"Breathe," Harrison said.

I took a shallow breath and then another. He undid the hooks on my bra and let it slip off my shoulders into his hands. He laid it next to my shirt and I nervously began to fumble with the button on my slacks but my fingers didn't seem to want to cooperate.

Harrison stepped around from behind me and turned the water off in the tub, and then tested the temperature with his hand. I managed to just get the button on my slacks undone, but couldn't bend enough at the waist to slide them down.

"I can't bend at the waist," I said.

Harrison turned and knelt in front of me.

"Put your hand on my shoulder so you don't lose your balance."

I reached out to take hold of his shoulder and realized my hand was trembling. I tightly gripped his shoulder to mask the trembling as he slid the zipper down. My heart was pounding against my chest so hard each beat caused a jolt of pain to shoot out from my cracked ribs. I took a deep breath and closed my eyes as he undid the zipper, then reached up and carefully slid my pants and underwear over my hips and down my legs.

"God," I said quietly without realizing it.

"Just step out of them now, one at a time," Harrison said.

I stepped out of my clothes, then he lifted each foot and slipped my socks off. I tried to take a breath but couldn't. I was beginning to tremble.

"Breathe," he said.

"I can't."

Harrison reached out and placed his hand on my leg just behind the knee. I looked down and saw that he was examining the bloodstains that covered my legs from ankle to knee. My stomach began to turn and I felt myself beginning to gag.

"I'm going to wash the blood off your legs before you get in the bath," he said.

Harrison looked up into my eyes and I nodded.

"Thank you," I whispered.

Any self-consciousness or vulnerability I had felt standing in front of him vanished. I was safer at that moment than I had felt with a man for longer than I could remember. Harrison had once saved my life by putting his own at considerable risk. I didn't think anyone would be capable of giving more than that, but I was wrong. He was doing it now. Fully clothed he was as naked as I was, sharing a trust I didn't know could exist between two people. I had lost that ability to trust as a five-year-old girl when my father walked out of my life. Harrison lost it the day his young wife was murdered.

Harrison took a washcloth and dipped it into the warm bathwater. He lifted my foot and placed it on his thigh, and he gently began to wipe away the blood in long, careful strokes down my leg.

When my first leg had been washed he set my foot back on the floor and rinsed out the washcloth in the sink, then repeated the process, cleaning away the stains of violence stroke by stroke.

He set the cloth in the sink, then stepped up behind me.

"Hold on to my arms and I'll lower you in."

I stepped into the water and let my weight sink into his arms as he lowered me into the warm bath. I lay back and let the water swallow me up. I took as deep a breath as my cracked ribs would allow, breathing in the strong earthy aroma of eucalyptus.

"I'll wait outside," Harrison said.

I looked up at him. In the candlelight, the scars on his face from Gabriel's explosion softened, and he appeared to be transformed into the blond beach boy of his youth.

"Please stay," I said.

He held my look for a moment, then nodded and sat down on the floor, leaning back against the door.

"I'll be right here."

I took a breath and closed my eyes, letting myself sink into the warmth of the water.

"Do you want to talk about it?" he asked.

"Williams?" I shook my head.

"I was thinking about your brother," Harrison said.

I opened my eyes and looked at the candlelight flickering on the tile of the bathroom wall.

"Someone loved him," I said softly, barely conscious of my own voice.

We looked at each other for a moment, and then I lay back and closed my eyes.

Forty minutes later his hand touched my arm and I opened my eyes.

"You fell asleep," Harrison said. "We should get you out of there and rewrap those ribs."

He took hold of my arms and helped me to my feet, wrapping a towel around my shoulders. As carefully as he had washed away the blood on my legs, he gently dried me off and began rewrapping the bandage just below my breasts.

"Tell me if this is too tight," he said.

I tried to say it was fine, because I either didn't care about the pain anymore or just didn't notice it. I wanted to ask Harrison a thousand questions, to take apart what was happening between us like it was a case we were working on, but I couldn't do any of it. I just listened to a sound I hadn't heard in a very long time—the beating of my own heart.

Harrison finished wrapping the bandage, then draped a robe over my shoulders, closing it around me.

"You should get some sleep," he said.

He walked me out of the bathroom and down the hall to my bedroom.

"Can you get into bed all right by yourself?"

I looked at the empty bed for a moment.

"I have a lot of practice at that," I said.

Harrison looked at me and I saw his eyes wander for just a fleeting second.

"I'm familiar with that feeling," he said.

I reached up and touched the crescent-shaped scar at the corner of his eye. He placed his hand on mine, holding it gently against his cheek.

"If this was . . ." I started to say before he stopped me.

"Yes," he said. "The answer's yes."

He closed his eyes and kissed my hand, seeming to lose himself for a moment, then his fingers slipped from mine, and he turned and left.

I stood absolutely still listening to the front door close, and the sound of the car starting and backing down the driveway. When silence returned so did the dull ache under the bandage around my ribs. I carefully sat on the bed, turned out the light, and lay down in my empty house.

9

The voices down the hallway wake me. I reach for my gun in the drawer of the nightstand but it's not there. I slip out of bed, walk over to the door, and press against it to listen. A man and a woman are yelling at each other. I can't understand the words because they're flying too fast, but I can hear the fear in her voice—that mixture of adrenaline and terror.

And then it stops, and the silence begins to gather and take on the quality of a scream. I open the door and step into the dark hallway. A faint light glows at the far end and I slowly walk toward it. I think I hear a sound, but it's only the silence. At the end of the hallway I stop, and then step into the light.

My mother and father are in the living room. He's holding her by the neck, her feet several inches off the floor. He turns and looks at me, then lets her go and she crumples to the floor like a bathrobe that has slipped off its hanger.

The ringing of the alarm yanked me out of the dream. I lay still for a moment measuring my breath. I didn't remember ever having the dream before. *Why now?* My hand touched the bandage around my ribs. Dreams and violence both come from places that are beyond our control. My daughter's screams in the night for months after the killer Gabriel touched our lives were testament enough to the connection.

The clock read nearly eight-thirty. I'd been sleeping through the electronic buzz of the alarm for an hour. I sat up, the broken ribs forcing me to make even the smallest of motions as if they had been carefully rehearsed. I looked into the dull light filtering into my bedroom through the curtains. The light wasn't right, and then I smelled the smoke that had settled over the city like a shroud.

I looked at my robe lying at the end of the bed and I was standing naked in front of Harrison again, his hands gently moving over my body. I tried to take a breath but could hardly manage it. A shiver ran through me and I closed my eyes, trying to hold on to that moment, but instead I saw the image of my half brother lying on the table at the morgue, a small bullet hole in the side of his head.

The phone on the nightstand began to ring. I let it go, trying to find my way back to the memory of Harrison, but it already seemed to be slipping away faster than I could hold on to it. I wasn't even sure it had happened. I reached over and answered the call.

"How you feeling?" Chief Chavez said.

"I'll have to give that a little thought," I said.

He hesitated a beat too long. "What?" I asked.

"We're on tactical alert. The whole damn county seems to be catching fire."

"That's not why you called me," I said.

"No. An officer is on the way over with your car to pick you up. I found something you need to see."

10

The hills above Pasadena hadn't begun to burn yet, but a fire to the east was laying down a heavy blanket of smoke over the city that turned the sunlight to the pale orange of a melon.

Chief Chavez and Harrison were in his office when I stepped inside. My eyes met Harrison's briefly, but he gave nothing away about the intimacy of the night before. A manila folder sat in the middle of Chavez's usually empty desk.

"Tell me that's Detective Williams's case file on my brother," I said.

Chavez nodded.

"How did you manage that?"

"Let's just say I didn't use your name," Chavez said.

"Any word on the Western Union clerk Lopez?"

Chavez shook his head. "Every media outlet has his picture. Every agency is looking for a cop killer."

Chavez pulled his chair back and I stepped around the desk and took a seat.

"It's not exactly what I thought might be in there," Chavez said.

I began to page through the file. There were the usual crime-scene reports from the riverbank where John was found. Coroner's report, preliminary autopsy, a few cursory biographical facts. Toxicology and the complete lab work were missing because they hadn't been finished yet.

"There's nothing here of any use," I said and looked at them both. "What was it you wanted me to see?"

Chavez motioned toward a brown envelope paper-clipped to the bottom of the folder.

"Take a look at that."

I opened it and pulled out a faded arrest report. It was dated 1987. I started to run down the lines of information.

"It's an arrest in a murder case," Chavez said.

My eyes stopped on the name of the suspect arrested.

"Thomas Manning," I said.

A mug shot was clipped to the back of the report, and I pulled it free and looked at the photograph.

"That's my father," I said, barely speaking above a whisper.

I quickly began scanning the rest of the report. "It refers to the River Killer murders."

"I remember them," Chavez said. "I made a few

calls to refresh my memory. Three young women were murdered, their bodies left on the banks of the L.A. River."

"Where on the river?" I said.

"Same general location as your brother. The murders were never solved."

In my mind's eye I saw the image from my dream the night before, only it wasn't a dreamlike image anymore. It was real. I was a little girl staring at my father choking my mother.

I felt a hand on my shoulder yanking me back to the present.

"Alex, you okay?" Chavez said.

I took a deep breath.

"Yeah, I'm okay."

"Look at the name of the counsel present at the questioning of your father," Harrison said.

I flipped to the second page of the report and found it in the middle of the page. "Gavin . . . He was my father's lawyer." I looked at Harrison.

"Your father was released within hours of his arrest, no charges filed."

I tried to let the pieces fall together in my head, but all it added up to were more questions than I had started out with.

"It can't be a coincidence that my brother was working for Gavin," I said.

"Unlikely," Harrison said.

"And if you carry that logic further, the fax my

brother sent probably had something to do with this. One or both of them must have been looking for something to do with that case."

"Or looking for someone," Harrison said.

I couldn't help but connect the dots that they had just laid out. My father had been questioned as a suspect in a serial murder case, and my brother died in nearly the identical place as the victims of that killer while working for the man who represented my father eighteen years before.

"A serial killer, and the murders of my brother and an LAPD cop. And the one connecting thread is my father," I said.

"That doesn't make your father guilty of anything, Alex," Chavez said. "Hell, you don't even know if your father is alive."

"No, but that's why you called me. It's probably what brought my brother and Gavin together, and now they're dead, and so is a cop who saw this file and was thinking the same thing we are. One way or the other my father is at the center of this."

"But how?" Harrison said. "Williams may also have just gotten a random hit on the name Manning linking your brother and father to the river."

"LAPD still considers your brother's death a suicide, and the coroner is probably going to agree," Chavez said.

"You think Detective Williams would agree if he could?" I said.

"Gavin still died in an accident."

"And the day my brother died, he tried to contact me for the first time in his life. There would have to be a pretty good reason for him to have done that, something that affected us both."

"Your father would be the logical reason," Harrison said.

I nodded. "But as what?"

"Only your brother knew that," Chavez said.

"Not only my brother—his killer knew, too."

"Have we found Dana Courson?"

"She lives in Studio City. There was no answer on her phone, no answer at her door. The public defender's office said she told them she would be out for a week. I left word for her to contact us if she calls in."

I looked at Chavez, whose soft, dark eyes were never very good at hiding even the most innocent of emotions.

"Your father was questioned in a murder case eighteen years ago," he said. "A bad arrest was made. My bet is it ends there."

"It didn't for my brother and Detective Williams," I said. "You think LAPD has made the connection between the River Killer and this?"

"If there is a connection," Chavez said. "They haven't made it yet if they're still looking for a cop killer."

"Can we get the complete case file on the River Killer?"

"LAPD has made it very clear that if you stick even a toe into your brother's or Williams's death, they'll arrest you for obstruction."

"All they have to know is that we're looking at an eighteen-year-old murder case."

Chavez shook his head. "Once they get their heads out of their asses, they may make the connection."

"Can you get the files?"

Chavez sighed. "I'll see what I can do."

I looked down at the mug shot of my father. He was years older in the picture than the last time I had seen him. The charming good looks that had fueled a dream of stardom had faded. The sparkle in the eyes was gone; the sharp lines of his face had softened. I tried to imagine what his life had been like after he left my mother and me, but I couldn't. Mug shots freeze a moment in time unlike any other photograph. The subject has no past, no future, just a single terrible moment in the white light of the camera's flash. The truth was, if I met this man on a street this afternoon, I wouldn't know who he was.

I took the file and stepped into my office while Harrison called the doctor who had attended to Gavin. I glanced at the mug shot of my father one more time, then closed the file and picked up the phone. I knew the number but, as I did every time I called, I looked it up in my book. Perfect daughters don't make mistakes.

"It's me," I said when she answered. "I need you to tell me something."

"It's one of those conversations, is it?" my mother said.

"No, I just need you to be honest with me."

"When have I not been honest with you?"

"That's not what I meant."

"Well, that's what it sounded like," she said.

"I'm sorry, I should have phrased that differently."

"You talk to everyone as if you suspect they've committed a crime."

I closed my eyes and took a breath.

"It's a bad habit," I said.

I thought I could hear the sound of a cigarette being lit, even though she swore she quit years ago.

"Okay, now what do you need to know?" my mother asked.

I thought I knew how to ask the question, but I suddenly realized I didn't. Or at least I didn't know how to ask without her thinking I was accusing her of something. I hesitated, and then asked it the only way I knew how. The way a cop would ask.

"Did my father ever abuse you?"

There was silence on the other end, as if the words had taken her breath away.

"How can you ask something like that?" she finally said, a slight trembling in her voice. "How can you?"

"I had a dream last night he was choking you."

"A dream? You accuse me of that because of a dream."

"Someone who is the victim of abuse hasn't done anything wrong. I'm not accusing you of anything."

"You think I'm the kind of person who would stay with someone who did that to them?"

"There is no kind of person who this happens to, they're only victims."

"Well, I am not a victim. I thought you would know that by how I raised you. . . . My . . ."

I let it rest for a second or two.

"I'm sorry, it was just a dream, but I needed to ask," I said.

"I don't know why I'm surprised. You spend your life walking through the filth of this world. God . . . never ask me something like that again."

I heard the sound of several deep breaths and then she hung up. I held on to the phone for a moment, staring at the redial button. I'd been to hundreds of abuse cases as a cop, and when asked for the first time in their life if they'd been abused, every victim answered my questions the same way my mother just had.

There was a knock on the door and Harrison stepped in. He started to say something, then glanced at the phone in my hand.

"Should I come back?"

I shook my head.

"Tell me something encouraging," I said.

"I just talked to the doctor who attended to Gavin," Harrison said. "There was nothing surprising in his death given the extent of injuries from the car accident."

"Did he talk to my brother?"

"No. A nurse thought she remembered a cop asking him a few questions, but she couldn't be sure."

"That would be usual after a fatal accident."

"Except she said it was a detective, not a uniform."

"Could she ID him?"

"She only saw him across the room in emergency, and he didn't talk to any staff."

We looked at each other for a moment, then I realized I was still holding the phone in my hand and hung it up.

"You okay?" Harrison asked.

I shook my head.

"I've spent my life walking through the filth of the world, according to my mother," I said.

"I was actually wondering about how your ribs feel," he said.

I looked up at him and his eyes met mine, making no attempt to let go.

"Thank you for last night," I said.

"You don't have to."

"I worked up the speech in the car on the way in, but I suddenly can't remember any of it."

I remembered doing the same thing in junior high school the first time I called a boy at home. I had hung up without uttering a single word.

"I'm a lieutenant, you're one of my detectives, it might not be such a good idea if we were to take it any further, particularly for you. You know how cops can be."

A voice in my head was screaming, *Idiot, idiot, idiot.*

"I think you have enough to worry about right now without any of this," Harrison said, letting me off the hook.

"I think about standing there last night, and what you did for me, your touch. . . . You make it very hard for me to act like a lieutenant."

The faint hint of a blush rose in his face. His reached up and touched the scar at the corner of his eye and smiled.

"I've never been with a naked lieutenant before."

His eyes held mine for a moment.

"When this is finished," he said.

The idea that I could be finished with what I was uncovering seemed a remote possibility. I glanced back at the phone and then at the report in front of me.

"Something else has happened, hasn't it?" he asked.

I nodded.

"If I don't need to know . . ." he started, but I cut him off.

"I had what I thought was a dream last night, but I think it was more than that."

"A memory?" Harrison said.

"Yeah. I think my father abused my mother," I said.

Harrison sat on the arm of the chair in front of my desk. "You're sure?"

I shook my head. I opened the file and removed the mug shot of my father.

"He's a stranger. I'm not sure about anything. But I don't imagine a therapist would consider the timing of the memory a coincidence."

"You talked to your mother."

I nodded. "It didn't go particularly well."

"She denied it?"

"Badly. Everything she said and didn't say to me suggests I'm right."

The wheels in Harrison's head turned for a moment.

"Even if it's true, that doesn't make your father a killer, particularly a serial killer," Harrison said. "They usually contain their rage from their everyday lives."

I nodded. "But it does make him violent."

I looked one more time at the mug shot, hoping to discover a detail, a window into some part of my father that would lead me in a different direction. It wasn't there. I looked out the window at the strange orange light from the smoke. The line separating reality from nightmare seemed to be getting thinner by the moment.

"I thought it was the dark I remember being afraid of as a little girl, but it wasn't," I said. "I think it was him."

11

Len Hazzard, the detective who led the investigation into the River Killer murders, had retired three years ago from Robbery Homicide and was living on the western edge of the San Fernando Valley in Chatsworth.

The Santa Anas were gusting to forty miles an hour through the canyons where subdivisions had replaced chaparral. The fires to the east of Pasadena had produced a surreal glow but no danger. Driving into the canyons was like entering a city under siege. Burning embers were falling out of the sky from a fire two miles to the north and starting spot fires on roofs. The tops of palm trees would explode in flames as if hit by a bomb. Cars packed with family valuables streamed out of neighborhoods while convoys of fire trucks poured in.

Harrison stopped the squad at a Highway Patrol roadblock and we showed our IDs, then turned into the subdivision. Detective Hazzard lived at the end of a cul-de-sac tucked into a rocky canyon. One side of the street was lined with palm trees that had been charred as black as charcoal.

Hazzard was standing on his front lawn wearing shorts and a Hawaiian shirt, holding an unlit cigarette and watching a slurry bomber make a run on a ridge a canyon away. He looked to be in his mid sixties, with thinning light hair, but was still powerfully built and tanned from hours in the sun every day. He shook our hands and invited us inside.

The inside of the house looked as if it had been decorated by a committee of VFW vets intent on fulfilling all their boyhood dreams through this one house. The upholstery matched the colors of NFL and NBA teams. Autographed sports memorabilia and baseball cards covered nearly every wall. I noticed a Yankees jersey of Babe Ruth's, another belonging to Jackie Robinson. From a quick glance at the rest of the collection, I imagined it was incredibly valuable. I wondered if I was the first woman other than a maid to set foot inside in a decade. We followed him into the dining room, where a large box sat in the middle of the table under a chandelier made of deer antlers.

"It's all here—every report, note, everything, I copied it all before I left," Hazzard said, staring at the box like he held a grudge against it. "I had it in the pickup when your chief called. It was going with me if I had to evacuate."

He looked out the window at the burnt trees across the street.

"I'll never be done with it," he said. "You have a case like that, Lieutenant? The one you can't let go of?"

I nodded.

A helicopter passed overhead, shaking the house.

"It's like the end of the fucking world," Hazzard said.

When the copter moved off, he turned to me. "Anything you want, it's yours. All I ask is that you keep me informed of everything, and if you make an arrest, I be there when you do it."

I nodded my approval, and he motioned to the chairs and we sat down.

"You arrested a Thomas Manning. What can you tell me about him?" I asked.

He appeared to study the name as if it were suspended in midair in front of him, then his eyes focused and he turned to me.

"Something's happened, hasn't it?"

I nodded. Hazzard waited for me to add more to the admission than a nod of the head.

"His son was found shot to death on the banks of the L.A. River," I said.

"Where on the river?"

"A few hundred yards north of the Fletcher Bridge."

The location clearly struck a chord with him and for an instant he appeared lost in memory.

"That's Northeast division. Why is Pasadena interested?"

"LAPD thinks it's a suicide."

"And you don't. Why?"

"Manning's son worked for a lawyer named Gavin," I said.

Hazzard began massaging the back of his neck as if he had to ease the name out of the past.

"Gavin was Manning's lawyer."

I nodded.

"Have you talked to him?"

"He died in a car accident the same day as Manning."

Hazzard got up from the table and looked out the window.

"We found the first victim, a twenty-two-year-old named Jenny Roberts, by the Fletcher Bridge."

He turned and walked over to the box containing the files and began riffling through it until he found what he was looking for, and then he placed a file in front of me. I opened it up to an eight-by-ten glossy, the kind actors use for auditions, of a beautiful young woman with shoulder-length hair, smiling at the camera.

The lines at the corners of Hazzard's eyes deepened as he stared at the picture. Lines that I imagined weren't there before he had seen her for the first time lying dead next to the river.

"Try forgetting that face," Hazzard said.

"What did you have on Manning?" Harrison asked.

Hazzard rummaged through the box again and removed another file.

"A month before she was killed, she filed a complaint against Manning alleging she had been sexually assaulted by him after an acting class he taught."

"Was he questioned in the assault?" I asked.

"Yeah. He was interviewed but there wasn't enough evidence to support an arrest."

"That's not enough for you to have arrested him on a murder charge," Harrison said.

"There were other complaints against him, similar incidents; he was a real piece of work. But he was never charged with anything. They're all in that box."

"But that's not why you arrested him," I said.

He shook his head.

"He knew one of the other victims?" I asked.

Hazzard nearly smiled, though he seemed unaccustomed to it.

"Chavez said you were a good detective," Hazzard said. "The second victim also took an acting class from him."

He tossed the folder onto the table in front of me.

"It's all there, everything you want to know about Thomas Manning. And it will get you exactly what we got: nothing."

"Was there a connection between Manning and the third victim?" I asked.

He shook his head. "Not a goddamn thing."

I stared at the folder for a moment as if it were the family album I never had.

"Was Manning the only arrest you made?" Harrison asked.

Hazzard nodded. "We had a possible witness to the killings, but he died."

"How?"

"He was a transient. We questioned him on two occasions. A week later he was beaten to death in the rail yards east of downtown."

I picked up the file on my father as another helicopter roared overhead.

"Did you question Manning about the transient?"

He shook his head. "Manning disappeared. We never found him."

"And then the murders stopped," Harrison said.

Hazzard nodded.

"Do you believe he's alive?"

"I'll believe he's alive until the day I see him lying on a slab."

"I'd like to take the files with us," I said.

Hazzard looked at the box for a moment as if it were a relative who had come for a weekend visit and never left.

"I've lived with those files for eighteen years. It would be a relief to be rid of 'em."

"I'll want to talk to you more," I said.

"As long as I don't burn to the ground, I'll be right here."

I slipped the folders back into the box with the rest of the files, thanked Hazzard, and started for the door with Harrison.

"You never said why you're interested, Lieutenant," Hazzard said. "Manning's son's death is still a long way from Pasadena."

I stopped by the door.

"What aren't you telling me?" he added.

"Two witnesses may have seen the man who killed Manning's son. A girlfriend who saw him leave the apartment with a computer, and a clerk at a Western Union office."

"And you're wondering if Manning has come back from the dead and murdered his own child?"

"The LAPD detective in charge of the case was murdered last night."

"Detective Williams. I saw the news."

I nodded. "I think they're after the wrong suspect."

"And why do you think that?" Hazzard asked.

"Because he told me he didn't do it just before he attacked me with a bat."

"You were the injured cop on the scene?"

I nodded. "I think the man who killed Thomas Manning's son also killed Williams, and I believe it's possible that that individual is connected to the River Killer."

"Why would a serial killer of young women suddenly kill two men?"

"He's trying to protect himself. I'm guessing that Gavin and Manning's son may have uncovered something about the River Killer."

"Do you have any proof of this theory?"

"The night Manning died he tried to contact me but wasn't successful."

"You tell LAPD this?"

"LAPD is looking for a cop killer. They don't want to know what I think," I said.

I glanced out the door. A shower of burning embers the size of golf balls were falling out of the sky, sending up puffs of smoke when they landed.

"I think you might be right about it being the end of the world, Detective," I said.

Hazzard looked out the window, his face a mask of intensity.

"Just a matter of time," he said.

I turned and looked at him. "You think Thomas Manning killed those girls, don't you?" I asked.

Hazzard smiled, but there was no joy in it. "I spend my days buying baseball cards and playing golf. What I think doesn't matter anymore."

I imagined Hazzard was one of the saddest men I'd ever met in my life. His Hawaiian shirt, golf clubs, and the sports memorabilia were Band-Aids holding together a lonely house and a psyche that had been assaulted by years of violence.

"Thomas Manning was my father," I said. "I'd like to know what you think."

A flash of surprise registered on Hazzard's face—something I would have guessed wasn't possible.

"You sure, Lieutenant?"

I didn't know the answer to that question. Until that

morning my father had existed in a memory that was as faint and harmless as a thirty-year-old television show. Now I was asking to replace that with the knowledge that my father could be a monster.

"I just want to know who killed my brother," I said.

Hazzard reached into a cooler I hadn't noticed under the table, took out a can of beer, set it on the table, and just stared at it.

"I hope that's what you want," Hazzard said. "Because I'd bet everything I own, your father murdered those young women."

12

It was near dusk when Harrison and I finished laying out Hazzard's case files on the conference room table and into some sort of recognizable order—evidence, interview records, search warrants, victims' histories, and suspect histories.

Photographs were pinned on a bulletin board in descending order from living candid shots to crime scene and finally to autopsy. Two of the candid pictures were professional head shots used by actors; the third was a snapshot that looked to be from a family album. All three women were blond, or at least dyed blond. The first victim, Jenny Roberts, was twenty-two years old. The second, Alice Lundholm, was only twenty. The third, Victoria Fisher, twenty-five.

All three had been sexually assaulted though no evidence of semen was present in Victoria Fisher. Each had then been strangled with a piece of yellow plastic cord. The crime-scene photos showed all three victims were naked from the waist down, hands bound behind their backs and lying facedown. All died within a period of six weeks. Two of them had taken a class taught by my father. No known connection to the third victim existed.

When we finished laying everything out Harrison sat down without saying a word. Even the simple act of sorting through paperwork takes on a weight when its subject is murder. It was easy to understand why Hazzard was relieved to have the case files finally out of his house. All I wanted to do was lie down and sleep. Living with these files in your house would have been like living with a black hole that, every day, took another piece of you.

"There's no reason to think Hazzard is right about your father," Harrison said.

I stepped over to the window and looked out. The first line of flames from a new brush fire was just visible on a ridgetop above Pasadena in the San Gabriels. I turned and looked back into the room. The one folder out of the entire box that remained unopened was the one containing information about my father.

"We also don't have a reason to think he's wrong," I said.

I took a seat next to Harrison and stared at the photographs on the wall. I could feel the tug of the investigation—inviting me to let go of the known world where people live day in and day out safely away from the shadow world tacked up on the wall. These three young women would know what I was thinking. They had been those people—safe and blissfully ignorant until they were yanked into the dark for a few terrible minutes.

I stared at the crime-scene pictures for a moment. At some point in every investigation you cross a line where what you discover from then on will forever change you. And I was staring at it. *Beyond this there's no turning back*, I said silently to myself. Hazzard knew all about that. He had crossed into this world and then tried to return to the old world. But the more normal he attempted to make his home, the more knickknacks he put on the walls, the farther away that world seemed to be from him. And now he was neither a cop nor a civilian.

"Were the victims put in this position before or after death?" I said.

Harrison scanned the autopsy reports. "After."

"Why?" I asked.

Harrison thought for a moment. "The killer didn't want her to look at his face. Or he didn't want to look at hers."

"He couldn't look them in the eye," I said.

I glanced at Harrison. "He was ashamed."

"The first two showed signs of hemorrhaging and abrasions from the cord used to strangle them. The third victim, only bruising, no damage from the cord."

"He used his hands on the third victim," I said.

Harrison nodded. "Why the change?"

"Victoria Fisher had dirt in her mouth, a tooth was

chipped, a split lip, some bruising on the face. She fought back," I said.

Harrison nodded and looked over the other two autopsies. "The first two victims showed no signs of a struggle; that could explain why there were traces of semen found on their clothes, and none on the third victim."

I stood up and walked around to the other side of the table, closer to the pictures. The usual distance time gives to old crime-scene photos wasn't present in these. They appeared fresh, as if they had just come out of the developing tray.

"Something's missing," I said.

Harrison shook his head. "You lost me."

"The fourth victim."

"There was no fourth victim."

"Exactly."

I saw in Harrison's eyes that he understood. "Why did he stop?"

I nodded.

"Serial killers don't stop," Harrison said.

"Not usually, not unless they've been caught or are dead. And we're assuming he's not dead because of my brother and Detective Williams. So there has to be a reason there were only three victims."

"He could have moved away."

I went through one of the piles of documents until I found a series of requests to the FBI spanning a period of ten years after the three murders.

"Hazzard spent years looking for hits on the FBI national database. He got two close matches, but arrests were made in both cases with no connection to Los Angeles."

"He could be killing in different ways that were unrecognizable to Hazzard. Over the last eighteen years there would have been hundreds of unsolved cases in L.A. County," Harrison said.

"Three victims, same body type, same ages, two killed the same way, the third strangled with his hands. All left in the same exact position. He wanted us to know it was him," I said.

"So why would he stop after he's gotten our attention?"

I walked back over to the windows. The smoke that had laid down a blanket over Pasadena from fires to the east was now rising in columns straight up twenty-five thousand feet, forming thick mushroom clouds that gave L.A. the appearance it was ringed by nuclear explosions.

"What if this isn't a serial killer? What if it was something else?"

"Such as?"

"The third victim wasn't an actress. Who was she?" I said, turning back to the photographs.

Harrison began going through her file. "A law student, single mother, worked part-time at the district attorney's office downtown as a clerk."

"She had a child?"

Harrison nodded. "A boy, four years old at the time of her death."

"Why her? How was she picked? The actress would have been easy. A predator wants to find beautiful young blondes, an acting school in L.A. is the first place he'd look. But a law student? How did he find her?"

Harrison quickly scanned another page of the file. "She was last seen leaving a restaurant on Melrose after dinner with others from the DA's office. No shortage of beautiful women in restaurants on Melrose. Wrong place, wrong time."

I looked over at the folder containing the files on my father.

"Where did my father teach the acting classes?"

He started to reach for my father's file, then hesitated and glanced at me.

"Go on," I said.

He opened the folder and began going through reports until he found it. "A theater on Santa Monica Boulevard near La Brea," Harrison said.

"Maybe two miles from where she would have been eating the night she died," I said.

Harrison replaced the report and closed the file. "You should sit down."

I raised my hand to my face and realized I was trembling. I looked at a chair but I couldn't move. As I tried to take a breath, the injured rib felt like a knife slicing into my chest. I looked across the table at the crime-scene pictures of the three young women lying on the banks of the river.

"Do you think my father killed them?"

I felt Harrison's hand on my arm and he guided me over to a chair.

"We're a long way from that," he said.

I tried to find another way to look at what was staring me in the face, but I couldn't. I closed my eyes and managed to gently get a breath of air.

"Someone identifying themselves as a cop took the surveillance tape from the Western Union office," I said. "John Manning's girlfriend thought the man who took his computer was a cop."

"You know something else?" Harrison said.

I looked at the bodies of the women one more time until I couldn't any longer, then got up and walked over to the window. The sun had dropped into the ocean; a dark orange shadow had fallen over Pasadena. The mushroom cloud of smoke rising out of the fire in the mountains had turned blood red.

"*War of the Colossal Beast*," I said.

"You lost me," Harrison said.

"It's a movie. A monster is destroying Los Angeles. My father played a cop in it."

Harrison joined me at the window, staring at the plume of smoke rising into the sky.

"The report mentions the name of a DA who was present at his questioning. See if you can find him. If my father did these things, I have to know," I said.

"We'll start with the third victim, Victoria Fisher. I want to know everything my father is alleged to have done the day she died. Talk to everyone my brother may have talked to."

Harrison nodded.

I walked back to the table and looked down at my father's file. If Hazzard had done his work properly, every known violent act my father ever committed would be here. How many were there? How far back did the history go? And if my own mother was abused, would I find her in these pages?

"Half of the Screen Actors Guild has played cops," Harrison said.

"I don't have nightmares about them," I said.

It was after ten when I finally sat down at the dining room table to open my father's file. I had talked to Lacy, as we promised we would every night. She hadn't heard about Detective Williams's murder, or my involvement, and that was just fine. I thought about calling my mother back but didn't.

Maybe we're not supposed to know the secrets of our own families. It might be love that brings people together, but it's the secrets they keep to themselves that sustain them over time. I didn't want to believe that, but staring at my father's unopened file, it would be easier to believe it.

I took a sip of wine along with a pain pill for my ribs

and began to learn who my father was. The first complaint against him came when I was eight years old. He had already been gone from my life for three years. A nineteen-year-old woman named Kelly. She was in a dressing room after a show when she heard a sound behind her and he was standing there. He told her to take off her blouse.

I felt a chill run up my back as I continued reading the complaint. My father didn't move, he didn't strike her, didn't touch her, he just stared at her and told her again to take off her blouse. The victim refused and he walked away as if nothing had happened. Nothing. Another actor found Kelly an hour later, still crying.

I reached for the wineglass and noticed my hand was trembling as I picked it up. I wanted to close the file, right then and there. Let the brush fires make a run down out of the mountains and take the house. I could walk away from it. It would be a small price to pay for letting these pages turn to ashes. I emptied the glass of wine and then poured another.

A woman named Jan was next, Chris after that. Then Anne, Morgan, and Perry.

I emptied another glass, and just as quickly filled it again.

None of them had been touched; none had filed legal complaints, only with the theater's management. But they were people to me now, with names. They were the age of my own daughter. And I knew that if they hadn't experienced fear before that day, they knew it from that moment on because of my father. Whenever a door opened behind them, whenever they heard a footstep, they would be afraid.

A makeup artist named Terry was the first one he touched. It was in the middle of a performance. She was in the dressing room going through her kit when she heard him enter the room. She began to turn when he reached out, put his hand over her mouth, and pulled her out of the chair. She tried to scream but couldn't, then just as quickly he let go and backed away, repeating, "I'm sorry, I'm sorry."

He touched two more women, mirror images of the first encounter that ended with an apology. I didn't look at their names. I wanted to open a second bottle of wine and turn the clock back to when my father existed as little more than an image on a television screen, but I didn't. I moved to the last report in the file—the only assault where police questioned him. Jenny Roberts, the first victim of the River Killer. The perfect young blond actress who did community theater and wanted to be on a TV series.

I had just finished an acting class. The other students had already left. The director, Manning, asked me if I wanted to work on a scene with him for an audition he had for a small movie role. We started walking out to the stage and I noticed he had slowed his walk and was a step behind me. Then he said, "Don't move."

I thought it was in the script, but I couldn't find

the line. His hand covered my mouth, and his other hand began to tear open the front of my shirt and touch my breasts. I tried to pull away but I couldn't, so I stood there and let him feel me until I felt his arm begin to relax. Then I drove the heel of my shoe into his ankle. He threw me to the stage floor and I began crawling away, screaming for help. He grabbed my ankle and began dragging me back across the stage on my stomach. I was screaming and crying. And then he let me go. He didn't say anything, he didn't move. He just stood there like he was surprised. Then he said, "I'm sorry, I'm sorry," and I got up and ran out the stage door.

I quickly scanned the report from the officer who had questioned my father. "She came on to me," my father said. "It happens all the time in the theater. Some people are unable to turn emotions off after intense work."

No charges were filed. He was fired from the theater a week later. A month after that, Jenny Roberts was found on the riverbank, strangled, her hands tied behind her back with a thin yellow cord.

I closed the file and pushed back from the table. It was nearly one o'clock. I poured the last of the bottle of wine into the glass and stepped out the front door. The dry air that had been flowing out of the desert into the basin was warmer than it had been earlier in the day. The smoke wasn't visible in the darkness, but the aroma of fire was there. I took a breath and it stung my throat. It was different than it had been when Pasadena was shrouded in orange light. Instead of just burning brush and chaparral, there was the sting of something else hanging in the air now.

Houses were burning—roofs, furniture, plastics, cleaning chemicals under kitchen sinks, fabrics, books, shoe leather. All physical evidence of lives lived was being consumed.

"It happens all the time in the theater," I whispered.

The words sent a chill through me as if I'd stepped into a cold room. All through my childhood I had pretended my father was a salesman trying to sell bicycles to cowboys. One day I dreamed he would come back. And now I hoped to God he hadn't.

13

Twice in the night I bolted out of sleep as I felt a hand reach around my neck and try to pull me into the darkness. Each time I sat up in bed and searched the dark corners of the room to make sure I was alone, then I lay down and tried to force myself back into a dreamless sleep that I knew wouldn't last.

The third dream was different. He didn't touch me this time, but he was there, standing behind me. I tried to fight off the dream, but it held a grip on me as surely as if he were in the room. Then I heard my mother. "It's okay now. It's okay."

The sound of her voice shook me from the dream and I jumped into consciousness. My ribs ached from lying on my side. The sheets were damp with perspiration.

The alarm clock read 5:10 A.M. I looked around the darkness and noticed the curtain blowing into the room. I lay back on the pillow and tried to think of something that would allow me to slip back to sleep. I attempted to picture my daughter, then to remember the touch of Harrison's hands as he gently washed my legs, but I could only hold on to either thought for a moment before the shadow of my father intruded, and another terrible question formed in my mind to push sleep further away.

Was I one of his victims?

Was that why I became a cop, to undo some terrible wrong that had been swept from my memory? Was that why my mother was so upset at the prospect of my wearing a badge? That inevitably the one investigation she knew I would have to undertake was my own past, a past she had spent a lifetime concealing from me?

I tried a breathing exercise that Lacy had learned from her PTSD sessions to relax, but my broken ribs made the exercise futile. I rolled onto my side away from the broken ribs and watched the gentle rise and fall of the curtains.

"Let it go," I started to say, then stopped. There was no letting go of this. Maybe this was what John Manning had known, and it was why he became an investigator just as I had. It was the thread that connected us, except he had chosen to solve the one mystery I had forever tried to bury: Who was our father? And that search probably cost him his life.

I got out of bed and walked back out to the dining room, where I had left the case files. There wasn't a sound anywhere. Not the wind. Not a distant car, a jet, anything. I realized I was shaking and eased myself down into a chair at the table and sat in the darkness. Tears began to well up in my eyes, and I wiped them away with the back of my hand. My brother had thought of me the night he died because he believed I needed the same answers he did.

Wind jostled the windowpanes. I heard the siren of a distant fire truck. A mockingbird began a wild singsong and then a crow let go with a series of shrieks.

I stood up and walked to the front door and stepped outside to get some air. The wind had shifted overnight and was blowing directly into my face. Smoke obscured the sky above. To the east over the nearest ridgeline, the orange light of fire glowed in the predawn. There were more sirens audible. The flashing lights of a fire engine appeared at the bottom of Mariposa. Other residents on the block were loading their cars with belongings.

I retrieved my phone from inside and hit the speed dial. Harrison answered on the second ring.

"Are you all right?" he said.

His voice was as reassuring as the feel of his hands on my legs. Fragile gray ash began falling out of the sky, covering the ivy on the hillside like new snow. The first wisps of flame were becoming visible, topping the ridge less than two miles away. A nervous deer came bounding out between two houses, its delicate hooves slipping on the pavement before it vanished into the shadows behind another house.

"The fire's moving right toward me. I think I'm going to have to evacuate," I said.

"I'll be right there," Harrison said.

"I think it's possible my father could be a killer," I said before I hung up.

By dawn the flames had crested the ridge to the east and began advancing. Three fire engines were parked in the cul-de-sac. My neighbors were packing their cars with pets, tax records, family photographs, and anything else that couldn't be replaced and would fit in an SUV.

I watched through the dining room window the exodus of my neighbors. I had gone through the house and piled anything I thought I couldn't live without in boxes by the garage door. The irony of my father's case files from a murder investigation sitting on top of family memories was not lost on me.

"I bet I'm the only one on my block saving a case file from a murder investigation along with all their baby pictures."

"You have a place to stay till the fire's out?" asked Chief Chavez, who had arrived shortly after Harrison, when he heard of the evacuation notice.

"I have an extra bedroom," Harrison said.

I glanced at him and his eyes revealed nothing more than an offer of shelter.

"Good, I don't want you alone," Chavez said.

"I'll be fine. I can get a motel room."

Chavez shook his head. "If your brother and Williams were murdered because they were a threat to someone, then that means whoever continues that investigation is also in danger."

"Me, in other words," I said.

Chavez looked out the door at the line of flames a mile from the house and shook his head in disbelief. "Do you really believe it's possible your father is the one they are looking for?"

"You mean, do I believe my father could have murdered his own son?"

His eyes appeared to reveal a reluctance even to consider the question so directly.

"Eighteen years ago my father ripped open Jenny Roberts's blouse and dragged her across a stage floor by her ankle as she screamed for help. A month later she was murdered. Does that make him a murderer? I don't know. Until last night, all I knew of him were a few images on the TV."

Chavez looked at me for a moment, hesitant to say what he was thinking. "Maybe you should walk away from this."

I shook my head and looked over at my father's file.

"I've already done that for most of my life. For an instant I had a brother in this world reach out to me. If I walk away, I'll lose him again."

"I don't want you alone. You stay with Harrison."

He gripped my hand and then walked out to his

squad, parked on the street. The sun was fully over the San Gabriels now, though from the amount of light coming through the heavy smoke you would never know it.

"I heard someone who lost his house in a brush fire say that no one is as free as the person who has just lost everything," I said.

I turned and looked at Harrison. "You believe that?"

He shook his head. "That sounds like something to believe when you have no other choice."

Tiny embers carried on the wind began hitting the side of the house as firemen began to deploy their hoses, preparing to defend the block. I closed the front door and stood looking into my house. So much pain had happened here. How could it possibly matter if I lost it? I wondered.

Tears filled my eyes and I rushed into the kitchen, grabbed a paper bag, and began walking through the house picking up things that I thought needed saving—salt and pepper shakers from the dining room table, a refrigerator magnet, a drink coaster, a pen, a book that I had never read, a pair of shoes, clothes from Lacy's closet that she hadn't worn in years, her princess phone.

When the bag was full I sat down on Lacy's bed and held it like it was a newborn. Harrison walked in a moment later and sat next to me.

"I don't know what half the things in this bag are,"

I said. "I was trying to find something happy to remember . . . I don't know."

I looked out the window at the smoke streaming by.

"There was a prosecutor from the DA's office present at your father's questioning. You want to start there?" Harrison asked.

"Okay."

I quickly packed the boxes of family records into my Volvo, closed all the doors and windows, then drove away from my home of twenty years, not certain it would be there when I returned.

14

The lawyer with the DA's office who had been present at my father's interrogation eighteen years ago was now working as an investigator out of the Antelope Valley office, sixty miles north of L.A. on the edge of the high desert.

This was as far as you could get from the center of the city and still be within the county. Tract after tract of housing developments spread out in every direction where desert used to be. Lawns replaced tumbleweed. Ninety-minute commutes redefined the limits of community.

From the parking lot of the DA's offices you could see extinct cinder cones rising out of the sand to the north. To the south, the column of smoke from the fire threatening my house climbed thousands of feet into the air, dwarfing the San Gabriels.

Outside of a few desert rats and dirt bikers, no one

came to the high desert out of choice. You came because it was the last place you could afford, or you came for work. In every sense it was the end of the road before leaving L.A. entirely behind.

The investigators' windowless offices were on the ground floor, far from the views of the lawyers three and four floors up. Frank Cross met us in the hallway and walked us back to his small office. Cross was a large man, over six feet, powerfully built, though far from fit. Why a former lawyer for the DA's office was now working as an investigator I suspected had something to do with his presence here at the outer edge of the system. His eyes had the tired look of a traveler stuck in an airport with no hope of ever reaching his destination.

On a wall of the office was a marker board with a list of open cases. A quick glance suggested the majority of them were spousal abuse, hate crimes, and property theft. Not the stuff investigators' dreams are made of.

"Your call said you wanted to talk about the River Killer investigation?" Cross asked.

"A portion of it," I said. "You took part in the interrogation of the only suspect ever arrested."

Cross's dull eyes appeared to focus.

"Manning," he said without hesitation.

"You remember?"

The corners of his mouth turned as if he had stepped on something sharp. "Do you fish, Lieutenant?"

"No."

He looked at Harrison, who responded without hesitation. "The one that got away."

Cross nodded. "The one you never forget . . . no one forgets."

"Was there a reason you were at the interrogation?"

"I was a cop before I became a prosecutor."

Cross closed his right hand into a fist and flexed the muscles of his forearm. Then he got up from his desk and walked over and closed the door to the office.

"Victoria Fisher worked in my office. I demanded to be there."

"You knew her?" Harrison asked.

Cross nodded. "I didn't know her well. She was clerking for us during summer break from law school."

"What can you tell us about Manning?"

He started to answer then stopped. "Why is Pasadena PD interested in this?"

"We're investigating another crime that may be linked to the River Killings."

Cross stood up from his desk, started to walk across the room, then paused mid-stride. He put his hand on the back of his neck and began to massage the thick muscles. "He's alive, isn't he?"

I didn't answer.

"Manning's alive, that's why you're here?"

"We don't know that for certain," I said.

"But you think he's killed again, otherwise you wouldn't be here."

"Has anyone else questioned you about this recently?"

Cross looked at me suspiciously and shook his head. "You have someone in mind?"

"His son may have been investigating the River Killings and was possibly murdered."

"He didn't talk to me." Cross appeared to replay the words in his head several times. "My God, you want to know if I think it's possible he could kill his own son, don't you? That's why you're here?"

Cross walked over to a filing cabinet, pulled out a set of keys from his pocket, and unlocked the drawer. He rummaged through it for a moment, then removed a videotape.

"He's a monster. It's all here. You want an answer, all you have to do is look and listen."

He gripped the tape tightly, as if trying to protect it. "Who else have you talked to?"

"The detective who led the investigation."

"Hazzard?"

I nodded.

"No one else, no one from the DA's office? Not City Hall? You're very certain about this?"

"Just Hazzard," I said.

He stepped around his desk and gently set the tape and an envelope down in front of me. "You don't make a copy, and I want it back."

I agreed, then reached over and picked up the tape. I noticed Cross's eyes follow it until I slipped it safely into the envelope and closed it tight.

Outside a fine coating of sand from the desert covered my Volvo. I got in out of the wind and set the envelope with the tape of my father's interrogation on the seat next to me.

"Cross is in a windowless office. Why do I feel like he's still watching us?" I said. "He's afraid of something, and it isn't just this tape, otherwise he wouldn't have given it to us."

Harrison looked around as the blowing dust obscured the surrounding landscape. The tiny particles of sand hitting the windows began to sound like rain.

"A former DA who's now working as a low-end investigator on the edges of the county."

Harrison thought for a moment.

"Maybe he's afraid of falling completely off the map," Harrison said.

I picked up the envelope containing my father's interrogation tape. "Or being pushed."

15

On the day Victoria Fisher was murdered my father spent the afternoon rehearsing a play at a small theater on Santa Monica Boulevard. The street had changed little in the eighteen years since the murder. For a few hours every night a crowd of well-dressed theatergoers visit the half dozen or so small theaters in what is known as the theater district. When the stage lights are turned off, and the patrons retreat in their BMWs and Saabs, the street is taken back by transvestite prostitutes and crack junkies on the prowl for a fix.

An assistant to the director of the theater met us at the door and led us onto the stage, where we waited. It was a small auditorium that seated perhaps a hundred and fifty. I walked back to the wings. A door marked EMERGENCY EXIT was just twenty feet beyond the wings. A short hallway led to dressing rooms farther back past the stage manager's office.

I heard the sound of the director's voice greeting

Harrison and started back out through the wings, but froze. *This is the place*, I said silently to myself. I replayed the actress's words in my head. Her descriptions matched everything around me as if it had happened just days ago.

I looked out through the curtains. The light from a single spot illuminated the dark stage. I heard his voice in my head.

Take off your blouse.

I stepped onto the wood floor of the stage. As I reached center stage I realized it was here where his hand had come around and covered her mouth and he ripped open her shirt. When she stepped on his foot and he released her she would have started crawling stage left toward the steps that led up into the darkness of the seats. I looked over the boards of the stage. She would have gotten a dozen feet, no more, before he grabbed her ankle and started to drag her back. I knelt down and placed my hand on the wood. It was worn and marked from countless productions. I imagined she tried to find the smallest crack or raised seam to take hold of with her fingers and stop him, but there was nothing that would help.

"Lieutenant."

I looked up and Harrison and the theater director were standing at the front of the stage, looking at me.

"What is it exactly you want to know?" the director asked. His name was Moore. He looked to be nearing sixty and holding on for everything he was worth to his youthful looks.

I let my hand linger on the cool wood for another moment, then stood up.

"You were interviewed by the police eighteen years ago about an actor named Thomas Manning."

"I remember it very clearly."

"Why is that?"

"Because it was the last day I ever saw Tom. He vanished after that. I had to take over the acting class he was teaching."

I had never heard my father referred to as Tom; I couldn't even remember my mother ever using the name.

"He was accused of molesting several actresses?"

Moore nodded. "I didn't learn about those things until he vanished."

"Did you believe them?"

The director paused dramatically, as if it were written in stage directions and we were working on a scene.

"I believe Tom was capable of anything, including greatness."

"You liked him?"

He shook his head. "Envied his talent. The rest of him . . ."

"What?"

Moore looked over the stage as if replaying a moment in time. "With a look he could make you feel as if you were nothing."

"According to the arrest report, you were the last person who could corroborate his whereabouts on the night of the murder."

Moore shook his head. "No, he left the theater after class with one of his students, an actress."

Harrison looked over the notes he had taken from Hazzard's files, then shook his head. "There's no mention of that."

"I told the detective."

"You're sure?"

"Yes. I don't know if they went any farther together than the parking lot, but they walked out of here together."

"Do you know her name?" I asked

He thought for a moment, shook his head.

"I'll have to make some calls, see if anyone remembers."

Moore disappeared into an office and returned ten minutes later. "I think this is her, but no guarantees." He handed me a piece of paper with a name and address.

"Has anyone else talked to you about this recently?"

"No."

I handed Moore my card as we left, the picture of my father gaining more, if not better, detail.

"Doesn't make sense that Hazzard would have missed a detail like that," Harrison said.

"Moore could be right—maybe they didn't get any farther than the parking lot."

"You want to talk to Hazzard?"

"Not yet. If he left something out, let's find out if there was a reason."

I handed Harrison the paper with the name and address. "Let's talk to her first."

I glanced back toward Pasadena. The smoke from the fire that was threatening my house now completely obscured the mountains to the east.

"What time was it my father left here?"

Harrison checked his notes. "Shortly after seven."

"About the same time Victoria Fisher was starting dinner at the restaurant on Melrose."

"Two miles from here."

The address was a small bungalow in Eagle Rock just west of Pasadena. A boy of about ten was rushing down the steps of the house carrying a backpack to a sedan parked out front. As the car drove away his mother appeared at the front door, waved, then glanced in our direction before stepping back inside. Candice Fleming was or had been her name on the day she walked out of the theater with my father eighteen years before.

"Did you see that?" Harrison said.

I nodded; it was a look familiar to any cop, but not in this kind of a neighborhood, or from a woman in a robe sending a son on a sleepover.

"It looked like she made us," Harrison said.

I opened the door and stepped out. "She did make us, but why?"

We walked across the street and up the steps to the front door. It was a small Spanish home. A large arched window was barely visible behind a bougainvillea that had climbed up the front of the house. As I reached for the bell, the door opened and the woman appeared behind the barred security door.

"Why don't you leave me alone," she said before I could identify us. "I've answered all your questions. I've always . . ." She let the rest go.

I held up my ID.

"I think you've made a mistake," I said.

She stared at the ID for a moment and silently mouthed *Pasadena*.

"Candice Fleming?" I asked.

She looked at me for a moment, then nodded and smiled as if she were selling toothpaste or hair products. "I'm sorry, I thought you were real-estate agents."

"I'd like to ask you some questions," I said.

She hesitated for a moment, then unlocked the door. We followed her into the small kitchen, where she poured herself a glass of wine and sat at the kitchen table. I noticed there was no wedding band on her left hand. I guessed her age at about forty. If she was still acting, I doubted she had had much success.

"What is this about?" she asked.

"Eighteen years ago you took an acting class from a Thomas Manning."

She looked at me as if I had just thrown cold water on her face. "That was a long time ago. What do you want to know?"

"He was a suspect in a murder."

She nodded. "I remember."

"On the night of the murder you walked out of the theater with him after class. I'd like to know what happened."

"Nothing happened. I got in my car and went home. I told the police this years ago."

"And that was it? You didn't see him after that?"

"No. I got in my car and went home."

"Has anyone else asked you about this?"

She shook her head. "All I did was take a class. Is there something wrong with that?"

She glanced at her watch. "I really have to be somewhere," she said and walked back to the front door.

As we stepped out I hesitated in the doorway and held out a card to her.

"If you remember anything else about Thomas Manning, I'd like to talk to you about it."

She glanced at the card before slipping it from my fingers. "Why would I remember anything about him?"

She looked into my eyes for a moment, then closed the door. We walked back to the car and stopped before getting in.

"Why is she lying to us?" Harrison said.

I looked back at the house. Through the vines of the bougainvillea I thought I saw her standing in the window watching us. "She sounded like she's protecting someone."

"Or hiding from them." Harrison looked at me. "There's a big difference between the two."

I opened the car door. "Not to her."

I glanced at my watch. It was nearing seven. Just about the same time my father and Candice Fleming would have been walking out of the theater.

The restaurant Victoria Fisher had eaten at with colleagues from the DA's office had changed names and ownership at least three times. We drove up and down the block, as my father was supposed to have done when he searched for a victim. This stretch of Melrose was unchanged in that respect. For a predator stalking beautiful young women, it was a candy store.

Harrison pulled to a stop on the 800 block of Martel, and I stepped out.

"Her car was found about here," I said.

It was a residential street, lined with trees and one streetlight between where her car had been found and the walk she had taken from the restaurant.

"A block-and-a-half walk from Melrose and the restaurant," Harrison said. "People in these houses would be used to the noise of people heading to their cars after too much tequila. It would take something out of the ordinary for anyone to look outside. You could step out of a car, or from behind one of these trees, before someone could react."

"And if you had practiced, you would know how to control a victim so they couldn't make a sound," I said. "My father ripped open Jenny Roberts's blouse and dragged her across the floor of that stage."

Harrison looked at me.

"Practice," I said.

I took one more look down the block at the tree-lined sidewalk. Victoria would have had a few glasses of wine, and be feeling happy after a dinner with friends. As she reached for her car keys, she may have heard the sound of shoes on pavement, or seen the movement of a shadow across her path. It was over before she knew it.

I took a few steps down the sidewalk and closed my eyes to imagine the darkness she would have been in. The sensation of a hand closing over my mouth was suddenly as real as if it were actually happening.

"Are you all right?" Harrison said.

He placed his hand gently on my back where the bandage wrapped around my ribs and I flinched.

I nodded unconvincingly and walked back to the car and my boxes of possessions and a single arrest report that were possibly all I had left in the world.

"What is it?" Harrison asked.

I shook my head.

"I'm not sure," I said.

I had never felt a sensation like that before, yet something about it seemed familiar. I looked over to the sidewalk across the street. Had my father been here? Did the pavement hold some fragment of memory like the sandstone of a fossil bed? Was that what I had sensed?

"All Victoria Fisher wanted to do was go home and kiss her son good night."

16

Victoria Fisher's parents lived in the same house where they had raised their daughter, just east of Ventura Boulevard in Studio City. It was the kind of house that could have been used in a 1960s television show. A porch, a small white picket fence, a bed of roses, and a perfect lawn. The bougainvillea and a cactus along the property line were the only giveaways that we weren't in a small suburb in the Midwest.

Harrison rang the doorbell and a moment later a trim woman with short-cropped gray hair opened the door. She wore a light silk Japanese-style shirt and cotton pants that had grass stains on the knees. I guessed her to be in her mid sixties. I started to identify myself but there was apparently no need. A mother who loses a child to violent crime will forever know the look of a cop versus a civilian.

"Has something happened to Danny?" she said.

I shook my head and identified Harrison and myself.

"We're here to ask you a few questions about your daughter."

Even eighteen years after the crime, a cop saying she wanted to ask about her daughter still struck her like a physical blow. Mrs. Fisher's shoulders sagged for a moment and her clear eyes moistened. She took a breath and gathered her composure. "You're Pasadena police. I don't understand."

"We're investigating another crime that could be related your daughter's death."

She hesitated for a moment, as if not wanting to invite us, and the pain we brought along, back into her life, then she motioned us inside. The interior of the house held no traces of the tragedy that had marked the family. It was light and airy, as if it had come in one piece from the pages of *House & Garden*. If the inside of a house could wear a mask to hide its true identity, this was it. Scratch underneath the robin's-egg blue paint and no telling what one might find.

She walked us through to the country kitchen and offered us iced tea as we took our places around the kitchen table.

"What can I tell you that we didn't tell a dozen policemen hundreds of times?" she said.

"There may be nothing, but sometimes the smallest detail can mean more than anyone realizes."

She considered this for a moment as if weighing the emotional cost of reopening the past. I started to follow up, but she interrupted me.

"What other crime are you investigating?" she asked.

"Someone who may have been investigating the River Killings was killed."

"Killed—you mean murdered?"

"It's one possibility we're following," Harrison said.

Mrs. Fisher glanced out the window. "If this has anything to do with Danny, I'd prefer a lawyer to be present."

"Danny?"

"Your daughter's son?" Harrison said.

She nodded. "Our grand— My grandson. My husband died three years ago."

"Why did you ask if something had happened to him when you answered the door?" I asked.

"He's bipolar, has bouts of paranoia. His medicine helps, as long as he's taking it."

"And he's not taking it right now."

"I don't think so."

"Why do you think that?"

"He disappears, sometimes for weeks, then shows up in places and situations."

She let the details slip away as she looked out the window and shook her head. "Well, you can guess what it's like."

"I'm a mother, too," I said. "We're not here to investigate your grandson."

"Has he been violent to himself or others?" Harrison asked.

"Why do you ask that?"

"We can alert other departments to look for him if he's a danger to himself," I said.

She considered the question for a moment.

"He's threatened suicide, but never overtly acted on it that I'm aware of."

"What about others?"

"He struck out at his grandfather several times. On a couple of occasions he assaulted strangers on the street, but that's been several years. You have to understand, it's the illness, not him."

"You raised him after your daughter's death?" I asked.

She took a breath that seemed to carry eighteen years of pain with it. "We tried. Can you imagine losing your mother to violence as a child? How that would change everything? How do you trust a world that would do that to you?"

"What about his father?" I asked.

"She got pregnant with Danny while on a trip through Europe during college. If she knew him, she never said who he was."

Mrs. Fisher smiled, or nearly smiled. "She was a good mother; she didn't need anyone else."

"Victoria was working in the office of a prosecutor named Cross. Is that correct?" I asked.

She sat for a moment as if she hadn't heard me, then she finally nodded. "I'd like to know what the connection is between all this and my daughter before I answer anything else."

"The individual whose death we're investigating was named Manning."

The look in her eyes changed from one of loss to

that of a mother still protecting her child. "I know that name."

"This individual's father was questioned in your daughter's death."

"I remember," she said.

The name appeared to bring back a flood of memories that began to overwhelm her. She shook her head at one of them—or all of them—and got up from the table and stepped to the window looking out over the backyard.

I gave her a moment, then walked over and stood next to her. The yard was awash with flowers of every shape and color. I imagined it was her way of dealing with the ugliness that had taken so much of her life from her. At least in the thousand square feet of soil that she could control, there would be a perfect world.

"I'm not here to do anything that would harm your daughter's memory, Mrs. Fisher. She was a victim in this. I wouldn't betray that."

Her eyes remained straight ahead, though I doubt she was seeing anything other than the thoughts she was wrestling with.

"It never ends," she said softly.

"I know," I said.

She glanced at me and took a breath. "I'm not protecting my daughter, Lieutenant. The dead are the only ones who are truly free."

She walked over to the kitchen door and opened it. "I have to show you something."

She stepped out and started walking toward the

garage as Harrison and I followed. The garage had been converted into an apartment. And then I knew what she meant.

"It's your grandson you're protecting, isn't it?"

She nodded. "Yes." She took a key out of her pocket and unlocked the door. "We built this for him when he was in high school."

She opened the door, reached inside, and turned on the light. It was a simple room: a bed in one corner, an old overstuffed chair, TV, stereo. Then I saw it.

"Look at the walls," Harrison said. "Even the windows."

Every available inch inside the apartment was covered with photographs, newspaper clippings, and pages and pages of single-spaced notes.

"What is this?" Harrison said.

I shook my head and stepped over to one of the covered windows. I started to read one of the pages, but it was very nearly unintelligible, except for one thing.

"It's all about his mother," I said.

"Like a shrine," Harrison said.

"It's more than that," I said. "He's doing something else here."

I walked over to the wall next to the bed. A clipping from a *Los Angeles Times* article reported the arrest of a suspect for questioning in the River Killings, and then his release. My father's name wasn't mentioned.

"It started about a year ago," Mrs. Fisher said. "He said he began to receive messages from someone claiming to know the truth about who killed his mother. He referred to them as notes from the dark angel."

"What kind of messages? Phone calls? Letters?" I asked.

"I'm not sure."

"You never saw them?"

"You mean do I believe they really existed?"

I nodded.

Mrs. Fisher remained standing at the doorway as if stepping inside was too much of an emotional leap. "I don't know if they were real or not. Danny said he was told if anyone else ever saw them he would no longer receive help."

"To find his mother's killer?" I said.

"Yes. It became the sole focus of his life—his obsession."

I walked over to the back wall of the apartment. A crude curtain hanging from the ceiling reached nearly to the floor.

"Pull it back," Mrs. Fisher said.

I slid the curtain back and saw what had been hidden. A series of circles drawn in ever-greater size spread out from the center until they covered most of the wall. There were hundreds of lines, some connecting, some not. In places there was writing. In others what at first looked like an area blacked out was instead line after line of handwriting so minute I couldn't read it. Harrison stepped over next to me and stared in wonder.

"This is . . ." He let the words go.

"Madness," I whispered.

"It's drawn like a solar system, or a universe," Harrison said. "Planets intersecting the different orbits, lines connecting one planet to another. All of it spinning out in ever widening orbits from the center like it's the sun."

"It could also be a family tree of sorts, a genealogy chart. All starting from a central point of origin," I said. "Look what's written in it."

"City Hall."

Harrison studied it for a moment. "Cross asked us if we had talked to anyone at City Hall."

Around the central circle were drawn a series of smaller circles, with names written in them.

"Look at the name in the second circle," I said.

"Cross."

I turned to Mrs. Fisher, who hadn't moved from the doorway. Her eyes pleaded with mine before she looked away. Harrison reached out and touched my arm to draw my attention to the third ring out from the center, where a number of circles had been drawn.

"T. Manning," I whispered. "My father."

I followed the same orbit my father's name was on around to another circle, with another name drawn inside. "The Iliad." A reference to Homer?

"He could be equating his journey to Homer's epic," Harrison said. "Any way we look at it, this will take days to decipher. If we can understand it at all."

"We can understand this," I said, pointing to two

more circles drawn on successive rings out from my father's.

"The names of the two other River Killer victims," Harrison said.

I walked over to Mrs. Fisher. "Do you know how long he has been working on this?"

She shook her head. "I found it several months ago when he disappeared for a week. He could have been working on it for years. I just don't know," she said.

"How long has Danny been gone this time?" I asked.

"Three nights."

Harrison made eye contact with me to make note of the timing. Danny would have disappeared the night my brother died.

"This doesn't make Danny guilty of anything, Lieutenant," Mrs. Fisher said. "He just wants to know why he lost his mother. He wants his world to finally make sense, that's all. He's been lost his entire life."

"Someone else trying to do the same thing may have been killed because of it," I said.

"Are you saying Danny's in danger?"

"It's something we have to consider."

She stared at the wall for a moment, trying to connect the various dots.

"I always assumed this was about the illness. I hated it because it was taking my grandson from me. And now you tell me this may be real." She shook her head in disbelief.

"I was prepared for any of the possibilities except that one," she whispered.

She reached up and wiped a tear from the corner of her eye, then stepped outside and sat on a bench next to the door. Harrison and I stood in front of the massive drawing for a moment in silence.

"Whatever the rest of this means, the one thing that's clear is where it begins," Harrison said.

"City Hall."

"The source of all evil in his universe," Harrison said. "Something happened there."

"Or he believes it did," I said.

"I wonder what Cross believes," Harrison said.

"We'll need a copy of this," I said, "and a watch put on the house in case Danny comes back."

Harrison nodded. I stepped closer to the drawing and looked at the small circle with my father's name in the center of it. *Were his secrets concealed in the labyrinth of lines and orbits covering this wall? Or did this take him even farther from me?*

"It's like trying to read a language that's never been written down before," I said.

Harrison stepped up next to me and wondered at its mad logic. "Until we can penetrate the drawing's code, none of this may make sense. Even then it may just be the ramblings of a paranoid manic depressive, making connections where there are none."

"It could also be someone with a dark angel," I said.

"If that dark angel exists at all."

"My brother and Detective Williams are dead," I said. "We have to assume that somewhere in this must be a sliver of truth."

Harrison's eyes began to follow the lines on the wall as if they were wires on one of the explosives he used to disarm on the bomb squad.

"There may be only two people in the world who can make sense of all this. One is a paranoid . . . the other apparently dropped from the heavens," Harrison said.

"I doubt the maker of this will trust anyone enough to share his secrets," I said.

Harrison nodded in agreement.

"So how do you find an angel?" he asked.

"You don't," I said. "They find you."

17

It was after dark when Harrison and I left Danny Fisher's garage and started back to Pasadena. Two uniformed officers were watching the house in case Fisher returned. A crime-scene investigator had photographed the drawing, section by section, so it could be pieced together into a full-size mosaic. The hundreds of papers tacked to the walls and scattered across the floor had been boxed and taken to headquarters. So far, there was no proof that Danny's "dark angel" existed.

If somewhere in those lines and orbits drawn on that wall Danny disclosed the identity of the River Killer, we didn't find it. The only thing I was certain of was that the world I knew so well just forty-eight hours before had begun to resemble the confused nightmare of Danny's map.

As we rounded the bend over the arroyo just west of downtown Pasadena I looked north toward the foothills where I lived. Where the lights of houses normally sparkled in the distance there was only the odd spot of orange flame in the darkness.

"Jesus," Harrison whispered.

I reached for my cell phone but stopped myself. Even if my house was still there, the surrounding phone and power lines would be down or gone completely. Making a call would do little good.

"I need to see if my house is still there," I said.

We exited at Fair Oaks and headed up toward the hills. Six blocks from my house two squads blocked the road. I recognized the patrol sergeant and he waved us through. A block farther on we passed the last streets that still had power and drove into the darkness.

There were no other cars moving, no people on lawns or sitting on front steps. Down a side street I saw the unmistakable shape of a horse standing in the middle of the street. Down another, the flashing lights of a fire chief's car cut through the dark and then disappeared.

At the bottom of Mariposa, Harrison stopped the car and I stepped out. Partly burned fire hoses were stretched across the street, still attached to the hydrant. Debris littered the streets as in the aftermath of a battle—roof tiles, wood, paper, puddles of waterlogged ash, a partly melted plastic lawn toy, the burned remains of a shoe. Somewhere in the dark I could hear the sound of a sprinkler spraying water with the steady beat of a metronome.

I walked out into the middle of the street and looked

up the sloping ivy-covered banks to where my neighbors' houses lined the street. In the darkness not a single silhouette of a roofline was visible.

"They're gone," I said. "All of them."

Harrison stepped up beside me.

"It could be different up at your end of the block," he said.

"Yes, it could be worse," I said.

I tried to take a breath but the air held a bitter taste that was different from the smoke of the morning.

"A lot of chemicals have been off-gassed," Harrison said.

"It's more than that," I said.

It was as if the air now held all that was lost in each of those houses. All the dreams, all the failures, all the moments that no one remembers that make up a single day, week after week, year after year. Like the phantom pains of an amputee, I could feel the missing homes' presence as surely as if they were still standing.

"The earth moves, the hills burn. Young mothers are murdered and twenty years later a son goes mad trying to understand why," I said. "And every year more people keep coming here thinking California is the promised land."

I looked at Harrison for a moment. "Damn this place."

I turned and started back to the car when my cell phone rang. It was Chief Chavez.

"The mother of Hector Lopez says he wants to turn himself in to you."

"The Western Union clerk?"

"Yeah. He must be afraid LAPD is going to kill him if he's caught by them."

"He's probably right," I said.

"His mother said he told you he didn't do it. He was just scared, that's why he hit you. He wants to prove it by surrendering to you. You believe him?" Chavez asked.

"He didn't kill Detective Williams. Where do I pick him up?"

"There's a Ralph's grocery store on Figueroa in Highland Park."

"I know it," I said. It was less than twenty minutes from where Harrison and I were standing.

"Park in the south corner of the parking lot. He sees that you're alone, he drives up and surrenders."

"Fine."

"I told her you wouldn't be alone."

"What did she say?" I asked.

"No. You're either alone, or no deal."

"So I do it alone."

"That's not going to work," Chavez said.

"There are two people who can identify my brother's killer: Dana Courson and Hector Lopez."

"We still haven't found Dana," Chavez said.

"I need Lopez, and I need him before LAPD gets him."

"That's what I thought you'd say," Chavez said. "Lopez will be there in an hour. We'll put a wire on you, and I'll have three units within five seconds of you."

"He's a Western Union clerk, not a cop killer," I said.

"Until he's in cuffs in the back of your car, he's both."

We agreed on a meeting place several blocks from the Ralph's, where I could be fitted with a wire, and then I hung up.

"Lopez?" Harrison said.

I nodded and looked back up Mariposa into the darkness where my house either did or didn't stand any longer.

"You want to drive up, take a look?" Harrison asked.

I shook my head.

"Whether it is or isn't there, I have a feeling it's already been drawn on Danny Fisher's map."

A few wisps of flame suddenly flared up in the darkness and then just as quickly died.

"Maybe everything has."

18

It was nearing ten o'clock when Harrison finished attaching the mike and transmitter. We were two blocks from the Ralph's, on a side street next to the 110 freeway. Three teams from tactical were already in position in unmarked cars within eyesight of the parking lot where I was supposed to pick Lopez up.

"This is a line-of-sight mike. You go anywhere we can't see you, we won't hear you," Harrison said.

"He's due in the parking lot in ten minutes. You should go," Chavez said.

I nodded and started walking over to the squad with the chief and Harrison in tow.

"The smallest thing doesn't feel right, you call us in," Chavez said.

I looked at Chavez and smiled. "Yes, Dad."

"Lopez gets out of his car, walks up to your passenger side, and puts his hands over his head. You get out and cuff him, that's the deal. He knows it, anything different . . ."

"I call you in."

"And get the hell out of there," Chavez said.

"He's not a killer."

"Humor me," Chavez said.

I smiled at him. "I always do."

Chavez drew a heavy breath, just as he had on every call we had made together for the last twenty years. The only difference was now I could see the cost of those breaths in the deep worry lines in his face, the graying of his hair, and the doubt that now resided just under the surface of his eyes where years before there had been only confidence.

"Remember, he walks to the passenger side, hands above his head," Chavez said.

"I remember," I said.

Chavez stood motionless for a moment as if searching for a reason to call it off, then nodded and walked away. I got in the squad car and Harrison stepped up next to the passenger window.

"You get the photograph out of my box of things?" I asked.

Harrison nodded and handed me the small photograph of my father I had taken from my brother's apartment.

"If Lopez recognizes him, that's it," I said.

"It's an old picture. You said it yourself, you might not recognize your father if he passed you on the street."

"Unless we find that surveillance tape from the Western Union office, it's all we have."

"I imagine that tape doesn't exist anymore," Harrison said.

"Then I hope Lopez says he's never seen this man in his life," I said.

I pulled out onto Figueroa and started driving the two blocks south to Ralph's. There were no Gaps or Starbucks along this stretch of road. Late-night worshippers from a botanica, the men in their best jeans and boots and the women in fresh white dresses, spilled onto the sidewalk. The smoke from a taco stand filled the air with the sweet scent of grilled chicken spiced with lime and peppers. This was the competing turf of two Hispanic street gangs. Graffiti tagged buildings and street signs. Every young man walking the street carefully watched me pass with the practiced eye of a combat soldier whose survival depended on his ability to see and understand everything around him.

"Test your mike," Harrison said into my earpiece.

"Do we know what kind of car he'll be in?" I asked.

"The mother wasn't sure."

The parking lot of the grocery store was less than half filled, cars spread randomly throughout. I turned into the lot and pulled over to the southern corner and waited. A few shoppers were pushing carts of groceries to their cars. Several young men who I imagined were gang members stood in the shadows next to the store, keeping an eye on their turf. A rusty van parked half a dozen spaces away from me was the closest vehicle.

Metro rail crossing gates stood open on the side street just behind the store.

I checked my watch. Lopez should be pulling up within the next five minutes.

"There's a car pulling in," Harrison said. "A brown Ford, single male Hispanic driving."

I followed it in my mirror as it passed behind me and continued on toward the front of the store.

"It's nothing," I said.

I looked around for the backup vehicles carrying our tactical teams. I made one parked across Figueroa. The second was in an alley directly across from me at the corner of an apartment building.

"Where's the third unit?" I asked.

"The north end of the parking lot," Harrison said.

The gates on the metro rail began to close and the warning bells began chiming.

"There's a train coming," I said.

"Say again," Harrison said.

"A train."

"Did you say train?"

"Yes."

The rumble of the approaching engine became audible over the clanging of the warning bells.

"Can you hear me over that?" I asked.

"Say again," Harrison said.

The train sounded its horn as it approached the intersection.

"Are you getting this?" I said.

Harrison didn't respond.

"Can you . . ." I started to say, then I saw movement in my rearview mirror. He appeared to be Hispanic, and was carrying a small brown paper bag at his side.

The train sounded its horn, blocking out all other sound, and the ground began to shake ever so slightly.

"I got movement behind me," I said, though I couldn't hear my own words.

The figure walked around the side of my car and stopped ten feet from my passenger window. In the darkness I could barely make out his features, but I could see enough to know it was Lopez. His lips moved but I couldn't hear the words over the sound of the train's horn.

"Put down the paper bag," I said as I stepped out of the squad with my hand on my Glock.

Lopez shook his head as if he didn't hear me. I pointed to the bag in his hand.

"Put it down and raise your hands," I said.

He nodded and I saw the flash of a smile. He started to bend over to put the bag down when the doors of the rusty van twenty feet away flew open and I saw dark uniformed figures rushing out.

"No," I yelled, but Lopez was already reacting.

"Drop to the ground," I shouted just as the train sounded its horn again.

Lopez glanced at me and began to turn toward the figures pouring out of the van. As he turned the paper bag fell out of his right hand and I saw the shine of silver.

"No," I started to yell when the first muzzle flash erupted in the darkness, followed quickly by three more. Lopez stood motionless for a brief second, then collapsed to the ground like a puppet whose strings had just been cut.

The sound of the train passed and I heard a mockingbird shriek in the distance. The odor of spent gunpowder hung in the air. One of the LAPD SWAT team approached Lopez on the ground with his weapon raised to the shoulder, ready to fire. I stepped around the back of my squad holding my badge out yelling, "Police, I'm police!"

"Clear!" yelled the lead man standing over Lopez.

On the pavement a few feet from Lopez was the silver can of beer he had been holding in his hand inside the paper bag. I rushed over to Lopez as the screech of tires seemed to come from every direction.

"We need a paramedic," I yelled, forgetting that I was wired.

Our tactical teams rushed up and surrounded us with their weapons drawn, not exactly sure what had just gone down. Within seconds of their arrival more LAPD units began pouring into the parking lot.

I heard someone say, "A beer, a goddamn beer."

Another voice said, "I saw a gun."

Lopez was lying on his back, one of his legs bent at the knee underneath him. His eyes held a look of astonishment, staring straight up toward the sky. On the front of his blue shirt four circular bloodstains were growing into one larger stain. I quickly patted him down. There was no weapon, no phone, not even keys in a pants pocket.

"Can you hear me?" I asked him.

He took a short, clipped breath and his eyes focused on my face.

"Do you remember the tape the policeman took from you?"

He blinked and I saw something approaching recognition in his eyes.

"Tell me what was on it," I said.

His chest heaved as he struggled to take a breath. I reached over and took hold of his hand.

"You're going to be okay. Do you understand?" I said.

Lopez's grip tightened ever so slightly around my hand. His eyes found mine and instantly I knew he understood I was lying to him.

"Did the officer who took the tape give you a name?" I asked.

His lips moved but he didn't make a sound. Then I felt one of his fingers gently tap my hand.

"Pow . . ." he whispered. "Pow . . . l . . . l."

He silently mouthed the name again, then his fingers gently lost all tension in my hand.

"Powell?" I said to him.

His eyes struggled to focus before darting upward and staring at the sky. I put my fingers on his neck to feel for the rhythm of his pulse, but there was only stillness.

"We need a paramedic now," I yelled.

I quickly placed my hands on his chest and began to put my weight into the compressions.

"Step away, Officer," a voice said from behind me.

"We need a paramedic!" I yelled.

"Step away now, Officer."

Out of the corner of my eye I saw Harrison step through the tactical team that surrounded me and kneel next to Lopez's head.

"I'm not getting a pulse," I said.

Harrison placed a hand on Lopez's neck as I continued compressions. After a moment he looked at me and shook his head. "There's too much damage."

I did two more compressions then stopped. Lopez's entire shirtfront was covered in blood.

"Step away now," said the same voice.

I turned and looked at the source of the voice, a man about fifty, dark suit, crisp white shirt, blue tie, a nickel-plated 9mm in a speed holster on his belt that matched the color of his hair.

"I'm Lieutenant Pearce, Robbery Homicide. This is our scene," he said. "I have paramedics on the way."

I rose to my feet and started toward him but Chief Chavez stepped between us.

"You're goddamn right it's your scene," I said. "Your men just killed a man armed with a can of beer. Do you know what you've done?"

"Alex," Chief Chavez said, his eyes catching mine just long enough to break the spell of the violence that had erupted. "Walk away," he said softly. "Just walk away."

I turned and looked at the LAPD SWAT team that had done the shooting. Three were huddled together in conversation; the fourth was sitting in the open door of the van, staring straight ahead, smoking a cigarette.

"His mother trusted us," I said, but none of them so much as looked in my direction. In their minds they had just gunned down a cop killer.

Chavez gently squeezed my arm and I turned and looked at him.

"We need to get your hands cleaned up."

I glanced at them and saw that they were stained with Lopez's blood.

"There's nothing else we can do right now," Chavez said. "We'll do everything we can to make this right."

I looked back at Lopez lying on the pavement, his eyes quickly dulling with death, staring up at an unseen sky.

"How do we make up for this?" I whispered.

I glanced back at two of the SWAT team members as they bumped congratulatory fists, then as I turned to walk away, I saw a face in an unmarked LAPD squad pulling away.

"What is it?" Chavez asked.

I watched the squad until it was out of sight, trying to be certain I recognized the face.

"Hazzard," I said. "Hazzard was in that squad."

19

It took an hour to drive from Highland Park to Harrison's small house on a rise in Santa Monica. I had passed on driving back up into the foothills to see if my home was still standing. It seemed oddly unimportant now.

We should have known that LAPD would be tapping Lopez's mother's phone. We should have known they would be there. And he should still be alive. Had Hazzard played me to get information that would help to find Lopez?

I had tried closing my eyes on the drive but each time I did I heard the shots echo in my head, and I saw Lopez crumple to the ground.

Harrison walked out onto the small deck that looked out toward the Pacific and handed me a glass of wine. The inland heat had given way to a cool ocean breeze on the coast. The sliver of the crescent moon was just cutting into the horizon out past Catalina.

"Every time I close my eyes I hear those shots, I see him fall. I didn't do my job very well tonight."

"You didn't kill him."

"I didn't save him, either. Hazzard played us. He gave us those files, and we handed him Lopez."

"Hazzard was Robbery Homicide. Most of those guys still carry their shield and weapon after they retire. He bleeds LAPD blue. We couldn't have done anything differently."

"We could have been smarter."

Harrison let the silence settle over us for a moment.

"Lopez said something to you, didn't he?" he asked.

I took a sip of wine and nodded.

"I asked him if the cop who took the tape gave him a name. I think he said 'Powell.'"

"Does that mean anything to you?"

"I think so, but I don't know why," I said.

I stepped back into the small living room that was furnished as sparsely as a classic Japanese wood-and-paper house from the nineteenth century. Bamboo floors, a few simple pieces of furniture. It had the feel of a sanctuary more than a house. A retreat from the world of cops and all that comes along with it.

On the mantel over the fireplace was a photograph of Harrison and his young wife looking into a camera held at arm's length. They were both smiling broadly, frozen for a perfect moment in time before her murder shattered Harrison's world. It was the first time I had ever seen her picture. She had shoulder-length jet-black hair, an Asian face that I guessed was Japanese.

Harrison stepped inside and I turned away from the photograph, feeling like an intruder. He walked over next to me, his eyes on the picture as I looked back out toward the ocean.

"Her parents met at Manzanar during the war."

"The relocation camp in the Owens Valley?"

Harrison nodded. "Her family lost their businesses, homes, everything."

He stared at the photograph for a moment, leaving another memory unsaid. "Her marrying a white guy was a challenge for her parents. Then their only daughter was murdered, and I couldn't even bring her killer to justice."

I started to reach out to touch Harrison's face but stopped myself. His eyes were far away, still wrestling with a past, torn apart by violence, that hadn't yet been pieced fully back together.

"You're a good man," I said softly.

"You would think that would matter, but it doesn't," he said.

"It did to your wife."

His eyes met mine and held them as gently as if I were being cradled in two arms. Without realizing I was doing it, I took a step toward him, and then it hit me.

"My God," I said in astonishment.

"What?" Harrison asked.

"Powell," I whispered.

Harrison looked at me for a moment. "The name Lopez said?"

"The officer who took the tape."

I ran it through my memory several times, trying to prove to myself that I was wrong. But each time I did, it became clearer, like a home movie coming into focus.

"It means something to you, doesn't it?" Harrison said.

I nodded, then stepped out onto the deck into the cool night air. Over the horizon the moon slipped out of sight into the ocean. The only light on the Pacific was a cruise ship lit up like a Christmas tree floating in the darkness.

Harrison walked up behind me.

"What is it?" he asked.

"Powell was the name of the cop my father played in the horror movie," I said.

"You're sure?"

I nodded. "What are the chances that someone would know the name of a character who's on-screen less than five minutes in an obscure B monster movie?"

"Not very good," Harrison said.

"I keep hoping that somehow he's dead, and all this can be explained another way, but every time that seems plausible, something happens to pull it back to the one obvious truth: He's alive, and he wants me to know it's him."

I caught a wisp of movement over my head—a bat hunting insects. I looked up and saw dozens of them darting through the darkness like pieces of crepe paper swirling in the wind.

"What does he want?" I said.

"I don't know." Harrison placed a throw over my shoulders, his hands resting gently on me for a moment.

"The tape," I said. I had forgotten about it.

Harrison shook his head.

"From Cross—the interrogation. I need to see it."

"Maybe it would be better to let it go for a few hours," he said.

"How do you do that?"

Harrison smiled gently. "I wouldn't know."

Harrison slipped the tape into the VCR but hesitated for a moment before he hit play.

"Do you want to be alone with this?" he asked.

I shook my head. "I can tell you what a policeman fighting a Cyclops sounds like, or an Indian who falls in love with a white girl, but I haven't heard his voice since I was a child. I need you to remember the things I might be reluctant to, or unable to, hear."

Harrison promised he would, then stepped back from the TV and pressed play on the remote. The screen was filled with electric noise for a moment, and then I heard the sound of a mike being rustled and the voices of several detectives uttering words I couldn't understand.

The image on the screen flickered and settled into a static, unmoving shot. At a table in a stark white interrogation room, a man sat looking at something or someone just off camera.

"State your name," said a voice that could have been Hazzard, though I wasn't certain.

The man at the table turned slightly away from where his questioner must have been sitting and looked directly into the camera.

"Thomas Manning," he said.

It wasn't the voice I remembered from television, but I knew it just the same. An octave lower maybe, less assured. It was the voice or a piece of the voice I had heard in dreams. The good looks that had fueled his ambition had faded, but his hair was still dark, his eyes as penetrating as pieces of coal on a field of white.

The off-screen detective asked if he had been read and understood his rights and my father acknowledged that he had.

"Did you murder Victoria Fisher?"

My father didn't hesitate. "No."

"Did you kidnap and murder Jenny Roberts?"

"No."

"Did you strangle Alice Lundholm and leave her body on the banks of the river?"

"I've done none of those things."

"You did rip open Jenny Roberts's blouse and drag her across the stage at the Players Theater."

"We were rehearsing a scene; that was part of it. She became frightened. I can show you the script."

"A month after that she was murdered."

"Not by me."

"You asked Alice Lundholm to take off her blouse?"

"She came on to me. It happens all the time in the theater. Some people are unable to turn emotions off after intense work."

He said the words with the practiced ease of an actor playing the same part in a long-running play.

"Why did your first wife file a restraining order against you?" Hazzard asked.

"You'll have to ask her."

"Did you abuse her?"

Every muscle in my father's body seemed to stiffen. He looked away from the camera and glared at his questioner. I knew the look. I had seen it in my dream the other night when he was standing in the hallway of our house holding my mother by her throat.

"As is my right, I'll wait for my lawyer to arrive before I answer—"

Hazzard cut him off: "What did you do to your wife?"

My father looked away from his questioner and down at his hands.

"In one year she made three trips to the emergency room. Why was that?"

The camera zoomed in for a close-up of his face as question after question began to fly.

"What did you do to her?"

He said nothing.

"Did you beat her?"

Silence.

"You twisted her arm, causing bruising . . ."

The list kept growing.

"You hit her . . . you choked her by the neck . . . you threw her against a wall . . ."

He didn't react. It was as if he had stepped into another room and was no longer hearing his interrogator's words. My father closed his eyes and began to lower his head.

"What did you do to your daughter, Mr. Manning?"

My father froze.

"Your daughter?"

He slowly lifted his head and glared into the lens.

"What did you do to her?"

The blackness of his eyes seemed barely able to contain the rage let loose inside. And then just as quickly it seemed to pass.

"I loved her," he said softly.

The questions continued but I didn't hear them. I don't know what else, if anything, he said, or what details he was asked. A minute passed, another, maybe ten, I wasn't sure. When I looked at the screen again, there was only static. Harrison walked over and turned it off.

"I'm not . . ." I started to say but couldn't finish the sentence. I got up from the chair and walked back out into the cool night. Where there had been lights from ships out on the ocean, now there was only darkness. Harrison stepped up behind me but didn't say a word.

"I think I missed some of that," I said. "Did you hear it all?"

"Yes."

"Did they . . . Did my father give any more answers after he spoke of me?"

"No, he didn't say a word. Hazzard kept asking questions until Gavin arrived."

Harrison picked up the throw and placed it over my shoulders again.

"What do you think?" I asked.

"I don't think a child should ever hear a parent in that situation."

"Do you believe him . . . my father?"

"That he loved you . . . yes, I believe that."

"What about the rest?"

Harrison shook his head. His hands pulled me against his chest and I could feel his heart beating against my back.

"I don't know," Harrison said.

"When we were on Martel where Victoria vanished, I had this sense that . . ."

"What?"

"I'm not sure how to say this without sounding like a frightened little girl instead of a Homicide lieutenant."

"You don't have to prove anything to me," Harrison said.

"Standing on that sidewalk I felt a hand close on my mouth. . . . I think it's possible I was my father's first victim."

I felt Harrison's chest rise against my back as he took a breath.

"He denied hurting you."

"He said he loved his daughter; that's not the same thing."

I started to turn to look at Harrison but I couldn't.

"And if he did something to his own daughter, is it such a leap for him to have murdered three women?"

A gust of warm wind blowing out toward the ocean swept across us. For a brief second the air held the scent of jasmine, but it didn't last.

"You should get some sleep," Harrison said.

"How?" I whispered.

I reached for Harrison's hand but it had already slipped from my shoulder.

20

The sound of gunshots jarred me out of sleep. It had been the same all night long. Four quick pops in succession, again and again and again. There was nothing else to the dream. Not Lopez's face, no muzzle flashes, no circles of blood on his shirt.

I was lying on the daybed wrapped in the blanket Harrison had placed over my shoulders. The light of dawn was just breaking in the east. I realized the sound I had thought was another gunshot was the ringing of my cell phone in the pocket of my jacket. I pulled the blanket around me and answered.

"This is Frank Cross," a man said. "You came to my office."

It took a moment to connect the voice with the investigator on the edge of the high desert.

"Yes," I answered.

"Have you looked at the tape?"

"Yes."

"It's not the whole story. There's more, much more. Can you meet me?"

"When?"

"Now."

"Yes, I can meet you."

"How far are you from the beach?"

"I'm in Santa Monica."

"At the bottom of Sunset there's beach parking. Park there and start walking south on the sand. When I see that you're alone, I'll meet you."

I started to ask a question but he was gone. I gathered my things and walked into Harrison's bedroom. In the half-light I could just make out the contours of his body under the white sheet. I started to take a step toward the bed to tell him that I was leaving, but stopped and left him to sleep.

It was just past five-thirty when I pulled into the parking lot at PCH and Sunset. A marine layer of clouds had shrouded the ocean in thick fog. There were half a dozen cars parked in the lot. Joggers were moving up and down the running path next to the beach.

I stepped out and walked to the edge of the lot overlooking the water. The air was heavy with the scent of brine and decaying matter. To the north the beach looked deserted, covered in places by a layer of drying kelp and tiny orange crustaceans that had been caught on the beach by the tide. To the south a few figures either walked or jogged along the expanse of dark gray water. I stepped over the parking barrier, slipped off my shoes, and began walking south.

I walked for ten minutes, stopping every few to look around, but there was no sign of Cross. I tried to replay Cross's words in my head, thinking I might have missed something, but each time I did I drifted instead to the night before, the touch of Harrison's hands on my shoulders, the beating of his heart against my back.

By the time I had followed him back inside he was asleep in bed. I sat and watched him—the rise and fall of his chest, the line of his leg under the sheet, the bend of his wrist and the curve of his fingers. Half a dozen times I stood up from the chair to slip into bed next to him, and each time I stopped myself, a voice in my ear whispering, "Don't go there." So I just watched him a little longer, telling myself that was enough. And each time I knew it wasn't.

Half a mile down the beach several figures were standing in a tight group staring at the water's edge. I picked up my pace, and as I drew closer I saw they were looking at something lying in the surf. Fifty yards out I could see a figure being rolled by a small wave.

As I reached the group, one of them turned to me. "It's dead," the woman said.

It was the remains of a large seal partly wrapped in kelp. A large open wound was visible on its back where a shark had struck. One of its big dark eyes stared ahead like a piece of glass.

I glanced at the other faces looking at the seal but Cross wasn't there. Farther down the sand the beach was deserted. To the north I saw a lone woman jogger. The others looking at the seal began to drift away and I waited for a few more minutes for any sign that Cross would appear. At six o'clock I started walking the mile back, trying to guess what he wanted to talk about on a deserted beach at dawn, and why he hadn't come.

I reached the parking lot and brushed the sand off my feet. There were a few more cars in the lot than when I had arrived. A surfer stood looking at the water as if he knew something the rest of us didn't.

I got in my car and sat looking at the gray water disappearing into the fog offshore. I had never understood people who found peace looking at the ocean. It always made me nervous—a repository of secrets. Not unlike the body of a homicide victim. You can understand how they died. You can do all the work of a cop and know the precise angle of entry, the caliber of the round, why the blood splatter had this pattern as opposed to another, or which blow, or stab wound, caused the fatal injury. But you can never know what they saw, or how fast they were breathing in panic, or what or who they thought about the moment before their death.

As I put the key in the ignition, a hand reached in the open window and took hold of the wheel. Cross was dressed in sweat clothes, the hood of a sweatshirt pulled over his head. His eyes, or rather the look in them, didn't appear to belong to the same person I had met in his office. There was panic in his eyes, maybe even fear. He walked over and sat on the guardrail overlooking the ocean and I followed.

I sat on the railing and waited for him to tell me why we were there. For nearly a minute he just stared out at the water.

"I knew Victoria Fisher," he said. "She worked in my office."

I wasn't certain whether he had forgotten that I knew this, or if there was more he was hinting at.

"I know that," I said.

Cross turned and looked at me from under the hood of his sweatshirt. He looked as if he hadn't slept in days.

"You have to understand the risk I'm taking, how you could be putting yourself, your career, at risk."

"You said on the phone that the tape wasn't the entire story."

He nodded and waited for a jogger to pass before he continued. "What do you know about me?"

"You were a cop, then a prosecutor, and now you're working as an investigator for the DA."

"On the edge of oblivion," he said. "Does that seem like an odd career path to you?"

I nodded. "I did wonder."

"I was a rising star in the office. There was talk that I might be the next DA of Los Angeles. That's a long way from Palmdale."

"And then a law clerk in your office was murdered by the River Killer."

"So goes the official account."

"What's the unofficial?" I asked.

"Two days before she died, Victoria Fisher was putting some court briefs together. Part of that day she spent in records. I think she found something that was a great threat to some very powerful people and she was killed for it, and it was made to look like the work of the River Killer."

"How do you know she found something?"

"She told me about it the day of her death."

"What did she find?"

Cross shook his head. "She was going to meet me the next day before work. She was killed that night."

"And you have no idea what it was she found?"

"California is the fifth largest economy in the world, Los Angeles its center, City Hall the keeper of its secrets. I've come close. For eighteen years I've been looking, and every time I sensed the truth was near, I was pushed away, my career in shambles."

"You have any proof of this?"

He shook his head. "Not a single document, no witnesses. Just the silence of a dead law student. Perfect in its conception."

"And difficult to believe," I said.

Cross looked at me and nodded. "When I was in uniform my patrol partner was Len Hazzard."

"I didn't know that."

"Why did Hazzard go on to become an elite detective in Robbery Homicide while I ended up chasing down bail skips and lizards in the high desert?"

"There could be any number of reasons," I said.

"True enough."

"If this is as complete a conspiracy as you say, how do you know I'm not a part of it?" I said.

"You're not LAPD."

"There are other agencies you could talk to. Why trust me?"

"Because someone in another agency isn't the daughter of the only suspect ever questioned in the murder."

The intricate circles and intersecting orbits of Danny Fisher's madness seemed for a moment like the simple lines of a road map, drawn with perfect clarity.

"You know who I am?"

"I was a good cop, an even better lawyer. We both want the same thing, Lieutenant. The truth."

"Do you know about Danny Fisher?"

Cross pulled back the hood of his sweatshirt and nodded.

"He's been missing for four days," I said.

"He's a mixed-up kid. It's not the first time he's run off; that could be about anything."

"Do you believe my father killed Victoria Fisher?"

He shook his head. "You tell me."

"I don't know," I said.

Twenty yards offshore a pod of dolphins broke the surface with their dorsal fins, chasing a school of small fish that began leaping out of the water, trying to escape their attack. Cross watched them intently for a moment in silence.

"They can leap into the air where they can't

breathe, or they can stay and be eaten. Not much of a choice."

I wondered if he was talking about the fish, or himself, or even my father. Cross pulled the hood of his sweatshirt back over his head and stood up.

"Help me," I said.

Cross just stared out at the gray water. "I can't even help myself, Lieutenant."

He started down toward the beach.

"Danny Fisher told his grandmother that he was getting messages from someone about his mother's death. He called that person his 'dark angel,'" I said.

Cross stopped and looked back at me.

"Danny makes things up. Be smart, Lieutenant. Walk away from it, as fast as you can."

I turned at the sound of screeching tires and a blaring car horn on PCH. When I looked back, Cross was down on the beach, running south along the water, disappearing into the fog.

21

I replayed the conversation as best I could for Harrison, but it did little to settle my uneasiness. If I was to believe in Cross's conspiracy theories, then I might as well accept as fact that Danny Fisher's tormented map could also be just as real. And if I bought into that, then all my years as a cop meant nothing.

But even if all the things Cross said were true, it still left three young women strangled to death along the river, my brother and a cop murdered, and my father the only possible connection to all of them.

Was Hazzard a piece of the puzzle, as Cross had implied? Did that explain his presence at Lopez's death? Or was he just a loyal officer taking part in a hunt for the killer of a fallen brother, even a misguided one?

Whichever answer was closer to the truth, the message Chief Chavez received overnight from Hazzard requesting the return of all LAPD files in my possession did little to clarify it either way.

As Harrison pulled off the 101 I could see a column of smoke rising in the distance from the fire that had passed through Hazzard's neighborhood days before and was now slowly moving into the Santa Monica Mountains. A few police barricades still blocked off streets where houses had been lost. A row of destroyed palm trees stood like thirty-foot-tall black embers.

The fire had moved through like a large hand spreading out over the landscape—a finger of flame stretching that way, another this way. Where one house was lost, the one right next to it stood intact.

On Hazzard's street a few trees and power lines had been singed, but no houses appeared to have been damaged. But the fire had left its mark, nonetheless. As the residents fled the flames, it was as if their fear had left a residue.

Hazzard's house, like the rest on the block, looked uninhabited. The hose he had fought the fire with was still stretched out across the lawn. The cedar fence around the side now looked like a row of burned matchsticks.

We parked out front and started for the front door. Three feet away we could see that it was open; the picture window in the front had a series of cracks in it. Harrison touched my arm and I stopped.

"Something's not right here," he said softly.

I hesitated for a moment, then reached for the door.

"What the hell have you done?"

We spun around. Hazzard was standing behind us, his hands covered in soot and ash, his eyes red and wild with anger.

"You talked to the boy, didn't you?"

"What are you talking about?" I asked.

"Danny Fisher. You talked to him. You filled his head with more madness."

"Danny Fisher's been missing since the day my brother was killed."

Hazzard looked at me for a moment then stepped past us and into his house. We followed him down a hallway and into a small office. It had been ransacked, the desk in the corner nearly destroyed in the process.

"What happened here?" I asked.

"Your brother wasn't killed. It was a suicide," Hazzard said. "Who else have you talked to?"

"I talked to your ex-partner Cross. He doesn't believe it was a suicide, either."

Hazzard closed his eyes and shook his head. "Do you have any idea how much damage you've caused?"

"Why didn't you tell me about him, or Danny?"

Hazzard took a breath. "If you've seen Danny's room, you know he's insane. And if you've met Cross, you'll understand that the only reason he has any job at all is because of strings I've pulled. And for these good deeds, I've become part of their wild conspiracies."

"You're protecting them?" I said.

"I was."

"You think one of them did this?"

Hazzard nodded. "There's no one else."

"The night Victoria Fisher died, my father left the theater with an actress. Why isn't that in your file?"

"Because they never got farther than the parking lot."

He took another deep, exhausted breath. "Your father didn't break in here."

"How do you know?"

"Because he's been dead for years, Lieutenant. The transient whose body we found after the last murder was probably him but we couldn't prove it."

"Why?"

"He had been run over by a train, probably multiple times. The body wasn't discovered for a week. He was buried as a John Doe because no identification could be made."

Hazzard's words felt like a punch to the stomach, but I tried to push them away.

"And you gave me the files because you wanted me to keep looking in the hope that I would lead you to Lopez."

Hazzard's eyes narrowed and the muscles in his jaw flexed. "He was a cop killer."

"Armed with a can of beer."

The walls of the room began to close in. I imagined the sound of a train moving over a track, my father crushed under its wheels. I moved as quickly as I could down the narrow hallway until I was standing in the living room.

"How can you be certain? For years you kept

checking databases looking for matches with the River Killer."

"It was how I made sure he wasn't alive."

I took a breath, my ribs aching again as if I'd just reinjured them.

"That doesn't change the facts of my brother's death," I said.

Hazzard walked over to the front door and looked out at the scarred landscape.

"At nine o'clock this morning the coroner certified the cause of your brother's death as a self-inflicted gunshot to the head."

He turned and looked at me. "Let the past stayed buried, Lieutenant, before anyone else is hurt. And I want my files back."

We drove out of Hazzard's neighborhood in silence until we reached the entrance to the 101.

"I thought I would go through my entire life knowing little more about my father than what I saw on television." But there was no putting the genie back in the bottle; alive or dead, he was becoming real to me.

"Could we really be this off track?" I said.

"Somebody took that surveillance tape, and they used the name Powell."

"And that leaves us right where we started."

I looked at the distant column of smoke from the

fire in the Santa Monica Mountains. "I want to go home and see if I still have a house standing, and if I do I want to take a long hot bath."

Harrison looked at me and smiled. "I'll help."

My cell phone rang and I answered. It was Traver.

"You got a message from Dana Courson," he said.

"My brother's girlfriend."

"Yeah. She said she'd meet you at her house at two o'clock."

I looked at my watch; we barely had time to get there.

"Did she leave a number?"

"No."

"Do we still have a unit watching her house?"

Traver checked. "It was pulled after the call came in. They told her not to go near the house if an officer wasn't present."

"Did she mention anything else?" I asked.

Traver checked his notes. "Yeah. She said she knows who Powell is. Does that mean something?"

I looked at Harrison. "It means the past isn't as dead as it seems."

22

It was ten after two when we stepped out onto the tree-lined street of ranch houses in North Hollywood where Courson lived. There was no car in the driveway. Half a dozen newspapers lay scattered on the porch where they had been thrown. A stack of catalogs and junk mail lay under the mail slot by the front door. I rang the doorbell but no one answered.

"If she's been here, she would have picked up the papers and the mail," Harrison said.

The curtains were drawn in the front of the house and, from what I could see, blinds shuttered the side windows. I checked the front door and it was locked, with no sign of forced entry. I looked back toward the street.

"Maybe she's come and gone," Harrison added. "If they told her not to approach without a cop present."

"She called us. She wouldn't leave," I said.

I stepped off the front porch and looked down the driveway to the back of the house.

"The door to the garage isn't closed," I said.

"She could have parked in the garage."

"Then why didn't she answer the door?"

We moved along the side of the house to the back. The gate to the backyard was ajar. A rectangular pool with a plastic cover stretched from the patio near the back entrance to a large bougainvillea and a banana tree that marked the property line. Harrison stepped over to the garage and pushed open the door. The air inside was at least a hundred degrees. A pungent aroma drifted out from inside.

"What is that?" I said.

"Gas," Harrison said, motioning to a mid-seventies yellow Volkswagen bug parked in the darkness. "That's why you smell the gas. They always leak."

"It's not just gas I'm smelling, there's something else." I flipped on the light switch but the light didn't come on.

"If she drove this, the engine would still be warm," Harrison said.

He walked over and placed his hand on the hood of the engine compartment.

"It's warm, but it could be just the heat of the garage. If it's been driven at all, it's not in the last few hours," Harrison said.

I stepped to the driver's-side window and the air became even more pungent with a sickly sweet odor.

"That's not gas I'm smelling."

I looked inside but couldn't make out anything in the darkness, and then I realized there was something moving.

"There's something in here," I said.

Harrison stepped over and had to cover his mouth with his hand.

"The glass looks like it's moving," he said.

I stared at it for a moment, letting my eyes adjust to the darkness. The inside of the window appeared to be moving, as if a current were flowing across the other side.

"Flies," I said. "The window's covered in flies, hundreds of them."

"Thousands," Harrison said.

He looked at me, then reached into his pocket, removed a handkerchief, and handed it to me.

"Cover your mouth," he said.

I put the handkerchief over my mouth as Harrison covered his with his tie. He looked at me and I nodded. "Go on."

He placed his hand inside his jacket pocket so he wouldn't add any prints to the handle, then reached out and opened the door. The odor swept over us like an invisible wave, followed a moment later by hundreds of flies streaming out from the car's interior. Harrison staggered back from the assault to his senses and I saw something on the seat fall toward us. I reached for Harrison as I heard the sound of tearing paper, and then the contents of a grocery bag spilled out onto the floor of the garage at our feet with a soft *thud*.

"Rotting groceries," Harrison said.

Several flies hit the side of my face and I turned and rushed out the door into the air, gasping for breath. My lungs struggled to be free of the odor of decaying food and I fought for breath as if I had just run a couple of miles. A fly caught in my hair buzzed next to my ear and I began shaking my hands through my hair, trying to get the last of them off me.

"What the hell was that?" Harrison said.

I turned and he was on one knee on the driveway spitting out a fly.

"She didn't leave those today," he said. "They've been in there for days."

I tried to understand what we were looking at. "If she didn't leave them, then what did she drive away in?"

"A second car," Harrison said.

I shook my head. "Why drive away in one car and leave a load of groceries in the other?"

"Panic," Harrison said. "Her boyfriend had just been killed."

When I had seen Dana Courson last she was pointing a gun at me and nothing about her struck me as someone in the grip of panic. She was scared but in control.

"I don't think so," I said.

I began to catch my breath and then stepped through the open gate to the backyard. Leaves and soot from the brush fires covered the sheet of plastic over the pool. An unfinished bottle of water sat on a table under a cabana. The back door was open to the kitchen. A head of lettuce was visible on the floor.

"There's something wrong here," I said.

Harrison stepped into the yard and looked at the door. When he saw the lettuce on the floor he drew his weapon and held it at his side. We approached the door and took positions on either side of it, and then Harrison pushed it open and we stepped in. Another bag of groceries lay on the floor—vegetables, fruit, and spilled containers of ice cream. More flies darted around, but nothing like the inside of the car.

A set of keys and a small shoulder bag sat on the blue Mexican tile of the countertop.

"She was bringing groceries in and was surprised by something—maybe the phone call about your brother's death," Harrison said.

I shook my head.

"She said he called her from the hospital after the accident. In the morning she went to his apartment. She found out about his death there, from the coroner investigator Chow and Detective Williams."

Harrison stepped past the groceries into the dining room with his weapon raised.

"Look at this," he said.

I stepped up next to him. Several of the chairs had been knocked over and the table pushed nearly to the wall. The glass covering a framed movie poster on the wall was broken.

"She fought back," I said.

The adjacent living room was empty, with no sign

that the struggle had spread there. On the far side a short hallway led to a bathroom and what were probably bedrooms. A series of photographs lined the walls on either side. Two of them had been knocked to the floor, shattering the glass. I pulled my weapon and stepped up to the closed door of the bathroom.

"What's that sound?" Harrison said.

"Running water."

I took hold of the handle, quickly pushed the door open, and raised my weapon. The faucet in the sink was flowing; the door to the shower was closed. I could see something dark through the clouded glass. I stepped forward to the sink as Harrison remained in the hallway covering the doors to the bedrooms.

"Anything?" he asked.

The water spiraling down the drain of the sink made soft gurgling sounds that almost sounded human. I looked over at the dark shape in the shower.

"There's something," I said as I stepped up to the shower and swung the door open. A dark terry cloth robe hung from a hook on the back of the door.

I stepped back into the hallway and we approached the doors to the bedrooms.

"We'll take them at the same time," Harrison said.

I nodded as he stopped at the first door and I took another two steps to the bedroom on the other side.

"Ready?" he whispered.

We swung the doors open and swept the rooms with our weapons. The air inside was strong with the odor of bleach. The drawn shades made it difficult to see. I reached for the light switch and flipped it on with no success. The circuit breakers must have been turned off.

I stepped into the room looking for the slightest sense of movement in the darkness. The bed appeared to be against the wall to my left. A chest of drawers was opposite that. Two steps in I stopped, letting my eyes adjust to the light level. On the floor a white bottle of bleach lay on its side. In front of the window, silhouetted by the dull light seeping through the blinds, was the shape of a person sitting in a chair. I raised my weapon.

"Don't move. I'm a police officer," I said.

The figure remained still.

"Dana Courson?" I said.

Again, no response. I glanced across the room one more time to be sure there was no one else present, then walked toward the figure. Three feet from her I could see the line of her arms stretched in back of the chair. The yellow cord around her wrists was just visible.

"Dana," I said softly, but there was only silence.

I reached out and placed my hand on her neck. The skin was slightly warm to the touch, but not because she was alive. I holstered my Glock, then stepped around the body to the window and cranked open the blinds. As I turned around Harrison appeared at the door.

He stared at the body for a moment, then looked down at the floor and holstered his weapon.

"Son of a bitch," he said softly.

The spilled bottle of bleach had masked the odor of death, which I now realized was filling the room. I looked at the body for a moment, trying to place myself in the details of the crime scene, avoiding her face to keep my emotions in check. Her jeans had been pulled down to her knees, her green shirt unbuttoned and open.

"You want to call LAPD . . ." I started to say, and then stopped as I looked at her face for the first time. "LAPD can wait a little longer."

"Why?" Harrison said.

"This isn't Dana Courson."

Her dark hair was shoulder-length. I guessed her to be about five-six. The decomposition that was beginning to swell her skin distorted her features slightly, but there was no doubt that this was not the woman I had met in my brother's apartment.

Harrison stepped around the body and looked at her, then turned and stared out the window. As much as he had tried since joining Homicide, he still wasn't able to entirely distance himself from each victim he saw. And if the victim was a woman, I knew that part of what he was seeing each time was the face of his murdered wife.

"You're sure it's not her?" he asked.

"I've never seen this woman before," I said.

"Then who is it?"

I shook my head. "I don't know."

I scanned the room quickly. On top of the dresser

was a small photograph in a frame. A woman with her arm around my half brother was smiling gleefully at the camera. It was the victim sitting in the chair.

"I think I've seen this before, in my brother's apartment."

"You're sure it's the same picture?"

I tried to remember what I had seen in the apartment, but it wasn't clear. So much had happened that events were taking on the feel of a film played at three or four times normal speed.

"I only glanced at it. I was looking more at the image of my brother than at the woman. Then I saw a photograph of my father that I remembered from childhood. It was just after that when Dana stepped out of the bedroom and pointed the gun at me."

I picked up the picture and stared at my brother's face.

"I remember his smile. It's the same as in the photograph at the apartment, a different frame maybe. She took the picture with her when she left my brother's apartment."

"But the woman you met in your brother's apartment who identified herself as Dana isn't the woman in the picture."

"No. She had shorter hair, and was at least five-eight."

Harrison walked over and looked at the picture. "You're certain?"

"Of that, yes."

I looked back at the victim in the chair.

"Who is she?" Harrison said.

"Wasn't there a shoulder bag sitting on the kitchen counter?"

"Her ID."

We rushed back to the kitchen, where she had set her keys and bag down on the counter. The groceries lying on the floor took on a whole new meaning after finding her body in the bedroom. The events were there to retrace in terrible clarity.

"He must have been inside already and came up from behind her as she turned to go back for the second bag in the car," I said. "She may have pushed the bag at him or he knocked it off the counter as he came toward her. Then he pulled her into the dining room and she fought back, breaking the glass in the poster and knocking the table and chairs aside."

Harrison stared at the contents of the bag spread out on the floor for a moment.

"It wasn't enough," he said softly.

Her purse was a small black leather bag in the shape of a pack. Inside were some Altoids, a small zippered bag for Tampax, lipstick and a nail file, a plastic toy in the shape of a sheepdog, some loose change, a cell phone, and a green wallet embroidered around the edge in purple.

Her driver's license was in a clear plastic sleeve. In the photograph she smiled broadly into the camera—the same smile that was on her face in the picture taken with my brother. I looked at her name and address, then handed it to Harrison. He studied it for a moment.

"Dana Courson?" Harrison said.

I nodded.

"The woman you met at your brother's apartment wasn't his girlfriend."

"No," I said.

Harrison thought for a moment, trying to put it together in his head.

"If she wasn't his girlfriend, who was she?"

"I don't know. She knew about his family history, his job . . . everything a girlfriend should know. I don't even think she was surprised about me," I said.

We looked at each other for a moment in silence.

"What the hell is happening here?" I whispered.

I ran it backward and forward, looking for a solution. My eyes stopped on the groceries on the floor. There were several pints of ice cream, fruit, vegetables, small candles that you put on a birthday cake.

"Who buys party candles after finding out her boyfriend is dead?" I said.

"No one," Harrison said.

"I don't think she knew John had been killed. Yet she's dead because her killer believed my brother told her something, or she saw something."

Silence settled over us with the uneasiness of a bad dream.

"So why did the woman I met in his apartment identify herself as Dana Courson?"

Harrison considered it.

"To get out of there without you knowing who she really was," he said.

I nodded. "That's why she took the photograph with her—so I wouldn't be able to identify her."

"None of which answers how she knew the things she knew, and why," Harrison said.

"Whatever she was doing there, she was up to her neck in it," I said. "She was afraid, and it wasn't just because I had surprised her."

"You think she made the call to bring us here so we would find the body?" Harrison asked.

"Somebody did, and they knew the name Powell."

"The name Lopez said before he died."

"Who may or may not be my father."

"But why call you? She could have called any cop."

"She didn't have to tell me the things she did in the apartment, but she did. She was trying to help without telling us who she is."

Harrison thought it through for a moment, but there was no putting this into a simple order. We walked back to the bedroom to look over the scene once more before calling LAPD. I hadn't bothered to look for a cause of death when we were in the room before so I examined her. The nails on her hands looked clean. If there was any tissue under the nails from her struggle with her attacker a sample should be easy to find.

Even though her pants were down around her knees and her shirt open there were no obvious signs of sexual contact.

"How many days do you think she's been dead?" Harrison asked.

"Sometime within a day of my brother, and before we put a squad on the house to watch for her. The receipt in one of the grocery bags should tell us nearly to the hour," I said.

There was a thin line of discolored and broken skin on her neck where the cord had been wrapped around. I suspected from the indentation in her throat that her windpipe had been broken as she was strangled. She would have lost consciousness within the first minute of the attack. Death would have taken another three or four minutes after that. And if we were right about what had taken place, she never knew why she was dying.

"Who made the call telling us to be here?" Harrison questioned.

"Someone who wanted us to know she was dead."

"But why? To help, or to take credit?"

I shook my head as Harrison took out his phone.

"What do you want to tell LAPD?"

I pictured Lopez crumpling to the ground like a rag doll. I wasn't going to let that happen again.

"We tell them a young woman was murdered who should still be alive," I said.

23

We stayed at the scene long enough to turn it over to LAPD and then left without giving them anything more than the vaguest of information to keep them from connecting it to my brother's death. In LAPD's ordered world I could easily imagine them finding my brother responsible in some way for her death—his suicide, then, the obvious result. I couldn't stop them from making the connection, but I wasn't going to help them.

If Hazzard had managed to create doubt in my mind about my father being alive or dead, Dana Courson's murder buried all notions that my brother's hand held the weapon that took his life. She was dead because her killer believed she was a threat, just as John had been. That she died not understanding why made the tragedy even more complete.

At the end of the afternoon I drove Harrison back to

Santa Monica. For the first time since the day of my brother's murder the Santa Ana winds had stilled, though forecasters were predicting "the event," as they called it, would begin again by dawn.

Harrison made a simple dinner and we tried to make some sense of what we didn't know. I watched the sun fall into the ocean, the thin layer of smoke from the fires still burning, turning the horizon the color of flame.

"We need to find the woman I met in John's apartment."

"Tomorrow," Harrison said. "I should rewrap your bandages."

I looked into his eyes and then shook my head.

"If my house is there, I need to know it," I said, almost unaware of my own words.

I wanted to walk through it, to touch my things. I wanted to stand in the middle of something that at least for the moment had the appearance of permanence. Even if I knew it was only an illusion.

"And I need to see it with my daughter."

"You still shouldn't be alone," Harrison said.

The last piece of the sun slipped below the edge of the Pacific.

"If it's gone, we'll come back here, or I'll stay at her dorm."

Harrison walked over, stepped behind me, and placed his hand on the wrap around my ribs.

"And I should still check these."

He slipped his hand under my shirt and gently tested the tension in the bandages, resting his hand on the small of my back before slipping away.

Lacy was waiting on the corner by her dorm as I drove into UCLA. I hadn't seen her since she left for school. I half expected her to have changed, but on seeing her I quickly realized that she had already grown up way beyond her years before she ever set foot on campus.

"I guess this couldn't wait," she said as we drove away.

I shook my head. "I really need to see if it's there, and I need to do it with you."

"I really need to be back here in a couple of hours."

I nodded that she would be.

Lacy started to say something, then stopped. "Why do you need to see it now? Something's happened, hasn't it? It's why you didn't call last night. You didn't call the night before, either."

We had promised we would talk every night when she left; this was only her first week in school and I had blown it.

"I thought it was a little much to call every night," I said, breaking the second promise we had made to each other: no more lies.

"It's more than that. You have that look."

So much for lies.

"What look?"

Lacy stared at me the way a parent would at a teenager they knew was lying.

"What happened?"

I would have to tell her something.

"An arrest went badly last night. LAPD killed our suspect as we were trying to take him in."

I pulled onto Sunset and headed toward the 405, trying to decide how much to tell her. A part of me still wanted to protect her from the uglier bits of the world, even though she already knew more about that darkness than most people ever would in a lifetime.

"I'm okay," I said. "Tell me about college."

As we drove over the pass to the valley she told me about her classes, the dorm, her roommate, the food, and the number of men who had already hit on her. I wanted her to be like every other college kid. But I knew she wasn't.

"No matter how hard I try, I know I'm different from everyone else," she said. "I haven't figured out how to tell a guy on the first date about being kidnapped and having a bomb strapped around my neck."

She wasn't searching for sympathy. She knew I understood. It was simply her reality—our reality. The idea of burdening her with any more right now seemed too much. The news about what kind of man my father was or wasn't, or if he was even alive, could wait, at least until I knew what that news was.

There was still no electricity in the neighborhood when we reached the bottom of Mariposa. As I started up the street past my neighbors' homes, the moonlight was just bright enough to illuminate what was no longer there. No walls on this lot, no roof on that one, nothing more than ash and brick on another, a lone picture window standing intact, smoke rising out of the charred rubble around it. Neither of us said a word.

I made the gentle curve and my lights swept the end of the cul-de-sac. The house to the north of ours had been reduced to a chimney and a water heater lying on its side. A house across the street was intact except for the south wall, which was gone, the wood frame exposed like the bones on the back of a hand. I pulled to a stop in my driveway and got out, leaving the headlights on. A charred lemon tree next door filled the air with a bitter citrus scent.

Lacy walked around to my side of the car and took my hand.

"I didn't think I would care this much," she said softly.

The hillside of ivy sloping down to the street had been burned down to the roots. The grass was little more than a blanket of ash. I stopped on the front walk as my heart began to pound in my chest. I thought I had prepared myself for any possibility, but I was wrong. The fire had swept around the house, leaving it untouched.

I walked back to the car, turned off the headlights, and removed a flashlight. At the front door I stood holding the key in my hand, staring at the lock for nearly a minute before slipping it into the slot.

Why, of all the houses on the block, would ours still be standing? I couldn't imagine. It certainly wasn't because what had taken place here over the years merited a level of grace that my neighbors didn't deserve. The pile of rubble next door belonged to a couple with two children in grade school. The mother was a teacher, the father an emergency room doctor. But it did nothing to protect them. The doctor would understand that. He saw it every day, just as I did. The good are hurt, and even die, while the bad walk away. It would be more difficult for his wife. The teacher in her would try to find the fairness in it so she could understand it. And the more she questioned it, the less sense it would make.

"Doesn't seem . . ." Lacy started to say but stopped.

I pushed open the door and we stepped into the entryway. Fine particles of what appeared to be ash drifted on air currents in the middle of the room. The air tasted almost metallic and was as lifeless as the sur-rounding landscape. The room was covered in powdery gray ash.

I stepped over to the dining room. A window that had blown in from the heat explained the ash. The screen on the window had melted and hung like strings of pasta. I started to take a step toward the kitchen and stopped.

On the top of the dining room table was a handprint in the ash, nothing else, just a print. It was bigger than my own by a couple of glove sizes. The fingers were long and thin.

"Oh, my God," Lacy said.

I switched on the flashlight and swept the room. There were footprints on the floor, moving all about the room. In the darkness I hadn't noticed, but the walls of the living room, the furniture, even the ceiling were covered in graffiti. The metallic residue I smelled was from the spray paint. Our house had survived the fire only to be trashed by vandals.

"Fucking assholes," Lacy whispered.

I turned off the light and was about to sit when I heard a soft bumping sound coming from the dark hallway leading to the bedrooms. I reached down and slipped my Glock from the holster on my waist and moved cautiously across the living room to the edge of the hallway.

"Go wait in the car and lock the doors," I said.

Lacy looked at me, wanting to argue, but didn't.

"You hear something that doesn't sound right, or I don't come out, you call nine-one-one and wait for a squad."

She nodded and rushed outside.

One hand on the flashlight, the other holding the weapon, I spun around and flipped on the light. The beam cut through the darkness to my bedroom door. The hallway had the look of a New York subway car that had been abandoned and left to taggers.

The same sound I had heard before, a soft thumping, was coming from behind my closed bedroom door. I shone the light on the floor, where a set of footprints disappeared into my bedroom.

With the light focused on the handle of the door to watch for movement, I walked to the end, past the bathroom and Lacy's room. From inside there was another soft *thump*, and then another as I took hold of the door handle.

Now, said the voice in my head. *Go.*

I pushed the door open as violently as I could. It hit the wall with a loud crack as I raised the flashlight and my weapon. Out of the darkness something flew through the beam of light toward me and I swung the Glock, my finger tightening on the trigger. It swept past me again and I felt a rush of air on the side of my face and then it hit the window with a flutter of wings.

In the circle of light from the flashlight I saw a small bird sitting on the windowsill, stunned from the impact. I gripped my weapon as hard as I could and swept the room, then relaxed and lowered it to my side. The footprints in the ash led to and from the window where the bird had tried to get out.

I holstered the Glock, turned out the flashlight, and walked over to the window and raised it. The bird made no attempt to fly out. I reached down and gently cupped it in my hands and lifted it out into the night air. The sparrow's head swung around as the bird got its bearings. It shook its wings free of dust and flew off into the darkness. In the grass along the back of the house I could just make out the footprints leading from around the corner.

I closed the window and looked over the room. The walls were the same as the hallway and living room.

The paint moved from bed, to headboard, to wall, to ceiling. The room was no more recognizable to me than the pile of ash that used to be my neighbor's home. I leaned back and looked up at the ceiling. I knew I should begin to go through the house, do an inventory, see if the vandals had stolen anything, but I didn't. I just stared at the slashes and swirls of orange and red and black paint.

"You bastards—" I started to say, but stopped myself. There was something else there, obscured or masked by the spray paint. It appeared to stretch across the entire length of the ceiling.

I walked over to the corner of the room where it seemed to begin and turned on the flashlight. It was like looking at a picture puzzle—find the rabbit in the witch's face.

"Letters," I said softly.

They looked to be written in pencil or gray marker. The first letter was *T*, the second *H*, each one at least two feet across. I followed it the length of the ceiling, the letters revealing themselves slowly until they formed the last word.

This is what it's like in my head.

This was no gang tagging or the idle fun of a bored teenager. But what was it? I stared at it for a moment, and then noticed there was more writing hidden under the paint. It looked to be half the size of the other words. And it was everywhere. It was all over the ceiling, the walls, the paint hiding it like camouflage, letter after letter of it, hundreds of words. I followed a line of writing across the ceiling and then down the wall, where it stopped above the headboard. As I looked closer I realized not all the writing spelled actual words. Most of it was just the swirl of the marker, like a child would do trying to imitate a parent's handwriting. But there was no innocence to it. Instead there was a frantic quality. Like the automatic writing of someone in the throes of religious ecstasy, speaking in tongues.

I directed the light onto the center of the ceiling and traced the script back down along the wall. Just above the headboard the gibberish turned to words again. It took me a moment to recognize the shapes of letters among the swirls of paint.

Help me, help me, help me.

I stared for a moment until I was certain I had read it correctly.

"Who are you?" I said into the darkness.

The swirls of paint seemed to come spiraling out at me. Then I recognized more words in the center of the ceiling.

"*Stop them,*" I whispered.

The words sent a chill through me. This wasn't just paint and lines of writing. It was the clearest picture of madness I had ever seen. My bedroom had become the interior of a disturbed psyche. I turned the flashlight off and sat down on the bed.

Was this my father's world? Were these the two voices in his head shouting instructions as he dragged a young actress across a stage? The first one filled with terror while the second, softer one begged for forgiveness. Was I looking at the horror he'd kept locked away for eighteen years until he could no longer contain the monster that had killed his own son?

Or was this the work of Danny Fisher's troubled mind? A call for help in the midst of chaos?

I looked around for something I may have missed—something definitive that would identify who had done this. The slashes and swirls of paint quickly became like a thousand voices shouting at me, demanding to be heard, and I couldn't quiet them. I tried closing my eyes, but it didn't help. I saw the image of my father holding my mother by the throat as her feet struggled to touch the floor.

"Mom."

I turned and Lacy was standing in the door.

"Are you all right?"

I nodded and Lacy walked over and sat down next to me.

"I think your room is untouched," I said.

Lacy took a long look around the room.

"Maybe it's time for a new house," she said. "Too much has happened here."

I looked over the mess that used to be my bedroom and couldn't help but think it reminded me of the wreckage that was my family history.

"I had a half brother that I never knew about," I said. "He was murdered four days ago."

Lacy looked at me in disbelief.

"I don't understand. How is that possible?" Lacy asked.

"My father . . ." I started to say, but I was no closer to understanding it than I was to deciphering the words written on my bedroom ceiling. I gripped my daughter's hand and shook my head.

"My father is a mystery," I said.

Lacy glanced at the ceiling for a moment. "This has something to do with it, doesn't it? This isn't just random."

I nodded. "I think it's what's left when all you have is secrets."

"Let's get out of here," Lacy said.

"I'll be out in a second."

Lacy held my hand for another moment, then walked out. I looked around the room, trying to think of one good memory to take away, but I couldn't.

I lingered to take one last look around, then followed Lacy out. As I stepped out the front door I heard my daughter's voice, barely above a whisper.

"Can you tell me your name?" she said.

In the darkness I could barely see the figure standing five feet from Lacy on the front walk, his arms held out wide at his sides as if he wanted to take hold of her. I pulled my weapon and raised it.

"Step away from her," I said.

Lacy looked at me and shook her head.

"Step away," I repeated.

The figure took a step closer to her.

"I said step away from my daughter."

He inched still closer, now little more than three feet from her.

"Don't."

He started to reach out toward Lacy.

"Mom," Lacy said, her voice rising.

"Step away from her," I said again.

He shook his head.

"Do it now!"

His hand stopped a few inches from Lacy. Danny Fisher was shirtless, the skin of his hands, arms, and chest stained with slashes of bright orange and black paint, giving the rest of his white skin an unnatural, ghostly appearance. His eyes were wide open with a wild look that I had never seen in a human being before. If he had slept at all in days it couldn't have been for more than a few fleeting hours.

"He's not going to hurt me," Lacy said, turning toward him.

Danny looked at my daughter as if those were the first words he had ever heard in his life. He then stared at his hands as if he had no idea how they had become covered in paint.

"Are you going to hurt my daughter, Danny?" I asked.

He opened his mouth to speak but nothing came out.

"No, he's not," Lacy said softly. She looked at him for a moment. "He wants to tell us something, that's why he's here, isn't it? He has a secret."

Danny's eyes filled with tears and he whispered something barely audible, then said it a little louder, and then again louder still.

"Stop . . . stop it . . . stop it . . . make it stop."

I lowered the gun to my side and he continued to repeat the words over and over.

"I'll make it stop, Danny," I said.

Lacy reached out and took his hand and he fell silent.

"Promise," Danny whispered.

"I promise," I said.

He looked at Lacy's hand holding his. Then he sank to his knees, wrapping his arms around his chest, and began to shiver as he rocked slowly back and forth.

"I'll get him a blanket," Lacy said, rushing into the house.

I holstered my gun, stepped over and knelt in front of him. His eyes were the color of a light blue gemstone; his hair was as blond as I remembered his mother's being in the photographs of her. I could see her features in the lines of his face. Victoria would have only been a few years older than her son when she was killed.

"I'm going to make it stop, Danny," I said.

He didn't appear to hear my words, then he began to faintly hum a song over and over. I didn't recognize it at first, but as he repeated it I realized what it was—a children's song. A game born out of the plague of the Middle Ages.

"It will be all right," I said.

He began shaking his head back and forth, the song getting louder each time. "*Ashes ashes, they all fall down.*"

"Who falls down? Who falls?" I said gently.

He stopped shaking his head. "Everyone."

I reached out and placed my hand on his knee. "Why do they fall?"

Danny's eyes found mine for just an instant.

"He's alive," he whispered.

"Who's alive?" I said.

His eyes held mine for a moment longer and then were gone, staring at a point in the darkness.

24

Danny's grandmother met us at the hospital where Danny was admitted for observation. He had said nothing as we drove him there. Was he talking about my father or the River Killer when he said, "He's alive"? I called Harrison and told him what had happened and that I would stay with Lacy for the rest of the night in her dorm.

On the drive back to UCLA I told Lacy as much as I knew of my half brother's life. But the details were those a cop would know, not a sister—age, occupation, and time of death on the concrete banks of what Angelenos call a river.

The only detail I understood as a sister was that we shared a father who had vanished from both of our lives, and that something was left incomplete in each of us. In the last few hours, maybe only in the last moments, of John's life he may have unraveled that mystery. That he had thought of me when he did would be as close as I would ever get to knowing him.

I left out the details of the investigation that pointed to the possibility that her grandfather was a killer. That he was a troubled man was as much as I was willing to say about him. I think she may have guessed much of it anyway.

For Lacy, an only child, to suddenly find herself connected to another person by blood was like turning a page in a book only to discover the next page was blank. The promise of something more had been filled and then lost all at once. And the questions she was left with were no substitute for the possibilities that had been so close.

Lacy's roommate stayed with a friend and I spent the night in the small dorm room, lying just a few feet from my daughter. For a brief moment it felt like she was a small child again, and the events of the world outside were unable to touch us. But the feeling didn't last—couldn't. Just before drifting off, Lacy said something that had dogged me since I first saw my brother's face in the refrigerated vault at the coroner's.

"I wonder how much he was like you," she said softly.

"He looked like your grandfather," I said, knowing that wasn't really what she was asking.

"He was an investigator. You're a cop. Your lives have been lived as if they were leading directly to this," Lacy said.

I stared into the darkness and knew she was right, or partly right. But what my daughter didn't understand,

and what I knew, was that the moment this was really leading to hadn't yet happened.

What sleep I had reminded me of the nights spent on boats with the roll of the ocean sweeping me in and out of dreams and leaving me more exhausted than before I had slept. Shortly before six I slipped out of bed and kissed Lacy on the side of the head before leaving.

It was already warm when I stepped outside. The promised Santa Ana hadn't begun to blow this close to the coast, but I knew looking back toward the mountains through the crystal clear sky that a morning this perfect, like most things in southern California, was an illusion and wouldn't last.

As I walked to the car I scanned my surroundings to make sure no one had followed Lacy and me to campus. A few students walked the paths. A campus security officer patrolled in his three-wheel scooter, but there was nothing to raise any alarms.

The drive back to Pasadena took about forty-five minutes, the traffic having not risen to the level of gridlock that it would reach in another hour. I picked up a bagel and coffee at Starbucks just off Colorado, then drove past the plaza to headquarters.

Patrol shifts were changing as I pulled into the lot. The first-year officers and veterans on the force who liked the action of nights were heading home. Those with families and a sense of their own mortality were just beginning their day.

I climbed the steps to the second-floor squad room, heading for my office, but stopped when I passed the conference room. Harrison was sitting alone inside, staring at the wall where we had assembled Danny's map of the universe. I stepped inside but he didn't turn, his eyes focused straight ahead at the map.

"How long have you been here?"

Startled, he turned and looked at me. He looked as if he hadn't slept. "Most of the night."

I was surprised by the flush I suddenly felt. My heart seemed to slip out of place in my chest for a beat or two. I closed the door behind me and walked over to him as he slowly rose from his chair. Our arms were around each other before I realized it and I closed my eyes and held him.

"I'm sorry," Harrison said.

"It's just a house," I said.

Harrison shook his head. "If they were just walls and floor and roof, it would be easy."

His eyes held mine. The blond surfer who had found sanctuary from a terrible crime by dismantling bombs was gone. For the first time he appeared as if he belonged in Homicide. I recognized something in his eyes that I had seen for years in my own in the mirror. If by holding on to the memory of a murdered wife he had kept alive a sense of hope, then trading that in for the fatalism of Homicide was no bargain.

"I should have gotten into bed with you," I said.

He reached out and took hold of my hand. "I should

have taken you. . . . Timing, as you learn on the bomb squad, is everything."

Harrison turned and looked at Danny's map.

"You've found something?" I asked.

"Maybe."

He walked over to the wall where the photographs of the map had been reassembled into the mosaic of the entire thing.

"If, as Danny said to you last night, 'he's alive,' it's only logical that he would have put that in here," he said.

I stared at the map for a moment.

"'If' is a big word when you apply it to the young man I saw last night."

"I remembered there were numbers in various places on the different rings."

I stepped up next to him and he pointed them out. There was no order, no apparent mathematical logic as the orbits of Danny's world spun out from the center in wider and wider loops. Harrison had discovered that numbers were drawn in several of the planetlike objects that were connected to the pinwheel arms of the galaxy that spun out from the center. There was a five, an eight, a six, and a three.

"They could mean anything; they could be symbols for something that's only in his head," I said.

"They could also be something very specific, something right in front of us," Harrison said.

I stared at the map for a moment and repeated the

number to myself silently several times.

"Fifty-eight, sixty-three," I said.

"What does that sound like to you?" Harrison said.

"It sounds like an address."

"That's what I thought."

"Without a street name, it's meaningless," I said. "It could also be eighty-five, thirty-six. How do you know the order of the numbers?"

"I didn't, so I tried them in every possible configuration. And then I began matching the different versions to every name or word I found on the map. Some were easy to eliminate, like your name, Manning, Hazzard. By three A.M. I narrowed it down to only the words that didn't seem to have any other place in this universe he drew."

I noticed a *Thomas Guide* sitting open on the table.

"You found it."

He nodded. "It's impossible."

He motioned toward the *Thomas Guide*. "Look at the open page."

I walked over and looked at the map it was open to.

"It's West Hollywood," Harrison said.

"A lot of actors live in West Hollywood," I said. Harrison nodded.

"What am I looking for?"

"*D* seven."

I found the coordinates on the map and began to run my finger over the streets until I found what he wanted me to see. I stared at it for a moment in disbelief, then looked back at the map.

"When I first saw it I thought he was making a reference to Homer and the journey he was taking, but I was wrong. It's a place," Harrison said.

"Fifty-eight sixty-three . . . Iliad."

25

Hollywood was just waking up as we pulled onto Sunset in Silver Lake and started west. The human wreckage from the night before was still being cleaned up. In a doorway a homeless man lay under a fire department's yellow sheet, his shoeless blackened feet twisted on the cement. Near the 101 a group of four runaways emerged from their sleeping place under the bridge in search of loose change and a meal scrounged from Dumpsters.

In another time Mary Pickford had built a studio on these same streets. Where D. W. Griffith had shot his masterpiece *Birth of a Nation*, four prostitutes sat handcuffed on the curb. One of them, who appeared to be little more than sixteen, had a black eye and a bloody knee under torn red stockings.

The address we had found on Danny's map was two blocks below Sunset on the edge of Beverly Hills. West Hollywood was an incorporated city a mile and a quarter square. The sheriff's department had jurisdiction, and not so lovingly referred to it as Boys Town. The annual Halloween parade could make New Orleans blush with envy.

I pulled off Sunset, dropped down the steep hill for two blocks, and made a left. In the middle of the block I pulled to a stop across the street from the address.

"The Iliad Apartments," Harrison said.

The name was written in elaborate silver script above the glass doors of the entrance. Bird-of-paradise plants that were twenty feet high framed the entry. There looked to be four floors. Through the glass doors I could see into the courtyard, where I assumed there was a pool. The building appeared to have been built in the late seventies.

"I suppose they thought the name would appeal to a gay clientele," Harrison said.

I nodded. "I don't imagine that's part of Danny's conspiracy theory."

A man walking a small black dog passed us, his sideways glance in our direction clearly making us as cops—a habit of residents born of less than friendly relations over the years with the sheriff's department.

"Victoria Fisher lived in the Valley, worked downtown, and died next to the river. Maybe this is something else, maybe it's nothing at all," Harrison said.

"Then why is it on the map?"

I looked over the facade of the building, trying to find some physical connection to the world Danny had drawn on his wall, and the one we had been chasing, but it eluded me.

"Are we looking at something from the past or the present? Is there even a difference? Are we going to find my father inside?"

"Danny said 'he's alive,' but he didn't say who *he* was."

I nodded. "But he said it at my house, after painting a plea for help all over my walls. Why would he come to me if it wasn't about my father?"

"Maybe the doctors will be able to get an answer from him at the hospital."

I shook my head. "As of this morning when I called his grandmother, Danny hadn't said a word. He's been talking to shrinks and taking different med protocols since he was fifteen. Why would he start talking to them now? I don't imagine he sees doctors as allies."

I stared at the building for a moment.

"I want to know everything we can about this building—ownership, management company, tenant records for the time of Victoria's death," I said.

We got out of the Volvo and walked across the street and entered the lobby. The elevators were to the right through a set of glass doors that we had to be buzzed through. Mailboxes and the intercom to the apartments were on the left. Mounted on the wall of the inner lobby next to the elevators was a plaster replica of a Greek torso. The faint scent of chlorine from the pool in the center courtyard hung in the air.

"I think you better look at this," Harrison said.

He was standing at the intercom, reading tenants' names listed next to the apartment numbers.

"Apartment three-oh-six."

I looked at the name next to the number. "Powell."

The name Lopez gave me just before he died, and the character my father played in the movie.

"Did Danny write the name Powell anywhere on the map?"

"I don't remember seeing it, but that doesn't mean it's not there," Harrison said.

The doors to the elevator opened in the inner lobby and a tenant stepped out. He was in his late thirties, dressed in a crisp dark suit, and was already working a cell phone. As he stepped through the doors into the outer lobby I asked him to hold the door and he looked at us suspiciously.

I pulled back my jacket and showed him my badge. "Pasadena PD."

That we weren't from the sheriff's department seemed to soften the look he gave us.

"Do you know a tenant named Powell?" I asked.

He shook his head and said a few clipped words into the cell phone, one of which was "script." I suspected he was an agent. We stepped into the inner lobby and took the elevator up to three. The apartment was at the far end around the corner. Sconces in the shape of Greek columns lit the pale rose-colored hallway. The carpeting was a deep burgundy and smelled freshly cleaned.

We rounded the corner and stopped at the apartment. I started to reach for the buzzer but stopped. The paint around the dead bolt had been scraped off and the wood indented.

"This door's been jimmied."

Harrison slipped his 9mm from his waist holster, knelt down, and examined the carpet.

"These carpets were cleaned within the last few days. This happened before that. The paint chips from the door have been removed," Harrison said.

He took a position next to the door with his weapon at his side. I rang the buzzer and listened for the sound of footsteps from inside, but there was nothing. I rang it again with the same result. I took hold of the door handle and it turned. Whoever had broken in hadn't locked it when they left.

"You want to bother with getting a warrant?" Harrison said.

I shook my head.

"I wouldn't know what to tell a judge," I said.

To enter without a warrant could put at risk any evidence we found inside, unless we entered because of concern for the occupants' safety.

"The jimmied door is cause enough," I said.

I slipped my Glock from its holster and turned the handle, then let the door swing open.

"Police officers."

We held our positions, waiting for any response, but none came. I stepped in first with Harrison right behind me and swept the apartment with my weapon. Light filtered in through vertical blinds that covered the far wall. The living room appeared clear. A small kitchen and dining area was to the left. A hallway on the right led to what I assumed were the bathroom and bedroom.

I reached around for the light switch and flipped it on. The apartment had been ransacked. Furniture had been overturned, anything that could be gone through or flipped over had been. Harrison moved toward the hallway and I followed. He turned on the light in the hallway and then cleared the bath and bedroom as I waited. He stepped back out and holstered his weapon.

"They're both the same as this."

I slipped my Glock away and looked around the room.

"This isn't just a burglary. Look at the furniture," I said.

The fabric on the couch had been sliced to shreds. The frames of chairs were smashed. A mirror on the wall was shattered. I walked over to the kitchen. The cabinets were open. Every glass, plate, and bowl—anything that someone could use—had been broken. I took out a pen and used it to pull open a drawer. The silverware had all been bent in half. An aluminum saucepan on the stove had been crushed. The inside of the refrigerator looked as if a baseball bat had been taken to all the contents. Even a roll of paper towels under the sink had been torn to pieces.

"What's this look like to you?" I said.

Harrison thought for a moment as his eyes went over the mess. "Madness."

I nodded in agreement. "But whose?"

I walked over to the hallway and stopped at the bathroom door. Two towels hung in shreds on a rack. A can of shaving cream had been crushed on the floor, dried foam clinging to the side of the bathtub. Toothpaste had been sliced open and squeezed out into the sink. Next to it lay a toothbrush with all the bristles cut off and left in a neat pile next to the tap. The mirror on the medicine chest had a spiderweb of cracks spiraling out from a blow to the center.

I opened it, hoping to find some medication that would identify the occupant. A bottle of aspirin had been filled with water, turning it into a white foamy mass that had solidified. A box of antihistamines had been crushed. There was no prescription medicine— nothing remotely personal.

I stepped over to the tub and shower. The shampoo had been spread across the walls, the bottle cut in half. A bar of soap had been sliced into flakes on the bottom of the tub. An ashtray with half a dozen butts mixed with the soap.

"He even destroyed the toilet paper," said Harrison, who was standing in the doorway.

I reached down and picked up a nail clipper off the floor. The tiny blades had been bent open.

"This reminds me of something," I said.

I turned to Harrison. "The methodical thoroughness of it. He didn't miss anything, except the lights."

"He would have needed them to see so he wouldn't miss something," Harrison said.

"It's like the interior of my house—every inch of it covered in paint or writing. Only here, the violence took over."

"Or Danny couldn't control it."

We looked at each other for a moment.

"So who lives here?" Harrison asked.

We moved to the bedroom and stood in the doorway. The blinds were drawn, as in the rest of the apartment. The sheets and blanket had been sliced into strips. The mattress was cut open, its padding and springs spilling out like a gutted animal.

"He probably did it during the day. There would have been fewer people around to hear anything," Harrison said.

The floor was littered with pieces of clothes, cigarette butts, and torn newspapers. Harrison knelt down and looked at the newspaper.

"These are all dated over a week before your brother was killed," he said.

I stepped over to the chest of drawers across from the bed and pulled open a drawer. What used to be socks, T-shirts, and underwear was now just a pile of shredded cloth. The rest of the drawers were the same.

"I think you should see this, " Harrison said.

He was kneeling on the far side of the bed next to a nightstand, holding two small picture frames.

"Whoever did this must have missed these. They fell behind the bed."

I stepped around the bed and looked. One was a picture of a small girl with dark hair in a blue print dress and saddle shoes. She was looking at something to the left of whoever was holding the camera, virtually no expression on her face—or at least no sense of connection to the moment the picture was recording. The other was a photograph of a boy holding a baseball mitt with a big smile on his face. I stared at them; the same sense of dread I had felt earlier began to send my breathing out of control.

"Oh, God," I whispered. "Danny was right."

"Your father?" Harrison said.

I tried to catch my breath but couldn't. Harrison took my arms and sat me down on the bed.

"How do you know?" he asked.

I stared at the photographs for a moment.

"Because I'm the little girl in that picture," I said.

Until then, I had clung to the possibility that my father was dead—that the nightmare I had been trying to stop had a different ending than this.

"He's alive," I said.

"That doesn't make him guilty," Harrison said.

I looked at the photograph of me for a moment and then closed my eyes.

"I don't remember the picture, but I remember the day it was taken," I said. "I hadn't until I saw this, but I remember it now."

I stepped cautiously into the memory as if onto a thin sheet of ice.

"I was four, maybe five years old. There was a neighborhood picnic. I was playing with friends and I ran over to our car. My parents were sitting inside it. I decided to sneak up behind it and surprise them. He had his hand on her wrist, and he was twisting it like he was taking a lid off a jar. She would shake her head, and then he would twist it further until she nodded yes at whatever he was whispering to her."

I took a breath, trying to slow down the memory but it continued to come. I remembered the smell of barbecuing chicken, the sound of a bat hitting a piñata and the candy spilling out. The yellow sundress my mother was wearing. How she held the arm my father had twisted behind her back for the rest of the party so no one would see the rising bruises.

"Someone other than my parents must have taken this picture," I said.

"You remember what you were looking at?" Harrison asked.

I glanced down at the picture for a moment and nodded. The room began to close in on me as surely as if I were my mother sitting in the seat of the car with my father's hand on my wrist. I walked out to the living room and opened the sliding glass door to the small balcony. The dry hot air offered little escape. I felt like I had walked into a crowded elevator with barely enough air left for a breath.

Harrison stepped out next to me. In the courtyard below, a Hispanic man was slowly skimming the black-bottomed pool. Something lying in the deep end glistened in the dark water.

"Whoever manages the apartment will have his records in the rental agreement," I said.

"I'll make the calls," Harrison said.

"We'll take the pictures with us, see if we can get a print off them."

Harrison nodded.

I turned and looked back into the apartment.

"If you could kill a physical place as if it were a living thing, and wanted to inflict as much pain as possible before it died, this is what it would look like," I said.

"You think Danny came here intending to kill your father?"

"He either couldn't do it or, not finding him, did this," I said.

Harrison looked over the room for a moment.

"What if there was a third person?" Harrison said.

I had been so focused on my father occupying this space that I hadn't considered another possibility. I played out the logic for a moment. "The same one who killed my brother?"

I shook my head. "Danny did this. Last night was his way of telling me."

My eyes ran over the carnage spread across the room, trying to find a connection to my father, and I realized there was nothing there except the mess that he had left behind, just as it had always been.

"I wanted Hazzard to be right," I said. "If my father was dead, I would know he didn't murder his own son."

"You don't know . . ." Harrison started to say something, then let it go. "What were you looking at in the photograph?" he asked.

I started to tell Harrison that I didn't know, but there was no stopping the memory that had been let loose. My heart began to beat out of control and I stepped back into the blue dress and saddle shoes. The day had been hot, like today. There were eucalyptus trees in the park where the picnic had been. I remembered finding my mother sitting alone in the car twenty minutes after he had twisted her arm, the scent of his aftershave lingering as she stared blankly out the window, her makeup streaked with tears.

"I was looking for a way to be someone else," I said.

26

None of the neighbors who were home remembered much about the tenant in 306. A young woman two doors down described him as middle-aged, average height, normal-looking. A tenant in 309 thought a young woman lived there, but wouldn't bet on it. The rest of the neighbors could add little to the description that made it anything other than useless. And no one had heard or seen anything that could pinpoint a day or time the vandalism had taken place.

It was approaching midafternoon when we pulled to a stop at 7928 Santa Monica Boulevard near the corner of Fairfax. Abraham's Property Management was on the second floor of an old Spanish building from the 1930s. The white stucco was now gray with age. The once ornate stonework and tile around the entrance was nearly black from the accumulated car exhaust of seventy years. The terra-cotta roof looked like a 3.0 aftershock would send it all sliding into the street.

An antique furniture store occupied the street level. Age being relative in Los Angeles, the front display window was occupied by a red coffee table in the shape of a kidney bean, a fondue pot, martini glasses, and Dean Martin cocktail napkins.

Harrison rang the bell and we were buzzed in through the heavy wrought-iron security door and walked up the creaky wooden stairs. There were two other offices on the second floor: a Chinese medical practice from which a strange blend of smells drifted out, and a travel agency that, from the brochures taped to the glass on the door, looked as if it hadn't booked a trip since the jet engine had replaced the propeller.

Inside Abraham's, a wooden counter with a swinging gate separated the waiting area from the reception desk and three offices. On the walls were photographs of various apartment buildings and a large map of L.A. with red stars on it marking the locations of properties they managed. A woman who was probably sixty but working hard to look fifty got up from a desk in the reception area and walked to the counter. She had dyed red hair that made her look oddly like Lucille Ball. Her dress was bright green, and her glasses hung on a gold chain around her neck. I imagined she had once been an actress who got no further than holding an extra's union card. A name placard on her desk read MS. WATERS.

She looked at us for a moment.

"You must be the policemen," she said loudly, traces of New York still in her voice.

In one of the back offices a man with the long beard of an Orthodox Jew got up from his desk, walked over, and closed his office door.

I showed her my badge, clipped to the waistband of my slacks.

"Which apartment building was it?" Waters asked.

"The Iliad Apartments, three-oh-six."

She walked back to a file cabinet, slid it open, then ran her fingers across the row of files until she found what she was after.

"One bedroom, carpeting, balcony, pool view, on-street parking, twelve hundred a month. Was rented sixteen months ago. Rent's been on time, pays with money orders, no complaints, nothing needed to be fixed."

"How many years back do you keep records?" I asked.

"Five years past the last month of rent paid," Waters said.

"How long have you managed the building?" Harrison asked.

She looked at Harrison and smiled, still believing that somewhere inside was the cute twenty-year-old actress who moved out from Queens to be a movie star. "Since the beginning of time, sweetie," she said.

"Have any of the tenants been there for eighteen years?" I asked.

She took a long, dramatic breath.

"I'll have to look."

"While you do that, I'd like to see the rental agreement," I said.

"We like to consider that confidential."

"I'd like to think that you're cooperating with a Homicide investigation," I said.

She looked at the file. "Homicide, in our building?"

"No."

She thought for a moment, though it was clearly only for effect.

"I once auditioned for *Dragnet*," she said. "They thought I looked too much like Maureen O'Hara."

"I can see that," Harrison said.

She flashed him a smile, then slipped the agreement out of the file and handed it to me. It was the standard form anyone trying to land an apartment would have filled out. I quickly ran through it for anything that would pinpoint the tenant as my father.

"Look at the name," I said.

"Powell," Harrison said.

An attached sheet held a bad Xerox copy of a New York driver's license. At first glance the picture held no part of my memory. But as I looked, the past began to emerge like a photograph in a developing tray.

The sharp lines of his face had softened. The dark hair had receded and grayed. There were probably another thirty pounds on his frame. It had all changed except the eyes. They were the same eyes I remembered seeing on *Bonanza* and in the Cyclops movie, as dark and intense as pieces of coal. My hand began to shake.

They were the same eyes I had seen on the day of the picnic as he twisted my mother's arm.

I started to ask a question but lost the words. I handed the copy to Harrison, then stared at the red star on the map of Los Angeles that marked the place where I found the answer I hoped I wouldn't.

Ms. Waters stepped back to the counter.

"The tenants in four-oh-two and the one in one-oh-eight have been there for eighteen years. I believe they're both retired couples," she said.

I tried to find my place again in the moment, but it eluded me.

"We'll need copies of these," Harrison said.

She nodded and took the files over to a Xerox machine on the far wall.

"It's him, isn't it?" Harrison asked.

"Him," I whispered to myself.

I realized my hand was still quivering so I folded it across my chest and tucked it under my other arm.

"Yes, it's him," I said.

A barrage of images and memories began rushing out of wherever I had kept them locked all these years. None of them was distinct, more like whispers from across a room, the words not quite understandable. But they were there, and they were of him.

I turned to Harrison and could see in his eyes the understanding of a fellow traveler to haunted memories. I looked at the rental agreement, trying to find a detail to pull me back.

"None of the personal history information is accurate. He was born in Maryland, not New York."

I could feel the quivering in my hand pass.

"He pays with money orders so there's no traceable bank account. I imagine the references and the past address are just as phony. If that license is genuine, then we can assume he's been in New York for a period of time."

I held on to the train of thought, afraid to let it go. The flood of memories began to slow to a trickle, but they were still there, just under the surface.

"He's still hiding after eighteen years, but he came back here," I said.

I turned and looked at Harrison.

"Why?" I asked.

"He rented it a year and a half ago," Harrison said, letting me finish the rest of the thought.

"About the time Danny began to hear from the angel," I said.

We looked at each other for a moment.

"There're things about my father that I've hidden," I said.

"You were a child, you didn't have a choice but to do that."

Ms. Waters stepped back to the counter with the copies.

"I nearly forgot, but you're the second person to ask about this apartment in the last week," she said.

I turned back to her. "Who else was asking?"

"She said she was an investigator."

"Not a police officer?"

She shook her head. "She showed me identification. It was about missing child-support payments."

"You showed her the rental agreement?" I asked.

Waters hesitated.

"Since a child was involved I thought it would be all right. But it wasn't who she was looking for," she said.

"Do you remember her name?"

"I don't, sorry."

"What did she look like?" I asked.

"She was pretty, pale skin. I think she had dark hair . . . maybe. James. I think her name was James. She left a card."

She returned to her desk and went through a drawer until she came up with it.

"This says Sloan Investigations, but I'm almost sure her name was James."

A gust of wind rattled the blinds on the window, sending hot air across the office. Waters stared at the window for a moment, then turned to us as we started for the door.

"Do you believe there's such a thing as earthquake weather?" Waters asked.

I shook my head. "No."

"I believe it," she said, turning back to the window. "Something bad always happens when it blows like this."

I didn't feel the wind on my face when we stepped outside, or sense the dry hot air wick away the moisture from my lips with each breath. I didn't hear the traffic, or see the first streaks of smoke in the air from more fires. I stood staring at the martini glasses and cocktail napkins in the window of the store below Abraham's Property Management as if I had just landed on a new planet and didn't know what they were. The world as I knew it, or at least the one I inhabited, was based on the conviction that my father had disappeared and then died.

A single xeroxed picture and a photograph of me in a bright blue dress had changed all of it. And now even my memories no longer seemed to belong to me. They were in his hands, just as my mother's arm had been that day.

A silent gust of wind sent a swirl of dust and dirt spinning past my feet before vanishing around the corner of the building. The sound of traffic on Santa Monica returned and I felt the dry air against my face. I stared at the papers in my hands for a moment.

Work it, I said silently to myself.

The wind rattled the glass on the display window in front of me.

"My guess is she's hiding," I said.

"I'm missing something," Harrison said.

"If she's who I think she is, she knows he's looking for her."

In the reflection in the window I could see Harrison play it out in his head.

"You think she's the woman in your brother's apartment?"

I nodded, then turned and walked over to the car. As I reached for the handle I saw the picture of myself in the blue dress sitting on the seat.

"What do you want to do?" Harrison asked.

"We need to find James."

I stared at the picture for a moment. "And I want to know what happened to that little girl."

27

There was only one Sloan licensed as a private investigator working in Los Angeles County. Sloan Investigations in San Pedro. We pulled onto the 110 freeway
and headed south toward the harbor.

San Pedro doesn't feel like it belongs in Los
Angeles, at least not the Los Angeles that most people
ever see. Its relationship is to the ocean, not the
sprawl to the north of it.

The big commercial fishing fleets had long since
vanished, replaced by the largest container harbor in the
country. The tight-knit Japanese and Mexican fishing
communities had drifted mostly inland, or traded in
their heritage for nine-to-five jobs. There was gang
violence now, and the possibility that someday a dirty
bomb would slip through undetected in a sea container
to spread terror.

We pulled off the 110 on Gaffey and drove six

blocks. Sloan Investigations was in a small strip mall with a taco stand and a dry cleaner on either side. We parked and got out. The heat of the Santa Anas hadn't reached the south coast yet. The air held the scent of the ocean along with grilled fish and dry-cleaning chemicals.

"Why would someone use an investigator way the hell down here for a job in town?" Harrison said.

"Because they are way the hell down here."

A little bell rang as we stepped inside. The receptionist was a heavyset Hispanic woman named Fuentes. A woman with two small children playing on the floor at her feet sat in the waiting area. She had a black eye, and the sad look of someone in need of more help than she was likely to find in a place like this.

I showed the receptionist my badge and she buzzed one of the two offices with closed doors beyond the reception area and showed us in. The owner and president of Sloan Investigations was a man in his late forties named Lester Sloan. He had a thin mustache that looked as if it had been drawn on the top of his lip with a Sharpie. A plate of half-eaten tacos sat on the desk. He was dressed in the kind of one-piece jumpsuit I remembered seeing Jack La Lanne wear as he preached physical fitness in the sixties.

"I'm looking for a woman investigator who may work for you," I said.

He wiped the *al pastor* sauce off his chin. I noticed a photograph on the wall behind his desk of Sloan standing next to a former manager of the Dodgers.

"Was she involved in a crime?" he asked.

"Not that I know of," I said.

"So you would say that this firm was also not involved in a crime," Sloan said.

"Not unless I find a reason to think so," I answered.

He breathed a visible sigh of relief, then spun around in his chair to the computer on his credenza and clicked the mouse and hit a few keys.

"I have only one female investigator working for me now. Andi James."

"Has anyone else asked about her?"

He shook his head as he turned the flat-screen monitor around. A Polaroid photograph and her investigator's license appeared. I stared at her face for a moment.

"Is that her?" Harrison asked.

I nodded.

"She works in town," Sloan said. "I had to be down at the harbor for another job, so I used her."

"I need her address and phone number," I said.

Sloan began to shake his head.

"She's a material witness in a homicide investigation," I said. "One of the victims was found tied to a chair where she had been strangled and stripped of her clothes."

"I'll get the address."

"And I'll need the name of the client," I said.

Sloan shook his head. "The retainer was paid with cash. They hired us over the phone. I don't know who it is."

He wrote James's address and phone number on a card, then handed it to me.

"Maybe she knows, if you can find her."

"What do you mean?"

"I haven't heard from her, and she hasn't returned my calls, in three days."

"Is that unusual?"

Sloan nodded. "It is if she's alive."

28

Dusk had fallen as we drove north from the harbor. As we approached the towers of downtown the winds were gusting to more than fifty miles an hour. In the distance bright flashes of green lit up the darkness where power lines arched and set off transformers. At Figueroa a semi-trailer truck had blown over onto the concrete median, where it balanced precariously. A traffic sign folded over by the wind was shaking like a dog trying to escape its collar. I thought for a brief instant I was seeing the world as my father saw it.

We turned off at Sixth and started east toward Andi James's address in the warehouse district. At Flower, a gust of wind had toppled a street vendor's cart, sending blocks of ice and brightly colored juices into the street. Women walking on the sidewalk kept a tight grip on their skirts. Pieces of trash and newspaper swirled along at street level, then disappeared skyward in updrafts.

At Grand I pulled over and looked south toward Seventh.

"What is it?" Harrison asked.

A pink handbill advertising tango lessons caught the car antenna then vanished with the next gust.

"He would have run past here," I said.

A block south, I could see the stone office building at the corner of Seventh.

"Gavin's office," Harrison said.

I nodded. I hadn't thought of it before, but this was the most likely direction he would have run.

"The streets would have been empty at that time of night," I said.

"Not entirely," Harrison said.

I nodded. There had been a killer present.

Across Grand a sedan slammed to a stop with a screeching of brakes and a man in a dark business suit pounded on its hood and began yelling at the driver.

"Even if someone had been driving by they wouldn't have stopped," I said. "Not for a shoeless man running down a deserted street in the middle of the night. They wouldn't have done any more than glance in his direction and look away."

I sat for a moment trying as hard as I could to imagine the feel of the pavement on my brother's shoeless feet, the sound of his breathing as he ran north, but I couldn't.

I looked across the street. A homeless man stood in a doorway trying to escape the wind. His face, beard, and clothes were the same color as the dark stone of the building he stood next to.

"He would have been invisible," I said.

Harrison was silent for a moment, his eyes focused on something across Grand.

"Maybe not to everything," he said.

"What do you mean?" I asked.

He pointed across the street.

"The Standard Hotel," I said.

"Look to the left of the building."

The gate to the parking garage began to rise.

"The parking garage might have a security camera pointed out toward the street," Harrison said.

I pulled across Grand and into the driveway of the garage below the hotel. On the ceiling of the sloping drive a camera pointed out toward the street. Harrison stared at it, calculating the angle and size of the lens.

"It might cover the nearest lane, maybe a little more," he said.

"Enough to see the car that was following him?"

"It's a chance," Harrison said.

"If he came this way, and hotel security has a tape . . ." I said.

Harrison stared at the camera for a moment. "That's a new camera. If the entire system is the same there wouldn't be a tape, it would be digital."

"I still get pictures developed at the drugstore; you lost me," I said.

"Images would be on a hard disk, not a tape. They can store endless amounts of data without recycling."

"Meaning they would still have it."

Harrison nodded.

The night captain of hotel security met us at the first level of the garage and walked us to the control room just beyond the laundry and employee locker rooms.

Harrison was right about the system—it was digital. The control room had a dozen monitors connected to cameras located throughout the hotel. The night captain pointed to the monitor showing the entrance to the garage.

"What night you interested in?" he asked.

I stared at the small monitor for a moment. A pedestrian walked by on the sidewalk, then the fleeting image of a car passed in an instant.

"Four nights ago, one o'clock on," Harrison said.

The captain spoke Spanish to the man sitting at the controls and he typed in the commands.

"It'll come up on this monitor here," the captain said, pointing to another screen.

The monitor flickered for a moment, then settled on the image of the empty street and the entrance to the garage. A time code in the corner of the frame counted out the minutes and seconds.

"Can you speed it up?" I asked.

The operator nodded and typed in another command. The minutes sped past like home video on fast-forward, though with no frame of reference, the image appeared static. Ten minutes in, a couple stopped directly in front of the camera and kissed, then walked on. A jogger passed three minutes later. A white sedan exited the garage and drove into the night, its taillights burning streaks of white into the image.

"What are you looking for?" the captain asked.

More seconds flashed by.

"Luck," I said.

Twenty minutes passed unchanged. There was a blur of a car on the street at twenty-three minutes. Twenty-four, twenty-five. Another car.

"Stop," Harrison said.

He stared intently at the monitor for a moment. "There was something."

"I didn't see anything," I said.

Harrison looked at the screen and nodded. "Take it back thirty seconds."

The operator reversed it. Thirty, twenty, fifteen seconds.

"There," Harrison said.

The operator shook his head. "I didn't see anything."

"I didn't, either," I said.

The security captain nodded in agreement.

"Take it back another ten seconds, then play it forward at normal speed," Harrison said.

The operator took it back and started it again.

"Can you freeze an image?"

"Yes."

I stared at the empty image of the street, waiting for it to change, but it didn't.

"What did you see?" I asked.

Harrison leaned in toward the monitor. "There."

I still missed it.

"Reverse it slowly."

The operator reversed it.

"Freeze it," Harrison said.

I looked at the monitor for a moment without seeing any change.

"The top of the screen," Harrison said.

In the top right corner of the image were two dark shapes that at first were unrecognizable.

"Socks," I whispered.

Harrison nodded. "He was crossing the street and ran through the corner of the image."

I stared at the screen for a moment, then closed my eyes and I was there. His breathing would have been out of control, the asphalt jarring every bone in his body, but he didn't feel it. There was only escape, a voice in his head saying, *Run.* Until he saw the yellow sign glowing in the darkness and he thought of me.

"If he was being followed at this point, the car should pass within a minute, two at the most," Harrison said.

I stared at the image of my brother's socks and couldn't escape the other horrible truth. Was our father running him down? A game of hide-and-seek, as if he were a child running through the backyard in his socks.

"Play it forward now, normal speed," I said.

The operator hit play and John was gone in two steps. Thirty seconds passed with no car. Another ten, then twenty.

The headlight momentarily burned a white hole into

the screen, then a white sedan cut across the top of the frame, only the left side visible.

"Back it up and freeze it when it's in frame," Harrison said.

The operator reversed it until the car was centered across the top of the picture.

"It doesn't show the plate," Harrison said.

Half of the passenger window was visible, but the reflected light made it impossible to see into the car.

"Can you tell what make it is?" I said.

Harrison shook his head.

"Looks like a Buick," the captain said. "LeSabre, I think."

The operator pointed to the corner of the windshield. "That's something."

"Move in on it," Harrison said.

The operator zoomed in on the windshield.

"Can you enhance it?" I asked.

The captain shook his head.

I stared at the corner of the windshield. There was something beyond it, a dull light shape in the darkness of the interior, but nothing more distinguishable than that.

"The best I can do is put it on disk," the captain said.

"We can take it to Caltech," Harrison said.

The image of my brother's socks on the pavement appeared again on the monitor.

"Would you like this image saved also?" the captain said.

I turned away and shook my head.

29

Andi James's address was a stark, gray, six-story warehouse three blocks from the river. There were no people on the streets here. No trendy bars. A small residential hotel sat on the corner a block away, its faded sign and red door looking like the grim make-believe of a Hopper painting.

We stepped out into the wind and crossed the street. The sound of a saxophone playing somewhere in the darkness drifted in and out with the gusts. James lived on the fourth floor. The windows in the building were all dark except for a few that flickered with dull light several floors up—candlelight.

"The wind took out the power," Harrison said.

In the darkness a trash can rolling in the wind was gathering speed, coming right toward us, and then it stopped.

The entrance to the building was a heavy reinforced door with two glass panels. A two-by-four was stuck in the jamb, propping the door open. The security buzzer for each loft would have been knocked out by the power failure. There were sixteen lofts on each floor. James was in 414.

We stepped into the lobby and I turned on the flashlight. In the darkness I could hear muted voices from one of the lofts. The air held the odor of a homeless man who must have sought shelter from the wind.

We followed the wall down the center of the building to the stairs and started up. Somewhere above, a door opened and footsteps began falling on the metal stairs, coming down, getting louder. Then another door opened and the footsteps were gone. James's loft was in the northwest corner of the building overlooking the street, secured by a heavy industrial steel door.

"Unless she opens it, we're not getting in here," Harrison said.

"If she had wanted to talk to us, she would have already," I said. "She doesn't know who to trust."

I took out my phone and dialed her number. From inside we heard her phone ringing. On the fifth ring a machine picked up. I recognized the voice as that of the woman I'd met in my brother's apartment.

"This is Lieutenant Delillo," I said. "It's time we talk. I'll meet you at your loft in ten minutes."

I hung up and Harrison leaned in close against the door and listened.

"Footsteps . . . I think you got her attention."

Harrison stepped back as the lights of the building

began to flicker on. On the other side of the door I heard the jangling of keys and then the dead bolt sliding in the lock. As the door opened James caught a glimpse of me and began to react.

"It's all right—" I started to say, but she was already rushing back into the loft in terror.

Harrison pushed the door the rest of the way open.

"I'm not here to hurt you," I said, stepping inside.

A bank of windows lined the wall looking out to the north of downtown. In the flickering light I tried to locate her in the large open room but I couldn't.

"I need your help," I said.

Harrison motioned to a door against the far wall. I stepped over.

"I can protect you," I said.

From inside I could hear her rapid breathing—the cadence of fear.

"Who is that with you?" James said, barely managing to put words together.

"My partner."

"How do I know?"

"You're the one who found Dana Courson dead, aren't you? And called me to set up that meeting so I would find her. You trusted me enough to call me. Trust me now."

There was silence on the other side of the door, then it slowly swung open.

She stepped into the room as the lights stopped flickering and stayed on. From the look on her face I doubted she had slept more than ten minutes in the last four days. The same revolver I had seen at my brother's apartment was clenched in both hands at waist level.

Instinctively she looked around the room to make sure there wasn't another threat before stepping away from the security of the door. When she was satisfied that she was safe, she sat on the couch, placed the gun on the coffee table in front of her, and drew her legs in tight around her.

"How did you find me?" she finally asked.

"The Iliad Apartments. We traced you to Sloan."

Panic began to rise again in her eyes.

"Had anyone else asked Sloan about me?"

I shook my head.

"Are you sure?" she demanded.

"Yes."

The panic in her eyes began to pass.

"I need to know who you were working for."

James took a breath and closed her eyes. "I think I was working for a killer."

She opened her eyes and looked at me but couldn't hold contact. "I think people are dead because of what I did."

"I need a name," I said.

"I don't know. We never met. I never even talked to him, but from the way he wrote, the words he used, I think he was a cop."

"How did you deliver information?"

"A Hotmail address. I sent the last information the day your brother died."

"Have you tried it since then?"

She nodded. "It's gone. The account was closed." She took a slow, ragged breath.

"Tell me about the job. Were you hired to follow my brother?" I asked.

James shook her head. "I was following Gavin."

"The lawyer."

She nodded.

"For how long?"

"A little over a week."

Harrison looked at me. "The date of the last newspaper in the Iliad apartment would place it just before that."

"You were following them the day they died?"

She nodded.

"Until the hospital. I lost John when he left."

"You know who they saw the day they both died?"

James shook her head. "Just addresses of where they went."

"Do you still have them?"

She nodded, then got up and walked over to the small kitchen and opened the refrigerator and took out a carton of milk. She poured it into the sink and removed a piece of paper sealed in a plastic bag. She walked back to the couch and handed me the list. "The ones where I think they met someone are highlighted."

There were four addresses. Two meant nothing to me, but the last two I knew. I handed the paper to Harrison and he studied it for a moment.

"A Chatsworth address. And Eagle Rock."

I nodded. "Hazzard and the actress Candice Fleming."

"You're certain of these?" I asked.

James nodded.

"And the others?" I asked.

"They were both buildings downtown, but I think they were about something else."

"How did you find the Iliad Apartments?"

"Gavin found it. I think he met the man in three-oh-six."

"Just once?"

She nodded. "I found out his name was Lewis Powell from the property company, but I still don't know who he is. I couldn't find any record of a Lewis Powell. It's like he didn't exist. And after your brother was killed, I stopped looking."

"How did you know the things you knew when I met you in my brother's apartment?" I said.

"I followed John and Gavin to a bar one night. After Gavin left I let John buy me a drink, flirted just enough to ask him about his work . . . family . . . I liked him." She let the rest go.

I stepped over to the window and looked out toward the San Gabriels in the east. A small line of orange flame cut through the darkness where a new fire had erupted. Harrison stepped up next to me and stared at the dark line of the mountains.

"Why didn't Hazzard tell us about this meeting?"

"I don't know."

I turned and looked back at James. "I don't think you should stay here. We can find you a safe place."

"Dana is dead, and she didn't know anything. How are you going to keep me safe?"

I started to answer but stopped myself. I couldn't protect her any more than I had protected Lopez. Who was I kidding?

"I have a place to go—no one will find me there, no one knows it."

Harrison started toward the door and I followed.

"Lieutenant," James said.

I stopped.

"There was someone else following Gavin and your brother."

"You're sure of that?"

"Yeah, and John knew it. He was trying to lose the other car when he had the accident."

I took out the xeroxed copy of my father's New York driver's license.

"Could it have been this man?"

She stared at the picture for a moment before placing him.

"The man from the Iliad Apartments?"

I nodded.

"It's possible, but I couldn't swear to it. I only caught glimpses of him."

She looked at the picture again, then handed it back to me.

"You know him, don't you?" James asked.

I nodded. "What make of car was following them?"

"A Buick. I didn't get a plate."

Harrison and I exchanged looks. The lights began to flicker again.

"I think I'll disappear for a while," James said.

Outside the wind had freshened and carried a faint trace of smoke. Harrison and I walked back to the car but didn't get in.

"Every step we take seems to bring me back to him," I said.

I glanced back at the warehouse and could make out the silhouette of James in her window watching us.

"I lied to her. I don't know who he is. . . . I'll drop you back in Pasadena and you can get started on the disk, and the addresses on that list."

I looked over the top of the car toward the orange glow in the sky above the mountains.

"Where are you going?" Harrison asked.

"Back in time."

30

I dropped Harrison in Pasadena, then took the 2 and began the climb toward the San Gabriel Valley. Tumbleweeds were flying across the freeway, piling up against the median until enough had gathered so the wind would take them all at once like a wave cresting a jetty.

A faint glow was visible just over the rise of the Glendale hills to the east where a new fire had started. The darkness occasionally lit up with a glowing ember streaking past the windshield.

Topping the rise leaving Glendale, the flashing lights of CHP and fire trucks blocked the road ahead. A flare was burning in the left lane next to a large deer that had been struck and now lay twisted on the road. Twenty yards ahead a truck lay upside down on top of the median, its load of thousands of oranges spread across the pavement.

A yellow fire department tarp covered the crushed

truck cab where the driver had died. As I passed on the right shoulder, oranges began popping under my tires, and the smoky air filled with the sweet scent of orange juice for an instant before the wind took it away.

At Foothill I turned west and drove into La Crescenta. A mile on I turned right. The homes lining the streets were modest, part of the first subdivisions to climb toward the mountains after the war. I took another left and then a right. At the corner of Carlotta I pulled over and stopped.

I had no memory of driving here before, but I had found it without even glancing at the map. Nothing looked familiar except that the ranch houses and split-levels looked exactly like hundreds of other neighborhoods that spread out across Los Angeles.

But I hadn't missed a turn. I knew that 3829 was two blocks straight up the hill on the right, and that there was a dry wash behind it, and that when the wind blew out of the mountains as it did now, the house would be filled with the scent of chaparral and eucalyptus. It was where we had lived with my father.

I pulled away from the curb and drove around the block to come at the house from the cross street. As I came back to Carlotta I switched off my lights and coasted to a stop as the house came into view.

The house was dark, not even a light by the front door. A FOR SALE sign was stuck in the small front yard where the ivy-covered hill sloped down to Carlotta. I opened the car door and stepped out. The air was filled with the scent of eucalyptus, as I remembered. At the edge of my vision I could see their dark shapes swaying in the wind next to the wash behind the house.

I walked across the street and stopped at the foot of the driveway. Details that I hadn't been able to see from across the street began to emerge. The house had shingled siding painted light green with white trim. There were no drapes on the front windows, as if the house were inviting me to come inside. I walked up the stepping-stones that led to the front door. Flyers advertising yard work were stuck under the mat. A Realtor's lockbox hung from the door handle. The house was unoccupied. The lockbox was broken. I turned the handle and the door swung open. I started to take a step but stopped when I heard the sound of my mother's voice.

"Be a good girl," she whispered.

I spun around, but there was no one there. It was memory I was hearing. I turned back and looked into the front hallway, then stepped inside. The air held the scent of cleaning products now, but what I remembered was something else. I took a step toward the empty dining room and stopped. It was perfume. My mother had worn it. I looked out into the living room and the fieldstone fireplace that rose to the ceiling. I reached out and flipped a light switch but it didn't come on. The power had been turned off.

I took a step and the scent of perfume returned. For an instant I wanted to turn and run out the door. My heart began to race, then a flash of memory lit the room and I saw her standing there looking out the window with her back to me. She was wearing tight stirrup slacks and a matching sweater. Her dark hair swept up on top of her head like an astronaut's wife.

She was whispering the same words over and over, holding something in her arms. I took a step into the living room and could hear her voice again, but there was an urgent quality to it now as she repeated the words over and over again.

"Be a good girl, be a good girl."

"Enough," I said out loud. Beads of perspiration were gathering on my forehead. The flood of memories began to come faster and I couldn't stop it. There were voices, a TV, all the sounds that make up a day inside a home, except none of them was distinct.

In a far corner of the house I heard the closing of a door. I turned and looked down the dark hallway leading to the bedrooms. The master bedroom was at the far end. The first door on my left had been my room. The walls of the hallway had been where pictures hung. I stared at the empty spaces and the images began to come back. The pictures had never been passed down to me, had vanished from family memory. And my father was in all of them—the wedding pictures, holding a sailfish in Mexico, my mother in a hospital bed with my father standing next to her holding his baby.

I walked to the end and stared into the empty space that had been my parents' room but there were no memories there. Not a sound, or a voice, or a picture of what their bed had been like. The reason I had come wasn't here. I stepped back into the hallway and stopped. The door to what had been my room was closed.

"Where is she?" I heard my father say.

I stepped up to the door, hesitated for a moment, then pushed it open. As it swung into the room, the past came rushing back. The walls were painted a bright yellow, a bed against the far wall, a dresser and rocking chair next to the window. The closet door was open. My mother was on her knees inside whispering the same words I had heard her saying by the window.

"Be a good girl, be a good girl."

But it was different now. It wasn't the gentle voice of a mother rocking a baby to sleep. She was pleading.

She repeated the words a few more times, then stood up. On the floor a five-year-old girl sat on a blanket staring up at her. I looked at the little girl's face and saw myself, but I had no memory of this. My mother said something I didn't understand, then she reached out with a trembling hand and closed the closet door.

I walked over and stared at the floor of the closet. I didn't remember this. Why would my mother have closed me inside a dark closet?

"What happened here?" I whispered.

I tried to work through it the way I would a crime scene, but I couldn't. The language of physical evidence wasn't enough. The bare, empty room was silent. I looked back at the closet, then took a breath and stepped inside.

"I know this," I said silently, and then I heard the voice in my head that had always been there, but I never understood the words. *Don't go there.*

The closet smelled of freshly dry-cleaned wool and shoe polish. I knew the feel of the soft blanket on the floor. I knew how far I had to stretch to touch each wall, and that the carpet in one corner was loose.

My mother was standing at the door looking down at me, her eyes betraying a wildness.

"This is our secret," she said and began to close the door.

I was sitting now. My hand followed the line of light across the floor as if I could hold on to it and keep it from vanishing as the door closed. With the *click* of the latch, the sliver of light on my hand was gone. I was still for a moment, then I heard my own breathing. It started slowly, as if I wasn't certain there was air in the darkness. Then my breathing began to race until it had the rhythm of a motor cycling again and again, trying to catch a spark.

The shattering of glass pierced the darkness beyond the door. I held my breath and listened. There was shouting, a single voice. I tried to understand the words but in the distance of memory only the meaning was understandable. Rage.

He was moving through the house, going room to room. A lamp was smashed in the living room, dishes thrown off the dining room table. I heard my mother's voice in clipped pieces. "No . . . no . . . it's my fault . . .

I'm the one . . . Don't . . ."

The wood of a dining room chair splintered, as if hit with an ax.

"God, don't," my mother said.

I heard the soft *thud* of a body being thrown against a wall and then he was moving again up the hallway. The glass in a picture frame shattered and then the door to the bathroom flew open and I heard the shower curtain pulled aside and then yanked from the rod.

He tried the door to my bedroom but the lock held. The whole house then shuddered as if a temblor had shaken the ground as he threw his body against the door. A piece of the frame snapped, sounding like a gunshot, but the door held. He hit it again and again, the cracks in the door frame opening farther each time. On the fourth charge the door gave way.

There was silence for a moment, and then I could hear him standing in the doorway, his breathing heavy with exertion. He stepped into the room and I stared at the faint line of light at the bottom of the door as he passed by the closet, walking over to my small bed. He began ripping at the sheets and covers, pulling them off like a dog digging at a burrow in the ground.

The bed hit the wall with a jolt and then I heard the sound of his voice. A low murmur, almost a growl. At first I couldn't understand the words, but then they emerged in repetition again and again. "Where are you? Where are you?"

His footsteps passed by the closet door heading toward the hallway, then stopped. I heard two clipped exhales, then nothing. Then another short violent breath. His shadow moved into the line of light at the bottom of the door. I covered my mouth with my hand, trying not to make a sound or take a breath.

The handle of the door began to turn. I started to reach for it, but the darkness in the closet that had been so frightening just a moment before closed around me like two large hands and pulled me back through dresses and coats hanging nearly to the floor until the faint light at the bottom of the door vanished and I disappeared in the darkness.

I heard the creak of the door's hinges as it opened. I could hear his breathing again, but this time short, shallow breaths, like he was running. He ripped at a hanger, pulling a coat down, but the light didn't penetrate the darkness surrounding me. He pulled down another coat and then another, getting closer, his breaths faster and faster as the hangers slid across the rod.

I backed myself into the corner of the closet, pulling my legs up tight against my chest, trying to get smaller and smaller. Another hanger was pulled away and I could see the edge of light getting closer to me.

Then a dull, heavy sound seemed to shake the air. My father's hand came through into my corner of darkness and then pulled away.

His footsteps were mechanical, like a machine that was broken and out of sequence. He crashed heavily into my dresser, smashing the mirror, then he was moving across the room, three quick steps and then one. The fabric of the curtain began tearing away from the window, then his body hit the floor and the room was silent.

I waited for a moment, listening for the smallest of movements, but there was only silence.

The darkness gently let go of me and I was standing at the door to the closet. My father lay on the floor by the window, his right hand still gripping the curtain that had partially torn away from the window. My mother stood in the middle of my room. A golf club slipped from her right hand and hit the floor. In her eyes I saw a fierceness I wouldn't have thought she was capable of. Her eyes found me and the anger vanished.

"This is our secret," she said, ". . . our secret . . . ours."

There was no fear in her voice, but there was no strength, either. The memory of my mother began to fade, then the past returned to its hiding place. I wiped away the moisture from my cheek and realized my hand was shaking.

I closed the closet door. Soft moonlight illuminated the empty bedroom. I walked over to the center of the room and looked down at the floor. A small dent the size of a coin's edge, or perhaps that of a golf club, lay under years of polish. I knelt down and ran my fingers over it and the shaking in my hands stopped. Was I to have been my father's first victim? Is that what she saved me from that night—and in doing so, what had it cost her? Was it that night that always separated us? Instead of pulling mother and daughter together, had it placed a barrier between us? A secret that eroded everything it touched?

I stepped over to the window and looked out at the dark shapes of the eucalyptus blowing in the wind beyond the back fence. *Work it,* I thought to myself. *Go over it like a cop would a crime scene.* But it was no good, I wasn't a cop inside this house. I was a little girl. My breathing began to spin out of control. The walls of the bedroom threatened to close in around me.

I ran through the house and out the door, not stopping until I was standing in the middle of the street, gasping for breath.

"You bastard," I whispered.

I looked back at the house that for years had been lost in my memory, but now stood like a fresh crime scene waiting to be worked, or maybe an open wound needing to be bandaged. I started to walk back to close the front door but froze as I stepped onto the sidewalk.

My legs were shaking and I couldn't move any closer. I slipped back into a memory as if there were no longer any distance between the past and the present. My mother was standing on the front walk, glancing nervously over her shoulder at the open front door. I was standing right where I was now. She was saying something to me and I was shaking my head. She said it again and I tried to move toward her but couldn't. She heard something inside the house, looked over her shoulder again, then turned to me.

"Run."

I tried to call to her but I couldn't speak. I tried to take a step, but my legs wouldn't move.

"Run," she pleaded. "Run as fast as you can."

I stepped off the sidewalk and could hear the soft fall of feet on the pavement, but they weren't mine. He was running in his socks, looking back at his pursuer, who was right behind him.

The memory of my mother slipped away. Did I listen to her? Did I run that day? Was I fast enough? Did I look over my shoulder and see the same man my brother saw the night he died?

"Run," I whispered. "Run as fast as you can, John."

31

I slept on the couch in my office but never for more than fifteen minutes at a stretch before the sound of hangers sliding across the rod in a closet yanked me back to consciousness.

If I had not understood entirely the world Danny had been living in since the murder of his mother, the view I had gained from the inside of a closet made it all too real. It was the feeling everyone in California has for at least a few moments after the ground shakes during an earthquake. Nothing you've trusted in your entire life will last. What is up is no longer up; what is down could be anything.

I had managed to cling to one truth as a mother. Parents love their children, even parents who disappear or fail. Not even the years in Homicide had shaken that belief. Even when investigating the death of a child at the hands of a parent, I knew that what had destroyed that family wasn't a lack of love. It was drugs, or alcohol, or one terrible moment that couldn't be taken back.

But what was I to believe now? As a cop I knew that memory was the most unreliable of all witnesses. It can be twisted and shaped by time and ensuing events until its connection to reality is held by the thinnest of threads.

As I watched the sun rise over the San Gabriels I knew only one thing for certain. The words Danny wrote on the ceiling of my bedroom were a warning: Nothing lasts.

When the morning shift started to arrive I walked back out to the Volvo and drove west toward Eagle Rock. The fires that had started the night before in the hills above Glendale had laid down overnight. The only smoke visible was on the horizon, hanging just above the Pacific, where it had been blown overnight.

Twisting through the streets of Eagle Rock, I stopped the car down the block from the small Spanish bungalow as a school bus approached from the other direction. Standing on the curb, Candice Fleming helped her son climb aboard the bus, then watched it drive away before walking back inside.

She had known my father. And she had lied to Harrison and me when we questioned her. Either one of those facts on its own could mean nothing, but together couldn't be ignored any more than the memories I had run from since I was that little girl in the blue dress.

I drove down the street and stopped in front of her house. I rang the bell and she came to the door a moment later.

"I told you everything I know," she said. "Leave me alone."

"Please," I said.

"I'm sorry, I have nothing else to say."

"Six days ago a lawyer named Gavin and an investigator came and talked to you here."

I recognized the look on her face as that of someone caught in a lie, but she quickly covered it up.

"What if they did? I told them the same thing I told you."

"They're both dead," I said.

Fleming began to shake her head. "I don't see how this has anything to do with me. I told you what I know, now leave me alone."

"The investigator's name was John Manning."

The name appeared to weigh her down; her shoulders sagged under her terry cloth robe.

"I don't have anything to say."

"I think you do, and I think you badly want to say it."

"You don't know me."

"I know what a secret can do to a person."

The air seemed to go out of her.

"Tell me about Thomas Manning and that night eighteen years ago."

She took a breath as she began to shake her head. "He's dead. What's the point?"

I took out the xeroxed copy of my father's New York license and showed it to her. "Take a close look at that face."

She looked at the picture, and I saw a flicker of fear in her eyes as she recognized the man she had known years before.

"He's alive?"

I nodded.

"Why are you doing this to me?" she said softly. "Why can't you just leave it alone?"

"Thomas Manning's son was murdered. What happened that night eighteen years ago has something to do with it. I'm trying to find out what."

She closed her eyes and looked down at the floor. "It's done and buried."

I shook my head. "No, it's not."

Fleming unlatched the door, then walked to the kitchen and I followed. She poured herself a cup of coffee and stared out the window without looking in my direction.

"I want to know what happened the night you walked out of the theater," I said.

She gripped her coffee cup tightly and shook her head. "I told you."

"No you didn't."

"Don't make me do this. Please."

"Do what?"

She shook her head in silence for several moments, then whispered, "Remember."

Fleming leaned into the counter as if it were the only thing keeping her on her feet.

"I think it's better we do this here than at the station, don't you?" I said.

She took a deep breath. "He said I would never have to talk about this, ever. He promised me."

"Who promised you?"

"The policeman."

I stepped over to the counter. "What policeman told you this?"

"Back then, a detective."

"Hazzard?" I asked.

She nodded. "He said no one would ever know."

"And you've kept this secret all these years."

She turned and looked at me and nodded.

"But he didn't tell you that secret would never go away, did he?" I said.

"Sometimes it feels like yesterday."

"What happened that night?" I asked.

She started to pick up her cup of coffee but stopped when her hand began to shake.

"I had heard about him from other actors in the class and from people in the theater."

"Manning?"

Fleming nodded. "There were stories that he had groped some actresses. Some people believed the stories, others didn't."

"You didn't."

She shook her head. "He was such a good

teacher . . . it didn't make sense. You wanted to be around him, you wanted him to like you."

"And he liked you."

I recognized the look in her eyes as shame.

"I thought so."

"So you left with him that night after class and you didn't go home alone."

She took a breath and looked at me. "I was only nineteen. I thought someone that talented could only be good."

"Where did you go?"

She walked back to the table and sat down, drawing her legs up and clutching them to her chest.

"We went to his apartment in Hollywood. He poured some wine. I told myself for years that it happened because I had too much wine to drink."

"But you didn't," I said.

"No. He was telling me about working in a movie. . . . Then he told me to remove my clothes."

She hesitated, remembering that night.

"'If you want to be an actress,' he said, 'remove your clothes.'"

She glanced at me as tears began to fall down her cheeks.

"I guess I went there because I thought . . . I tried to leave, to fight him off, but . . . He raped me." She lost her breath for a moment. "When he was done with me I rushed out without my shoes. I walked home in bare feet."

The image of my brother running in his socks hit me and my breath caught short. I stepped away from the table and looked out the window for a moment until it slowed.

"Do you know what time you left?" I asked.

She shook her head. "It seemed like a long time. I know I didn't get home until almost midnight. Then I didn't tell anyone—not even my closest girlfriends. A few days later the police came to ask me some questions and I thought everything was going to be all right."

"Hazzard?"

She nodded. "I told him what happened."

"And it wasn't all right?"

She shook her head. "He said since I went to his apartment voluntarily, I couldn't prove that he raped me. He told me never to talk about it, ever. That it would only complicate the murder investigation, which was more important than what had happened to me."

"He couldn't have committed the murder if he was in his apartment with you," I said.

She lowered her head and nodded. "I thought my silence would help to punish him for what he did. . . . It didn't, though."

"And you've done what Hazzard said. You didn't tell the lawyer Gavin—no one."

She shook her head. "The other policeman asked, too, and I told him the same thing."

"What other policeman?"

"He came a day or two after Gavin. I don't remember his name. He was black."

"Williams?"

Fleming nodded. "I think so."

She rested her head on her knees and began to rock slowly back and forth.

"I thought one day it would feel different, like it never really happened."

She looked up at me and shook her head. "I was wrong. . . . He had no right to tell me what he did," she whispered. "He had no right."

32

I stayed with her until she had said everything she needed to or could manage. None of the details changed, but with each telling her emotions became sharper as the pain worked its way from the past to the present.

As she opened the front door Fleming stopped me.

"Why you?" she asked. "Why after all these years and all the policemen in this city are you the one?"

I could hear the words in my head as I answered. They were about a blue dress, and the sound a golf club makes as it leaves a small dent in a wood floor, but they weren't the words I said to her.

"I took the call," I answered.

The drive back to Pasadena should have taken a little over fifteen minutes but I wound my way through surface streets, stretching it out to nearly an hour. If I had had doubts before that my own father was capable of killing, they were gone now. But had learning of his raping a young actress cemented that possibility, or was it the alibi that cleared him of suspicion? Was he any less of a monster if he was guilty only of rape? Was the damaged woman I had left in Eagle Rock less of a victim than Victoria Fisher? And where did that leave me? Was that day in the closet the end, or was it the beginning?

Harrison and Chavez were waiting for me when I walked back into my office.

"Your phone was off," Chavez said.

"I was talking to Candice Fleming."

Harrison handed me a cup coffee and I walked over to the window. The sun had begun to bleach the blue from the sky. A thin line of smoke hung horizontally across the mountains like a boundary line on a map.

"What do we know about Hazzard?" I said.

"Highly decorated, retired as the highest-ranking detective in Robbery Homicide," Chavez said.

"He may have suppressed evidence that could clear my father of suspicion for Victoria Fisher's murder."

"You're certain?"

"That he suppressed evidence, yes. Whether it would clear my father, I'm less sure. There are questions about the time line."

"What evidence?" Chavez asked.

I turned from the window.

"The night Victoria Fisher died he raped Candice Fleming."

The words seemed to sting Chavez, whose role had always been to protect me. On some level he still wanted to believe I was that naive rookie cop he had met all those years ago.

"She told you this? Your father did this?"

I nodded.

"You believe her story?"

"Yes."

"Why?"

I looked at Harrison.

"A little girl in a blue dress told me last night."

Harrison's eyes registered understanding but Chavez shook his head.

"What does that mean?" the chief said.

"My father's violence began in my house when I was a little girl."

Like someone who has just been told of the death of a family member, Chavez looked like he had taken a physical blow. The muscles in his jaw tensed, then he sat down on the edge of the desk.

"I'm okay," I said.

He tried to nod but it was a pale imitation at best. "Maybe you're mistaken about this."

I walked over and sat on the edge of the desk next to him.

"I don't think so. . . . But you're right, maybe."

"Maybe's good," Chavez said. He took my hand and gave it a squeeze, then let go.

"I need you to find out something," I said.

"Anything."

"Detective Williams talked to Fleming before he was

killed. He must have known something about what happened eighteen years ago. It might help to know what it was."

He nodded.

"I'll make some calls," Chavez said, then stood and walked out.

On the wall of my office was a smaller version of Danny's map of the universe. I walked over and stared at it for a moment in the vain hope that everything might become clear. No luck.

"Caltech should have an image for us from the security camera by midday," Harrison said.

"Maybe someone over there should take a look at this, too," I said.

"Someone in chaos theory," Harrison said.

"There's nothing here that can help us. This is a picture of the world inside Danny's head."

"You mentioned a time line," Harrison said.

"My father took Candice Fleming to his apartment in Hollywood after they left the theater around seven. It would have taken at least twenty minutes to get to his apartment. They had some wine and talked." The picture of my father as the hapless bicycle salesman on *Gunsmoke* flashed in my head, but I couldn't hold on to it. With each new piece of information, the past I had always clung to was quickly vanishing. "Fleming could have been there an hour, or two or three; she couldn't say."

"And Victoria Fisher left the restaurant on Melrose around nine," Harrison said.

I nodded.

"That's not a very big window of opportunity."

I tried to work back through the autopsy report but the details eluded me. "Was there any semen present in Victoria Fisher's body or on her clothes?"

Harrison shook his head. "Just the first two victims."

"Which would be consistent with an attacker who had just raped another woman a short time before."

"Or who had been fought off."

"What if there was another reason?"

We thought about it in silence for a moment.

"Victoria's and your brother's killer was neither your father nor the River Killer."

"Cross's conspiracy theory."

Harrison nodded.

"On the day my brother died, he and Gavin made four stops, the first at Candice Fleming's. Their last meeting was with Hazzard. What about the other two addresses? Did you match them?"

"Their second stop that day was at the County Courts building."

I tried to fit that into the puzzle but couldn't.

Harrison nodded. "I couldn't make sense of that, either. The third stop was Parker Center."

"Police headquarters."

"Where Robbery Homicide works from."

"Which brings us back to Hazzard."

I walked over to the door. The detective squad room was filled with the sounds of police work—keyboards, printers humming, phone interviews. I closed the door and looked back at Harrison.

"So I can either believe the time line works and my father is a killer, or . . ."

We let the idea sit for a moment.

"Or a highly decorated detective in the most elite unit in LAPD, and possibly people in the district attorney's office, are involved in the murders of at least three people," Harrison said. "Four if you include Victoria Fisher."

"And the police assassination of Hector Lopez."

"Not much of a choice."

The implication settled over us.

"It might be better if you step away from this," I said.

"For whom?"

"I don't have a choice with this; you do."

Harrison tried to smile. "Someone has to rewrap your bandages."

"We keep this between us—no one else."

Harrison nodded.

There was a knock on the door and Chavez stepped in. He started to say something, then saw the looks on our faces.

"Something's happened."

I shook my head. "Just working out the details."

Chavez closed the door and leaned against it, crossing his thick arms over his chest. "It's a bad career move to lie to your chief."

I forced a smile. "Only if you're caught."

He looked at Harrison. "It's even worse if you're not a lieutenant."

"I can always go back to the bomb squad," Harrison said.

Chavez let it go for the moment. "Detective Williams spent seven years with IA before joining Homicide."

"Internal Affairs."

"You need anything else, you talk to a Captain Larson."

"What division does he work out of?"

"Downtown."

I looked at Harrison.

"Parker Center."

33

Parker Center was the headquarters LAPD built to honor the legacy and integrity of its legendary chief William H. Parker. When he arrived on the scene in the 1950s, L.A. was an open city with enough corruption in and out of the department to rival that of any large eastern city.

He built a modern department that was the model for police across the country until a petty criminal named Rodney King went for a drive with too much malt liquor in his system. The cracks that opened that night in the foundations of Parker Center were deeper than the ones caused by the officers' batons on Rodney's head, and have yet to be completely stitched back together.

Larson agreed to talk to us, but not on the record, and not in the office. An outside agency asking questions about a recently murdered detective was not in his career's best interest. An officer who had fallen in the line of duty was the one sacred cow left standing after the scandals had done their damage to the department. The fact that I was the one asking the questions, the woman cop who had walked away with a bump on her ribs when their detective had his throat cut, did not go down well in any squad room in any division across the city.

Harrison and I stopped outside a small restaurant off Alpine in Chinatown just before noon. The few hints of smoke that occasionally drifted on the wind gave way to the intense aromas of ginger, garlic, and brewing tea inside. The railroad car–like seating area ran straight back. The diners all appeared to be Chinese. There was no sign of an Anglo cop anywhere. A thin waiter in a red vest approached us, said something in Cantonese, and pointed vigorously to the back of the restaurant and motioned for us to follow.

We walked the length of the seating area and into the long galley kitchen where the cooks, standing over woks, smoking cigarettes, stopped what they were doing and stared at us. The waiter motioned toward a door at the back of the kitchen and we walked into an alley where an unmarked squad car was parked.

Larson stepped out of the driver's side and looked around, making sure he wasn't being watched. He looked to be well past the age where being anything other than an Internal Affairs officer was an option. He had thinning hair and moved like a man never sure his foot was going to meet ground on the next step. I started to introduce myself but he interrupted me.

"I was under the impression we were doing this alone," he said, not once looking at Harrison.

"We are alone. This is my partner."

"I don't like witnesses to meetings that never happened."

Like most Internal Affairs officers, he trusted no one, particularly other cops.

"Who knows you're here besides Chavez?"

"No one."

"And you're certain you weren't followed?"

I nodded.

"You have questions about Williams?"

The back door of the restaurant opened and a waiter poked his head out and said something to Larson in Chinese. He shook his head and the waiter nodded, then disappeared back inside.

"This is how it works," Larson said, turning to me. "You're here because of Chavez, no other reason. He tells me you're not to blame for Williams's death. I accept that, but not enough for me to be here any longer than necessary. You ask me a question, I answer it, you get nothing beyond that, no freebies."

"Twenty questions?" I said.

"Take it or leave it."

Larson glanced over at the open door of his squad as if he were about to bolt.

"You worked with Williams?" I asked.

He nodded. "I was his supervisor for four years before he moved on to Homicide."

"Did Williams make any inquires with IA either the day he was killed or the day before?" I said.

Larson gave away a look of surprise for just a moment. "Yeah, the day he was murdered," he said.

"Did it have anything to do with the River Killer investigation eighteen years ago?"

Larson shook his head. "No."

"Did it have anything to do with the questioning of a rape victim named Fleming, or a suspect named Manning?"

He shook his head, glanced at his watch. "Anything else?"

"Did he inquire about a Homicide detective named Hazzard?"

Larson looked at me with a mixture of surprise and concern. "How do you know this?"

"Did he?" I repeated.

"Yeah, he asked about Hazzard, from when he was in patrol, before he made detective."

"What kind of investigation?"

"OID."

"Officer-involved death."

Larson nodded.

"Were any other officers involved?"

"His partner, but just as a witness."

"Cross," I said.

"Yeah," Larson said. "It was routine. The findings

of the investigation were that Hazzard acted in accordance with guidelines involving use of deadly force."

"Was Williams ever involved in investigating Hazzard when he was with Internal Affairs?"

"I think we're done here," Larson said, turning back to the car.

"What are you afraid of?" I said.

Larson stopped. "Name it."

Harrison glanced at me briefly.

"Robbery Homicide?"

The name seemed to make Larson wince.

"What do you think LAPD is, Lieutenant? A scout troop? It's a tribe. And in that tribe there are other tribes—some powerful, some dangerous, some both. I'm a Band-Aid the department puts on wounds so the public feels better, that's all. I do my work, I go home and have a drink, then I get up and do it all again the next day. Consider that career advice, no charge."

"Did a lawyer named Gavin request information about the same OID investigation the day before Williams did?"

The look on Larson's face was all the answer I needed.

"Is it possible to see that report?" I asked.

"If a request is made through official channels, I believe you'll find that no so such report still exists." Larson's joyless face became even grimmer. "Give my best to Chavez. And don't contact me again."

He walked to his squad and quickly drove away without looking back. Harrison and I stood in silence for a moment, Larson's words settling uncomfortably over us.

"What does a twenty-year-old investigation that cleared Hazzard have to do with the death of Victoria Fisher, your father, or three deaths years later?"

I shook my head. "Maybe everything."

We walked back through the restaurant onto the sidewalk out front. Passing slowly by was an LAPD black-and-white. The driver, wearing dark wraparound sunglasses, looked in our direction for a moment, then stared straight ahead as he drove past.

"What did that look like to you?" Harrison said.

The squad car paused for a second as it turned the corner, then disappeared.

"An exclamation point."

Regardless of what we thought we knew when we walked through the doors of the restaurant, we walked out with an entirely different set of questions.

Across the street a man walked out of a poultry store carrying two headless chickens still weakly flapping their wings.

"You suppose the chickens know something we don't?" Harrison said.

"What was Gavin's and my brother's next stop?" I asked.

"The County Courts building."

34

It was a short drive up over Broadway to 210 W. Temple, the Los Angeles County Courts Building. We stopped in a space reserved for police vehicles and watched as a steady stream of jurors filed back into the building after lunch. In a justice system responsible for a population greater than forty-two of the fifty states in the nation, the building gave the appearance that it was bursting at the seams.

"Why a court building?" Harrison said.

It hadn't occurred to me until that moment, then it seemed all too obvious.

"It's not just a court building," I said, and stepped out of the car. "It's also the district attorney's headquarters."

"Where Victoria Fisher worked," Harrison said.

"If Gavin and my brother went through those doors, security will have a record of where they went."

Inside, hundreds of jurors were waiting their turns to step through the metal detectors. No one got beyond the lobby without a pass, juror badge, or official ID. We showed our IDs to a deputy and were directed to a bank of elevators reserved for non-courtroom floors.

Being a county facility, security was provided by sheriff's deputies, not LAPD, but there was no shortage of uniformed officers and detectives present on their way to or from court or the DA's office, all of whom seemed to glance in my direction as if there were a large target taped to my back. We stepped off the elevator on the eighteenth floor and stopped at reception.

We showed our IDs once again and gave the receptionist my brother's and Gavin's names and the date of their visit. She entered the information in the computer and quickly got a result.

"They signed into room eighteen-twelve-seven."

"Which is?" I asked.

"Bureau of Central Operations Administration."

"Do people within the department need to sign in here?"

"Only visitors."

"Is the name Hazzard listed either that day or the day after?" I asked.

The receptionist scanned the columns of names and shook her head. "Nothing here."

Walking down the hallway to the office was like falling down a rabbit hole into the worst nightmares we have to offer. In this room, crimes against children; in that one, gang violence; in the last room on the right, sex crimes.

We stepped inside and were clearly eyed as police officers by everyone within our field of view. We gave the receptionist the information and she checked the logs on her computer.

"They weren't here to see anyone; it was a freedom of information request for documents," she said.

"About an OID investigation?"

She shook her head. "Documents related to specific investigations remain in that department's records."

"Can you tell me what the file was they requested?"

She nodded and hit a few keys. "It was a personnel record, a Victoria Fisher."

"I'd like to see the documents they requested."

She passed along the request and a few minutes later a black woman in her late fifties named Robinson stepped into the reception area.

"I'm sorry, the file you requested is no longer available."

"I'm sorry?" I said, thinking I had misunderstood.

"That file is no longer available."

"What do you mean by 'available'?"

"Files this old are still only on paper. When we say they aren't available, between you and me, it means we can't locate them: They could have been moved years ago to records, they could have been misfiled, God only knows."

"Six days ago this same file was requested. Was it available then?"

"I could check the copy logs to see if any duplicates were made."

She stepped away to another desk and returned a moment later with a puzzled look on her face.

"Apparently it was—one copy was made. Gavin was the name on the request. The file must have been moved within the last few days," she said.

"Where did it go?" I asked.

She smiled the way an aged grandmother would who has been asked the same question over and over again year after year.

"That would depend on why it was moved," she said.

"And you don't have that information."

She smiled brightly. "Honey, when I don't know something, I just assume it's been done for a reason and move on."

"Good advice."

Robinson walked away and I stepped back to the receptionist. "How far back can you track requests for information?"

"We switched to this operating system about four years ago. Anything before that would be on disk; five years before that it's all paper."

"Would you check to see if anyone else has requested this file at any time?"

She nodded and hit a few keys and began scanning information. Several pages in she stopped.

"About a year and a half ago, another civilian request."

"What was the name?"

"Fisher," she said.

I looked at Harrison. "Danny."

I thanked the receptionist and we stepped back into the hallway, trying to fit the new pieces of the puzzle into what we knew so far.

"A boy trying to uncover the mystery behind his mother's murder requests his mother's personnel file. Then a year and a half later the son and lawyer of the suspected serial killer request the same file."

A detective stepped out of a doorway down the hall and leaned against the wall, looking in our direction.

"Why just one copy?" Harrison said. "A single piece of paper?"

We looked at each other for a moment.

"The fax."

I glanced down the hall and the detective was gone.

"This is what it's like in my head," I whispered, then looked at Harrison. "You remember the definition of madness about repeated action?"

"Someone who repeats the same thing over and over expecting a different result."

I nodded and looked back down the hallway. "It could also be a definition of hope."

I picked up my phone and punched in the number for Cross's office. It rang twice and was picked up by an operator.

"Investigations, Palmdale. How may I direct your call?"

"Investigator Cross," I said.

"I'm sorry, Investigator Cross is out of the office this week."

"Are you sure?"

"Yes. Would you like to talk to another investigator, or leave your name and number?"

I quickly hung up. "Cross is out of the office all week."

"Which is strange, since you just saw him two days ago," Harrison said.

From around the corner I heard the sound of footsteps echoing on the marble floor and then silence.

"If paranoia was a crop you grow," I said, "I believe we just stepped into a field of it."

As we passed the reception desk and walked to the bank of elevators, I noticed the receptionist picking up the phone. Two floors before the lobby, the elevator stopped and two plainclothes detectives stepped in and quickly turned their backs, without making eye contact, blocking our exit.

As we reached the lobby one of the detectives reached inside his jacket, pulling it back just enough to reveal the weapon on his belt. The doors opened and the detectives paused just long enough for a sense of threat to rise in my throat, and then they walked away.

Outside the courthouse the wind was blowing out of the desert again. Pieces of paper and plastic bags blew along the curb like they were caught in the current of a river.

As we approached the Volvo I realized where I had seen one of the detectives on the elevator with us.

"The lead officer at Lopez's shooting—I think he was just on the elevator with us."

"Pearce," Harrison said.

"Funny him being in that elevator at the same time as us."

Harrison's attention was on something across Temple.

"It gets funnier," Harrison said.

I looked across the street. The sidewalk was filled with people who had left the courthouse and were heading to their cars.

"What is it?" I said.

Harrison shook his head. "I think I just saw Cross."

35

Danny had been moved from the hospital in Pasadena to County USC and its lockdown psych ward. Pulling up outside County, it was easy to understand how the PI Andi James had lost my brother the night she was following him.

What Barnum & Bailey is to circuses, County USC is to medicine. It was built back when it was assumed one facility could handle all of Los Angeles's medical needs. Its large white edifice looms over the surrounding neighborhood to the east of downtown. The large open wards feel as if they were lifted from a page in a Dickens novel. On any given day it handles more patients than almost any hospital in the country. One out of every twenty-seven babies born in the United States arrives here. The treatment of high-velocity impact wounds is a specialty in the emergency ward.

Inside, the people waiting for treatment reminded me of the crowd in a large open-air market in East L.A.

There were a dozen different languages being spoken. Old men in cowboy hats in wheelchairs, young pregnant mothers in labor, fever-stricken children all waited their turn for treatment behind the gunshot and car-accident and heart-attack victims.

The psych ward, in contrast to the chaos around it, was quiet. Or at least the kind of quiet produced by tranquilizers. We checked our weapons with the deputy at reception, then were led into the general ward, which was nothing more than a very large room with beds pushed up against the wall. A few patients stared at a television in the corner with no sound. Others sat or lay motionless on their beds. A few walked back and forth, trying to pass the hours of boredom.

An orderly passed us into the lockdown area and directed us to the desk in the center of the ward. A nurse was walking past each locked room, glancing through the windows in the doors at the patients inside. The resident on call met us at reception and introduced himself. As we walked to Danny's room, he started to fill us in on his condition.

"He's had moments of lucidity, but they don't last more than a few minutes at a time, and then he retreats into extreme paranoia, bordering on the fantastic."

"He's got reason," I said.

We stopped at the door.

"At two this morning he was convinced there were eyes in the walls watching him. He had to be restrained. We're trying some new protocols that will hopefully balance things out for him."

"Has he talked about an angel or dark angel?"

The doctor shook his head. "He hasn't talked to us at all. I don't believe he looks at us as being the good guys."

"If he sees you as the enemy, we'd like to see him alone."

The doctor nodded his approval. "You can try, but I'd be surprised if he talks to you."

The doctor unlocked the door and Harrison and I stepped in. The room was not much bigger than a cell. The walls were painted a dull yellow. Anything that could possibly be harmful to patients or others had been removed.

Danny was wearing white hospital scrubs, standing at a small sealed window that looked out toward the west and the towers of downtown. When the doctor closed the door, Danny turned around and looked at us.

"Do you remember me, Danny?" I asked.

He looked at me blankly, giving away nothing. "I'm crazy, not stupid. I remember you."

He looked at Harrison. "I don't know him, though."

"He's my partner, Harrison."

"How do I know that?"

"Would you like to see my ID?" Harrison said.

"Anyone can get an ID."

"I can wait outside if you prefer."

Danny smiled, shook his head. "You pass."

"Do you mind if we sit down?" I asked.

"Mi casa es su casa."

As we stepped over and sat on the bed, I noticed Danny took exactly half a step away from us for each one we moved closer.

"I want to talk about your map and some other things."

"You talked to my grandmother, didn't you?"

"I couldn't talk to you, you weren't home."

"My grandmother's old. I think she has Alzheimer's."

"A year and a half ago you went to the district attorney's office and asked to see your mother's personnel file."

He shook his head.

"No I didn't," Danny said, taking a step away. "I don't know what you're talking about."

"You went to the courthouse, signed in, and found a file. Do you remember? It was something to do with an old police investigation, twenty years old."

"I don't know what you're talking about. I think you should see a doctor."

He folded his arms across his chest and pressed himself against the wall.

"It's important that I know what's in that file."

"Why?"

"Because the man who killed your mother also killed my brother."

Danny exhaled sharply, then looked at me. The dull sheen of the narcotics' effects appeared to vanish from his eyes.

"So you're like me?" he asked.

For an instant I was back in the closet listening to my father pull the hangers across the rod.

"Yeah, I'm like you."

"Do you have dreams?"

I nodded. He let his arms fall to his sides and closed his eyes.

"I remember everything," he whispered.

He opened his eyes and they were full of tears.

"I remember the night she didn't come home. They let me stay up watching out the window for her headlights to turn into the driveway, only they never did. When she wasn't there in the morning no one said anything until the phone rang and my grandfather answered it on the second ring. That's when the secrets started—people whispering, talking about me like I wasn't in the room. But I heard everything, just like now."

"Do you remember it, Danny?"

He spoke just above a whisper.

"I remember. It said they all fell down."

"Who fell?"

The clarity in Danny's eyes began to slip back into the dullness of the drugs and he didn't appear to hear my question. I looked at Harrison and shook my head.

"He said that before at my house. It's like the game kids play, Ring Around the Rosy . . . but I don't know what it means."

"They all fell to the ground, but one of them," Danny said.

"Who didn't fall, Danny?"

"Them, one of them, wouldn't fall."

Harrison tried to find a crack in the words that would bring some understanding but it eluded him.

"You've got to tell us more, Danny, that's not enough," I said.

"They were all supposed to fall, but he wouldn't."

"Why? Who wouldn't fall?" I asked.

"I told you, he, he, hehehehehehehehehheeeee!"

Harrison shook his head in exasperation.

"Don't think I didn't see that," Danny said.

"Do you know the name Hazzard? Was he there when they wouldn't fall?"

"Hazzard's a policeman."

"That's right."

Danny looked at me, struggling to retrieve the information from his confused mind. "Hazzard? I remember that name. He was helping to find my mother's . . . You're a policeman."

The words appeared to exhaust him and he slowly sank down to the floor. I walked over and knelt in front of Danny, trying to draw him back from the haze of the drugs.

"I need your help, Danny."

"Do you remember everything, Lieutenant?" Danny asked.

The sound of the golf club striking my father jarred me like a clap of thunder.

"Almost everything, " I said.

He put his hands to his head as if the memories

inside were pounding to get out. "Me too."

His eyes drifted across the room and he appeared to be slipping away.

"What happened to the file, Danny?" I asked, trying to bring him back.

He shook his head. "You won't find it."

"Why won't I find it?"

"I told you, I remember everything, just like you."

"Tell me where it is," I said.

He pointed to his head. "Here. That's where it is."

"In your head?" I said.

"Yes . . . that's where it is."

He sat motionless for a moment, his eyes beginning to wander in the haze of meds. We helped him to the bed and laid him down. The muscles in his face began to relax; I could see the boy of five standing at his bedroom window waiting for the lights of his mother's car to sweep the driveway. I placed my hand lightly on his forehead.

"She loved you very much," I said, but he was already as far away from the small dull room and his sad memories as the drugs would take him.

The sun was going down when Harrison and I stepped outside County USC. As we walked to the car I noticed a large column of smoke rising to the west of L.A. and spreading out in the shape of an anvil.

In the block walk to the Volvo, the column of smoke had begun to turn the light the deep orange and red of the sunset. There were multiple sirens wailing in the distance.

"Danny's seen that file. 'They all fell down' is too specific; he's trying to tell us something but he can't figure it out in his mind."

Harrison nodded. "But what?"

An LAPD black-and-white came around the corner and gunned its engine as it sped past us.

"So much for Cross's vast conspiracy rippling through the highest levels of the halls of power," I said. "Twenty years ago cops didn't find other cops guilty in OID investigations unless there was no alternative. All it would have taken was for the IA officers not to look beyond the surface."

"Someone must have," Harrison said.

I nodded. "An ambitious law student working in the district attorney's office named Fisher, who found something she shouldn't have, and hid it in the only place she could think of until she figured out what to do with it."

"And it stayed hidden until Danny and Gavin and your brother found it," Harrison said. "Without that evidence we have nowhere to go with this."

"And without Danny, we can't find it."

I looked back at the hospital. The light reflecting on the windows made it appear that a fire was raging inside. The pager on Harrison's belt went off and he checked his message.

"Caltech has an image from the car."

36

The sun had set by the time we arrived in Pasadena at the Caltech campus. The smoke that had turned the sky the color of a blood orange now hung in the wind, carrying tiny particles of ash and soot that gathered in the corners of my eyes.

As we pulled up and stopped at the computer science building I noticed a gray sedan in the rearview mirror stop a block away.

"What is it?" Harrison said.

I checked the mirror again. The figure in the car hadn't made a move to get out.

"It's possible we're being followed."

Harrison glanced in the side mirror. "We must be doing something right."

I opened the door and stepped out, glancing back at the sedan. "That all depends on their point of view."

The computer specialist working on the disk from the parking garage was a doctoral candidate who appeared to be little more than twenty years old. He wore the standard uniform of the nerd genius of the school: a T-shirt that read BYTE ME, shorts, and sandals. He explained that the program he had used was originally designed for spy satellites, and then was adapted for use with deep-space pictures from the Hubble telescope.

As the image of the car began to appear on the screen Harrison tried to explain what was I seeing and how many pixels it took to create but it still made little sense to me.

"This was the first generation," the kid said.

I stared at the image of the car passing the garage entrance.

"I'm interested in the windshield. It looked like there was something visible in the shadows," I said.

He nodded, hit a few keys. "That's what I thought at first, but this was all I got." He hit a few more keys and the dark shadows began to lighten.

"I don't see anything," I said.

The kid nodded. "There's nothing there to see in the shadows. We're looking in the wrong place."

He hit a few more keys and the image began to refocus. "What you were seeing wasn't in the shadows, it was in the glass of the windshield."

"A reflection?"

He nodded.

"I think this is what you were looking for," he said.

The whiz kid's eyes darted back and forth between us, and a faint smile appeared on his face. "I solved something, didn't I?"

I let the idea settle, trying to understand what exactly we had found and what it meant—how it fit into the puzzle that now covered twenty years. I pointed at the screen just to the right of center on the windshield. "What is that?"

The kid did his best to hide his excitement at having solved God knows what in his imagination.

"Yeah, this is really cool," he said.

He worked the mouse and the keyboard again and the image on the screen shifted and gradually came into focus. The distinct shape of a hand appeared to float in the darkness, the thin white line of an unlit cigarette dangling between the fingers.

I stared at it for a moment and imagined the same hand picking up the gun that was placed against the side of my half brother's head.

"What does the cigarette say to you?" I asked Harrison.

"He's nervous. He could be trying to calm himself with a smoke."

I stared at the fingers. The cigarette dangled loosely, the way it might if the person had a cocktail in the other hand.

"That doesn't look like nervousness to me," I said.

Harrison nodded in agreement. The kid shifted in the chair and cleared his throat to get our attention.

"You see something else?" I asked.

He stared at the screen as if trying to decipher an image of a distant planet. "It's just an idea."

"Go on."

"It's not lit. When my father quit smoking, he'd hold a cigarette like that for hours sometimes."

Harrison looked at me in surprise. "The first meeting with Hazzard, when he was standing outside watching the fire approach."

"He had a cigarette in his fingers," I said.

Harrison nodded. "It was unlit."

"Would you put that image on a disk?" I asked, and got up from my chair.

The kid nodded and slipped a disk into the computer.

"It's a murder case, isn't it?" he said.

"Why do you say that?" I asked.

He looked us both over and smiled. I got the odd sensation that I was being dismantled and put back together like I was part of an equation.

"Isn't it obvious?" he said.

A flash of understanding way beyond his years played out in his eyes, then he turned back to the computer.

Obvious, I thought silently to myself.

We carried death in our eyes, the way we moved, our language, even our dreams. And the more we tried to disguise it, the more obvious it became.

"Yes," I said. "That's exactly what it is."

37

Outside Harrison and I sat in the car for a moment, neither of us saying what we were now clearly thinking. A cop killed my brother, Detective Williams, and Dana Courson. The same cop who set my father up for a series of murders he didn't commit. And the only proof we had was a file that no longer existed, and an image of an unlit cigarette on a security camera.

"What do you want to do?" Harrison asked.

"You mean short of taking Hazzard's confession?"

In the rearview mirror I saw the same dark sedan that had followed us pull away from the curb and drive toward us.

"I think we must have hit a nerve," I said.

I lowered my hand to my waist and rested it on the handle of the Glock as the sedan approached from the rear, pulled alongside, and stopped. The tinted passenger-side window slowly opened, and I saw Cross sitting behind the wheel.

"I don't like being followed," I said.

"We're on the same side, Lieutenant. I'm just covering our backs. We need to talk."

"Something wrong with the phone?"

Cross nodded. "You bet. There's a parking garage up ahead on the left. Follow me."

I glanced at Harrison, then did as Cross said, following him into the dark garage.

We wound our way up to the third level and parked alongside Cross. The rest of the level was nearly empty. He slid across to the passenger seat and rolled down the window.

"You were outside the courthouse," I said.

"I'm not the only one."

"LAPD."

Cross nodded. "I don't make a habit of sitting in parking garages."

His face was lined with exhaustion. The hair under the baseball cap he wore was streaked with sweat.

"You tell me what you think you know, and I'll tell you if you're on the right track," Cross said.

"IA investigated Hazzard for the killing of a suspect when you were both in patrol; you were his partner."

Cross nodded. "He was cleared."

"Did you ever see the final report?" I asked.

"No, I was a rookie. Back then you did your job and shut up."

"You were questioned as a witness."

"I was handed a statement and told to sign it. I never even read it."

"What happened?"

Cross shook his head. "I don't know, I wasn't there."

"I think the document that Victoria Fisher found had something to do with that investigation."

He nodded.

"We need to see it," I said.

Cross suppressed a nervous laugh. "It's gone, *whoosh*, into the ether. It never existed. It won't help, forget it."

I looked at Cross for a moment. "What haven't you told us?"

Cross took a breath. "I think you would be better off just walking away, Lieutenant. There's nothing you can do."

"Why?"

"Hazzard killed Victoria Fisher, then pinned it on your father and made sure he disappeared so no arrest would ever be made. No arrest, no questions, it all ends."

"He claimed the body of a transient on the railroad tracks was my father?"

Cross nodded. "The investigation ended, nothing is provable. A perfect crime."

"Except it isn't perfect," I said.

"Why?"

"Thomas Manning didn't kill Victoria Fisher."

"Without proof it's meaningless." He looked at me for a long moment. "What do you know?"

"Thomas Manning couldn't have killed Victoria

Fisher because at the time of her death he was inside his apartment raping a young actress."

Cross stared at me in shock, then sank back into the seat.

"Two places at once can't be done."

"That's right."

"You're sure?"

"I've talked to her."

Cross stiffened and sat forward. "That leaves only one possible scenario for what happened to your brother."

I nodded. "Hazzard."

"Can you prove any of this?" Cross asked.

I shook my head. "Not without the fax my brother sent me the night he was killed."

Cross sat back. "What are you doing here at Caltech?"

"We have an image of the car my brother's killer was driving the night he died."

"Plates?"

I shook my head. "Just a make and the killer's hand holding an unlit cigarette."

Cross looked at me for a moment then stared out into the darkness of the garage.

"That's not enough," he said.

"It's almost enough."

Cross began to shake his head.

"Almost can't do nothing but get you killed," he whispered. "You think LAPD is just going to walk in and let you gut them like this?"

He took a deep breath. "You never talked to me, we never met, and I've never heard any of the things you just said. If asked under oath, I'll put my hand on the Bible and swear to it."

He slid behind the wheel and sped the length of the garage and disappeared down the ramp.

A moment later the sound of squealing tires came roaring around the corner behind us. We turned, reaching at the same time for our weapons as an SUV drove past us, the front seat full of college students. My hand relaxed around the handle of the Glock, and I took a breath.

"You want to try pushing Hazzard?" Harrison said.

I shook my head. "Not until we have somewhere to push him."

I drove back down the ramp, stopping the car as we emerged onto the street. There was no sign of Cross. Across the commons, clusters of students walked to and from class.

"What are you thinking?" Harrison asked.

"Science," I said, as two clusters of students walking in the same direction became one group, then split into three groups, each heading in a different direction.

"How do you find structure in events that appear unrelated?" I said.

I looked at Harrison, who glanced over at the groups of students I had been watching.

"In bomb disposal you work backwards from a presumed point of detonation. Make connections that must be present for the device to work even if they aren't visible."

"If the fax was the page from the report, let's say that's the point of detonation. Where do you go from there?"

"You work back from the last point of contact, or in this case anyone who's seen it." Harrison played it out in his head for a moment. "Hazzard, your brother, your father if they talked to him, Gavin, possibly Detective Williams, and Danny."

"I wouldn't count on Hazzard coming forward."

"Which leaves Danny or your father."

I let the idea settle for a moment, or tried to.

"Which one?" I said. "The hapless bicycle salesman, the love-struck Indian, or the Cyclops victim?"

Harrison looked at me, doing his best imitation of understanding.

"There're some things I haven't told you about my father and me."

"I imagine those are private," Harrison said.

"If my father had wanted to come to me with this, or was capable of coming to me with this, he would have by now."

"You're still a cop," Harrison said. "He's spent the last eighteen years hiding from them."

"And the eighteen before that hiding from me," I said.

Harrison turned and watched an intense young student walk by, lost in conversation with himself.

"Which leaves Danny," Harrison said.

"Something's happening, probably right now, and we're missing it."

"We could bring Hazzard in, hold him for as long as we can."

I shook my head.

"It wasn't Danny," I said.

"You lost me," Harrison said.

"Danny may have seen the file, but he wasn't the one who requested it at the DA's office."

"Why?"

"You have to be of age to receive records like that. He wasn't lying, it wasn't him."

"He was a juvenile."

I nodded.

"His grandmother requested the file," Harrison said.

38

Danny's grandmother was waiting for us when we pulled into the driveway. I had called ahead but didn't give her any details except that we had talked to Danny in the hospital.

She led us back into the house and we sat down at the kitchen table as before.

"He won't see me," she said. "I've tried several times, but . . ."

"He will when he's stabilized," I said.

She took a deep breath and shook her head.

"I'm sorry about what he did to your house, if that's what your visit is about. I would be more than willing to pay for any damages—"

"That's not why I'm here."

"I don't understand why he did that to you."

"The only suspect in your daughter's murder ever arrested was my father, Mrs. Fisher. That's why Danny did what he did."

Fisher stared at me for a moment in silence. "Your father?"

"Yes."

She stood up and walked over to the window and looked out.

"Why did you come here?"

"I'm here because the private investigator who was murdered was my brother."

She turned and looked at me.

"We believe he found evidence that points to the real killer of your daughter."

"And you're going to tell me it wasn't your father."

"That's what we think it suggests."

She shook her head. "Why didn't you tell me this before?"

"Before, I thought it was possible that my father was guilty, but I wasn't sure."

"I don't want anything to do with this. How dare you come to my house and use a disturbed boy to prove you're not the daughter of a killer. I want you out of my house."

She started walking toward the door.

"You may already have something to do with it," I said.

She stopped at the edge of the dining room and looked back.

"Who killed my daughter?"

I glanced over at Harrison.

"We think your daughter was murdered because she discovered something at the DA's office involving a police investigation," Harrison said.

Mrs. Fisher went over the meaning of the words in her head. "You're telling me a policeman killed Victoria?"

Harrison nodded. "It appears to be the most likely possibility."

"Can you prove this?"

"A year and a half ago you requested your daughter's personnel file from the DA's office," I said.

She gave a measured nod. "Danny asked for it. I didn't want to fuel his paranoia, but I thought there might be something in there to help him know his mother, how wonderful she was."

"Did you look at it?" I asked.

"I tried . . . I looked at her ID picture . . . I couldn't look at the rest."

"Did you copy everything in the file?"

She stepped back over to the kitchen table and sat down. "Yes. Danny was very specific about that. He wanted everything."

"Do you know where it is?"

She nodded. "Danny took it into his apartment for a day or two, then gave it back to me. I haven't looked at it again. It's in the office in the other room."

"We'd like to see it."

She nodded and started to get up but stopped. "I don't understand. What does a personnel file have to do with my daughter's death?"

"She may have hidden what she discovered in that file

until she could figure out what to do with it."

Mrs. Fisher leaned back in her chair and took a breath. "And it's been there this whole time."

I nodded. "Was there. Her file is missing. I'm assuming it's been destroyed. Your copy is all that's left."

"With whatever evidence was in it?"

"Yes."

Fisher sat in silence for a moment as if trying to digest a new chapter in a book. When she appeared to have examined it enough, she turned and looked at me with the fierce eyes of a mother still protecting her daughter.

"What did your father have to do with this? Why was he arrested?"

"My father abused my mother and had a history of assaulting pretty young women like your daughter. I haven't seen my father in a very long time."

I didn't add any details about the attacks, though from the look in Fisher's eyes I doubted any of it would have been a surprise.

"The detective said he was dead, if I remember."

I shook my head. "He's alive."

"I'll go get the file," Fisher said.

She walked out of the room and returned a few moments later with a thin folder and set it on the table. I opened it and began to go through the contents—a performance evaluation, a copy of her employee ID, her employment application, and a tax document.

"It's not here."

Harrison quickly went through it also, but I hadn't missed anything.

"It would make sense that Danny would have removed it," Harrison said.

"Is there anywhere in the house or his apartment where Danny may have hidden something—a special place he might have talked about?" I asked.

Mrs. Fisher looked out toward the darkness of the garage.

"Danny didn't share his secrets, at least not with me. I wouldn't know where to begin to search, but you can try if you like." She turned and looked at me. "I suspect you may have more experience with keeping secrets than I do, Lieutenant."

We walked out to the garage and opened the door to Danny's apartment. The walls had been stripped of the pieces of newspaper and handwritten notes he had taped everywhere. Every piece of furniture, every possible hiding place had been gone through by crime-scene techs. The room had the feel of a tree that had been stripped of its leaves and branches by a windstorm. All that was left that identified it as a place where someone once lived was Danny's intricate map covering the back wall.

"I wish you could have taken that away also," Fisher said.

She stared at it for a moment, then turned and walked outside. Harrison and I began to go over the room again, but it quickly became clear that the few possible hiding places left held nothing.

"We may as well be looking for a needle in a pile of needles," Harrison said.

"He tried to tell us when we were at the hospital what we are missing," I said.

I stepped back to the door and looked at Danny's map.

" 'They all fell to the ground, but one of them,' " Harrison said, repeating Danny's words.

He stared at the map for a moment. "If there's a connection pointing to something, it's beyond me."

I reached for the light switch but stopped.

"Or we just weren't listening," I said.

" 'They all fell to the ground,' " Harrison said, shaking his head. "I don't see it. It just doesn't point us anywhere."

"Maybe we're missing it because it doesn't sound like something that can help us. What else did he say?"

Harrison replayed the conversation at the hospital in his mind.

"He told us it was 'here, that's where it is,' as he pointed to his head," Harrison said. "And inside his head is the one place we can't go."

I glanced at the spiraling orbits and swirling lines of words on the map, and then Danny's words seemed to fall into place.

"Maybe we don't have to," I said.

"Danny's told me twice where it is, I just didn't understand."

I looked at Harrison.

"I thought it was just a picture of madness. But that wasn't it. It was a message, it has to be, those words are too specific."

"What words?"

"The ones he painted on the ceiling of my bedroom. '*This is what it's like in my head.*' He left it at my house. That's why he went there."

39

Electricity had been restored to most of the neighborhood, though that mattered little to my own block, where there were no longer any homes but my own. The glow of flames was visible in the distance in several directions. The scent of burned citrus still drifted on the wind from the scorched lemon tree on the next lot. I slipped the key into the lock and pushed the front door open.

We stepped inside and shone our flashlights. The sight of what had happened to the inside of my house was still a jolt as I looked around. I thought I was beyond feeling or caring but I was wrong. Harrison stared in silence at the ash-covered furniture and the paint swirling across the walls.

"We should look at the message Danny left," Harrison said.

Walking down the hallway where my family pictures

had once hung, I began to feel like I had stumbled on an archaeological site. It wasn't my house any longer. The memories once contained in these walls no longer felt as if they were mine, but rather just another part of a world that had vanished into the past.

I pushed the bedroom door open and Harrison stepped in and looked up at the ceiling. He stared at it long enough to make out the words, then looked around the room.

"Where do people hide things of value in houses?" Harrison said.

"Sock drawers," I said.

I walked over to my dresser and pulled open the top drawer. The clothes inside were untouched by the gray ash that covered everything else. The whites and colors were as startling to look at as an open wound. I swept my hand through the clothes but found nothing there. I pulled open the next drawer and the next until I had gone through them all, but it wasn't there.

I looked over to the closet, but didn't say anything for a moment. A set of footprints was visible near the closet.

"Check the door," I said.

If he had guessed or understood anything about my past, he gave no indication of it. Harrison went over to the door and stopped. The knob was covered with a thin layer of ash that had been undisturbed.

"It's not here. This hasn't been opened."

"We're looking in the wrong places," I said. "You hide *things*—rings or jewelry—in drawers and closets.

We're looking for a piece of paper that he wants us to find."

"Like a note you leave someone if you're going to be out," Harrison said.

I turned and rushed down the hall to the living room and crossed over to the kitchen.

"This is where you leave a note," I said.

I checked the small kitchen table by the window but there was only a set of silverware, salt and pepper shakers, and a napkin, all covered in ash. On the kitchen counter ash covered the phone book, and a pad of paper next to the wall phone was untouched. A half-filled wineglass, a coffee cup, and a few plates were scattered across the counter, but nothing else. I felt Harrison's hand on my shoulder and he pointed the flashlight the length of the kitchen.

"The refrigerator."

In the circle of light a single sheet of paper hung on the refrigerator door, held by a small yellow magnet in the shape of a pencil.

"Did you or Lacy walk into the kitchen when you were here before?"

I shook my head. "I don't think so."

Harrison shone the light across the tile floor. There were two sets of prints in the ash.

"Someone else has been here. Shoes are different sizes," Harrison said.

"Could have been a fireman checking gas lines," I said, not really believing it.

I stepped over and shone my light on the paper

hanging next to a note, barely visible under the ash, that I had written to myself—*Call Lacy*.

I slipped the paper out from under the magnet and pointed my light on it. It was a legal-size xeroxed copy. In the upper left corner was the letterhead of the Los Angeles County District Attorney and the official government seal. Below was a statement, several paragraphs in length. Below that two signatures appeared.

"It's a witness deposition," I said. In the upper left corner was a date.

"Eighteen years ago," Harrison said.

I slipped my reading glasses out of my pocket and began to read. It was handwritten, not typed, and had the appearance of being done in haste.

Me and two friends, Darren and Walter, were walking home from a party when the police car stopped us.

What time?

Just a little before midnight.

Had you done something to get stopped?

You don't have to do anything to get stopped in L.A., lady. You just have to be breathing and black. We weren't gang members. We didn't break the law. Darren was an honor student. He was going to go to college in the fall.

What happened after they stopped you?

The cop told us to fall down and me and Walter did, but Darren wouldn't because we hadn't done anything. I think he was just tired of being treated like he had been stealing car stereos and selling dope from the day he was born. I didn't see all that happened after that 'cause my face was on the ground. The cop told him again, and when he didn't move the cop grabbed him around the neck, picked him up off the ground, and started choking him. All I saw was Darren's feet in the air, kicking like he was being hung. He was making these sounds like a baby, and it went on and on until his feet were just hanging there. The cop dumped him on the ground next to me and I looked at his eyes and knew he was dead. There wasn't no fight, he just wouldn't lie down on the ground because we hadn't done anything, and the cop killed him with his hands.

What about the other cop?

The other cop just stood there the whole time like we was nothing. They said Darren resisted arrest, that he fought back. They lied.

Did anyone from the Internal Affairs Division ever question you about this?

Not a cop, a lawyer, no one. It was like Darren never existed.

I stared at the piece of paper for a moment, trying to calculate the amount of misery it had caused, but it was beyond me.

"Everyone who's touched this is dead. . . . In Danny's mind he confused it with a nursery rhyme," I said.

The statement was taken from a Germaine Washington.

"Look who took the statement," I said.

"Victoria Fisher."

"Do you remember what day she died?" I asked.

"September twentieth, I think," Harrison said.

"This is dated two days before that."

"If we search Homicide records I imagine we'll find that Germaine Washington died shortly after this by a random gunshot or an unsolved drive-by shooting. Unless, of course, he stepped into the back of a police car one day and just vanished."

"It should be easy enough to match the details to that of the OID investi—" Harrison stopped himself, remembering what Larson had told us in the alley behind the restaurant. "What OID investigation?"

We stood in silence for a moment looking at the deposition, trying to understand fully what we were seeing, and more important, what we weren't.

"Why didn't Victoria put Hazzard's name on the document?" I said.

"Fear. She was accusing a cop of murdering an unarmed suspect. Maybe Germaine Washington didn't know a name."

"But Victoria Fisher did, otherwise there would be no reason for the interview."

I let the idea settle for a second. "She didn't include a name because she was afraid of the other cop who just stood there and did nothing."

"Cross," Harrison said. "He claimed he wasn't

present at the scene and signed a statement that was handed to him."

"According to this, he lied."

"Which makes him just as culpable," Harrison said.

"It's more than that," I said. "It makes him dangerous."

We looked at each other for a moment, sorting out the pieces.

"If Victoria didn't know that Cross was the other cop, what would be the first thing she would have done with this?"

"She would have showed it to Cross."

"And he picks up the phone and calls Hazzard."

"And Hazzard makes her death appear to be the work of the River Killer."

"Cross was telling the truth about a conspiracy . . . of two people. Himself and Hazzard."

The ash covering every inch of the inside of my home began to feel like it was part of the same lie that had buried the truth about Victoria Fisher's death. You could see everything in front of you but the details were obscured just enough to make the thing unrecognizable.

"My brother went looking for the truth about our father and stumbled on this."

I looked down at the footprints in the ash. Danny's were clearly marked by the imprint of the athletic shoes he had been wearing. The others were flat, leaving no imprint other than the shape of the shoe and its size.

"Who else was in my house?" I said.

"Hazzard or Cross?"

I shook my head.

"If it was Hazzard or Cross, they wouldn't have left this for us to find."

I stepped back into the living room and realized the extra set of prints had moved around the house. I looked in the hallway and saw that they led to Lacy's room. I stared at the blank footprints in the ash and then an old uneasiness returned.

"My father."

"We don't know that," Harrison said.

I nodded my head. "Yes we do. He's the only one left. What was he doing here?"

Harrison motioned to the paper in my hand. "He could have been looking for that."

"If he knew about this, he couldn't have known it was here." I followed the footprints to my daughter's door. "That's why he was here."

My heart began to race. "He wanted to look at his granddaughter's room."

"It could have been you he wanted to see," Harrison said.

I shook my head. "I don't think so."

I looked down at the imprint of his shoes, and the sound of his rage on the other side of the closet door was as real as if it had just happened.

"I was a little girl, maybe five. My mother hid me in a closet to protect me from him. I listened to him throw her about the house as she tried to stop him, and then he came for me." I looked at Harrison.

"My father didn't come here looking for me."

I glanced at the footprints one more time, then walked back outside as quickly as I could. Harrison stepped out a moment later and we stood in silence. The shifting wind had taken away the scent of burned lemon. I hadn't noticed before but the sounds that usually accompanied the night were also gone—no coyotes, no insect buzz, no birdsong or distant TV. The fire had taken it all.

"What do we do with this?" Harrison said. "Without names on it, how much value does it have?"

I looked at it for a moment, trying to connect all the acts of violence that had spun out from this piece of paper like the orbits in Danny's map.

"It's not all we have," I said, and turned to Harrison as one of those orbits became terribly clear. "They made a mistake . . . we made a mistake."

Harrison shook his head.

"It's Andi James, the PI at my brother's apartment, who could ID the man she saw there. And she still can."

A pained understanding appeared in Harrison's eyes.

"We told Hazzard it was Dana Courson," I said.

"And they killed an innocent thinking she could ID one of them."

"Oh, God," Harrison whispered as he realized something else. "We made another mistake."

I started to ask what, but stopped as I knew what we had done. "Candice Fleming."

Harrison nodded. "We told Cross."

40

It was almost ten o'clock when we stopped in front of Candice Fleming's Spanish bungalow.

"No lights," Harrison said.

We had tried calling half a dozen times on the drive over and each time the line had been busy.

"You would think a light would be on if someone is on the phone."

I stepped out of the car and scanned the street. The only movement was a man walking a dog halfway down the block; the only sound, distant traffic and the wind moving through a stand of palm trees.

We started up the front walk, watching the dark windows of the house for any movement. As we approached the steps Harrison touched my arm. The front door was ajar and swaying in the breeze.

I pulled out my Glock, rushed to the door, and pushed it open. Leaves had blown in the door and were scattered across the living room floor, but everything else seemed to be in place.

"Something's burning," Harrison said.

I crossed the dining room to the kitchen. The blue flame of a burner on the stove glowed in the darkness under a cooking pot that was beginning to smoke. Harrison walked over and turned off the burner.

"Macaroni and cheese," he said.

Alarm bells began ringing in my head.

"That's kid food. She was cooking for her son," I said.

"Where are they?" Harrison said.

I turned and looked into the darkness of the rest of the house.

"Check and see if the car is in the garage," I said.

Harrison stepped out the back heading to the garage and I rushed out of the kitchen to the hallway leading to the bedrooms.

"Candice?" I called, but there was no response.

The room on the right was a small home office, the door open. I raised my weapon and reached around and flipped on the light. The room was empty. I checked the bathroom with the same result, then stopped at the master bedroom door when Harrison returned from outside.

"Her car's in the garage," he said.

I quickly pushed open the door and stepped in, and Harrison switched on the light. A pair of jeans and a T-shirt were on the bed. A pair of black two-inch heels lay on the floor beneath them.

"She just got home from work and was starting to change," I said.

I turned and rushed across the hallway and pushed open the door to her son's bedroom. The small bed was unmade. A few piles of clothes were scattered across the room along with a number of model cars and trucks and helicopters. There were posters of Angels and Lakers players on the walls, and a large crayon self-portrait with the words "Peter, the Great." It was every little boy's room I had ever seen, and that only made it worse.

"They're both gone," I said.

My stomach began to turn with the realization that something I had said put them at risk.

"We'll need pictures of them both," I said. "See if you can find her purse or wallet."

Harrison nodded and left, and I walked over to the bed and sat down. The bedspread was a print of a rain forest with animals hanging from the trees. A pair of sneakers lay on the floor next to the bed, exactly as his mother had done in her room. A T-shirt had been tossed on the end of the bed and I reached over, picked it up, and held it to my face, taking in the sweet scent of a little boy.

As I set the shirt back on the bed I looked across the room and my eye stopped on a section of wall painted to look like a bear. In the center of the bear's paw was the doorknob for the closet. The air in the room seemed to vanish as I took a breath. I rose and walked over to the closet.

"Peter," I said softly.

I reached out and closed my fingers around the knob, turned it until the bolt cleared the jamb, then slowly opened it. I watched the line of light from the room slice across the darkness on the floor of the closet, stopping on two small sock-clad feet that flinched as the light touched them.

"It's all right, Peter, I'm a police officer," I said as gently as I could.

The feet drew back from the light, trying to cling to the darkness in the corner. I slowly knelt down in the doorway as Harrison stepped back into the room. I motioned with my hand for him to call for help and he silently stepped back out.

In the back corner of the closet a small hand reached out of the darkness and pulled a foot out of the light. From the darkness I heard him fighting to quiet his breathing.

"You're safe there," I said softly. "I won't move. I'll stay right here until you say it's okay."

I waited for a response but none came.

"If you run your hand along the edge of the light, you'll see it's still safe."

A moment later his small fingers emerged slowly from the darkness and moved along the edge of light as if testing its strength.

"You see, just like before, no one can see you, or

hurt you there. . . . I know about this because I'm a police officer. It'll be our secret, we won't tell anyone."

The sound of his breathing began to slow.

"Promise," came out of the darkness.

"I promise," I said.

Slowly a hand crept out into the light, a little bit at a time, until his entire hand was visible.

"Your mom was making macaroni and cheese. You like macaroni and cheese?"

His fingers withdrew into the darkness for a moment, then came back to the light, where he began to run them back and forth over the floor of the closet.

"Yeah," Peter said.

Harrison stepped to the doorway and nodded that help was on the way.

"Did your mom ask you to stay in here until she got back?" I asked.

His other hand tested the light, but he didn't answer. I glanced at my watch to try to estimate how long it had been since whatever happened to his mother had taken place. We couldn't have missed it by more than half an hour.

"Is your mom in a secret place, too, or can you tell me where she is?"

The top of his blond head became visible as he leaned into the light and rocked back and forth.

"She went with the man."

Each passing second began to sound in my head like a clock picking up speed. And with each click she was slipping farther away.

"What man, Peter?"

His little hands tightened into fists and withdrew into the shadows. How far had he taken her in just these few seconds?

"What man?"

"The man who came to the door," he whispered.

I reached out and placed my hand a few inches from the edge of the light. "And that's when you came to hide here?"

"Yeah," he said, but it was little more than a squeak. Then his hand slipped back into the light and his fingers stretched out until they just touched mine.

41

We were driving west on Mulholland as I checked my watch. Another unit had arrived five minutes after Harrison's call. Seven minutes after that Peter slipped out of the darkness of the closet and I held him long enough for his grip to relax on my arm.

How many minutes had it taken to get here? Another ten? I hadn't looked when we left the house. Each second that passed became a heartbeat pumping blood out of an open wound.

As we rounded a curve, the dark line of the ocean became visible in the distance and we pulled to a stop at the top of a gravel road that disappeared down the valley side through thick vegetation. A short driveway led to a house on the right, which appeared to have lost power. Cross's home was the only other one on the street, another hundred yards out of sight around a corner in complete darkness.

I eased my foot off the brake and coasted until we

reached the turn. Twenty yards ahead, surrounded by large oaks and chaparral, was the house. The headlights lit a tall brick wall topped with metal spikes that appeared to wrap around the property.

"A fortress," Harrison said.

I shut off the car, stepped out, and started walking down the gravel road until the driveway came into view.

"It's not a fortress anymore," I said.

The iron gate that stretched across the driveway had been smashed. The ornate scrollwork and bars looked as if a tank had driven through it. I looked around the corner of the wall into the courtyard. A large white sedan was parked inside.

"It's a Buick," Harrison said.

"The car that followed my brother."

He nodded. "If this belongs to Cross, he killed John."

We rushed up to the Buick. Its front end was undamaged.

"This didn't drive through that gate. Someone else was here," Harrison said.

I looked in the car, and sitting on the front seat were several long coils of yellow cord.

"Oh, God," I whispered, and then began running across the courtyard toward the front door. The entry was nearly hidden in shadow, but I could see that the front door was partly open. I swept the windows facing the entrance with my weapon—nothing moved inside. It was like looking into the lifeless eyes of a corpse.

"Go," I said, and Harrison was through the door.

"It smells like the ocean," Harrison said.

Broken glass, sand, and water covered the floor where an aquarium had been smashed. A three-foot-long yellow eel as thick as my fist was moving slowly across the gray slate tile, slapping its tail, opening and closing its mouth as it gasped for water that was no longer there.

"Cross," I yelled.

Not a sound came back. The kitchen was to the left, past the fireplace; a hallway led to the right and the bedrooms. I stepped into the living room. I motioned toward the hallway and Harrison nodded. I took three steps and stopped, my stomach in my throat.

"Jesus," Harrison said.

A clump of long, sandy brown hair was lying on the floor. I walked over. The hair looked to be eight or ten inches long.

"Just under shoulder-length," I said. "Candice Fleming."

I knelt down and examined it. "Pulled out at the roots."

Down the hallway was another clump of hair in front of a closed door. I pushed the door open, then swung around, raising the Glock. Inside, the coffee table and couch had been pushed back, creating an open space on the rug large enough for a person to lie down. A sheet of heavy clear plastic had been laid down.

I walked over and looked down at it, playing out what I was seeing in my head.

"He put the plastic down to keep any rug fibers from

sticking to her clothes, and to catch any blood or bodily fluids."

Harrison knelt down and examined it. "It's clean. It hasn't been used."

I looked over to the broken window.

"He either took her somewhere else in the house, or . . ."

"Someone stopped him," I said.

"She could still be alive."

"Then what happened to Cross?"

We ran back outside and looked at the smashed gate and then back at the house.

"What does this look like to you?" I asked.

Harrison's eyes moved across the grounds, stopping and taking in details.

"The gate is crashed, then two entries are made into the house—the window and the door. This wasn't the work of a single person."

"Something a tactical squad would do in a rescue," I said.

"Or a killing."

I looked at Harrison. "We have to find Hazzard."

42

What I had learned since finding Danny's message on the door of my refrigerator was that my father did not kill Victoria Fisher. But the door to that nightmare hadn't been closed. Two young women had still been murdered by the River Killer, and whether by design or actual circumstance, my father was connected to them.

Harrison had hit it on the head at the theater when he called my father's assaults on the two students dress rehearsals for a full performance. Was it part of this? Or did this chain of violence end with Cross and Hazzard? Which of my father's roles had returned from the past?

A large silver pickup that I didn't remember seeing before was parked in Hazzard's driveway. I drove slowly to the end of the cul-de-sac past his house. No lights appeared to be on. Nothing was visible in any of the windows.

I pulled to a stop behind the pickup and stepped out. For an instant the wind held the scent of a rosebush, but then it shifted and the bitter remains of destroyed homes replaced the sweet, pungent air.

"Look under the truck," Harrison said.

There was a puddle under the front of the truck, and a dark line of fluid running down the driveway to the curb. I walked around the side of the pickup. The front grill had been heavily damaged. The pattern of the denting matched the contours and lines of the gate at Cross's house.

"Call for backup," I said, and Harrison took out his phone.

Inside the cab a bone-handled hunting knife lay on the passenger seat. On the floor were small pieces of yellow cord. I pulled out my Glock, stepped up to the corner of the garage, and looked around to the front windows. In the dark interior of the living room something was there. Not visible, but there just the same.

"There's movement," I said.

The blackness appeared to be shifting in and out like a tide, but whatever I had seen was already gone.

"The back," I said, but we were already moving, nearly there. A bonfire in the middle of the yard illuminated the back of the house with a warm glow.

"His things," I said.

Hazzard had emptied his house of his prized signed hockey sticks and jerseys and balls and bats and set everything on fire.

"He's burning his bridges," Harrison said.

A figure was standing at a bedroom window on the second floor, in the darkness. His face appeared more like a mask than that of a living, breathing soul. Circles of shadow surrounded his eyes, the set of his jaw as rigid as if it were carved of wood or bone. I could see his mouth moving ever so slightly, as if he were whispering a secret to someone just behind him in the darkness.

I heard myself say, "The house," but I was already running to the back door as Harrison kicked it open. Somewhere inside music was playing.

"The Stones," Harrison said. "He's playing the Rolling Stones."

A stack of unwashed plates filled one of the sinks. The odor of fried food and spilled beer hung heavily in the air.

"He's falling apart," I said.

We moved across the kitchen to the living room.

"The music's coming from the second floor," Harrison said, but I didn't hear a word. Candice Fleming was crawling across the carpet, short lengths of yellow cord dangling from her wrists.

I rushed across the living room and knelt next to her as Harrison covered the stairs.

"You're all right now," I said.

She didn't react to the sound of my voice, just continued to crawl, her eyes fixed on the door and her escape. I reached over and placed my hand on hers. "Your son is fine. I found him."

She stopped moving, her fingers digging into the carpet as if it were soil in a garden.

"Peter stayed right where you told him to. You did the right thing," I said.

"Peter," she whispered.

I nodded.

She started to reach out toward me, then saw the cord dangling from her wrists and I could see panic beginning to return in her eyes. I took her hand and tried to pull her back.

"We're going to take those off you. It's over."

She shook her head.

"Yes it is, but we have to get you outside. Can you walk?"

Fleming looked at me, her eyes still partially in the nightmare inflicted on her.

"Delillo," she whispered.

"That's right."

I got Fleming to her feet and walked her to the front door.

"Run to my car. Other policemen are coming; they'll take care of you."

The panic in her eyes vanished and she stared at me with unmistakable clarity.

"He was a policeman," she whispered.

She turned and ran into the night as I rushed back to the stairs where Harrison waited. A half dozen steps led to the second floor. I eased up the stairs until the hallway came completely into view. It looked as if a windstorm had blown through it. Shattered glass littered the floor, strands of wire and pieces of broken picture frames hung on the walls where pieces of his collection had been.

The music was coming from the room at the end of the hallway fifteen feet away. A faint light was visible along the bottom of the door. There were two other doors, one on either side between where we stood and the far end.

"Take the left door, I'll take the right," I whispered, and Harrison began to move, the broken glass on the carpet snapping under his feet with each step.

Harrison stopped at the first door and swung into the room with his weapon raised, then stepped back into the doorway and shook his head.

"Cover the far door," I whispered, and Harrison raised his gun.

I pressed myself against the wall on the right and inched along. The door was another six feet. Half a dozen steps with glass snapping under each step and I stopped. Harrison nodded that he had me covered, and I reached out and tested the handle—it was unlocked. I turned the handle as gently as I could until I felt the latch release, then I pushed the door open and brought the Glock up to a shooting position.

Half a step into the room I caught the smell of beer, and then the door swung violently back toward me. I tried to react, but it was too swift. The door knocked me back against the frame and then started to close on me. I tried to bring up the Glock but the door closed on my arm, pinning it just above the elbow. Pain shot up into my shoulder and my legs buckled. If the Glock was still in my hand I couldn't see it through the narrow opening or feel it in my fingers.

"Tell your partner to stop, or I shoot you right now," Hazzard said from the other side of the door. I could smell the beer on his breath through the opening where my arm was caught in the door. I could see the barrel of his revolver as he pressed his hand to the edge of the door. What little I could see of the room appeared to be mostly empty and used for storage.

"I don't think a man who just saved a woman's life is going to shoot me," I said.

Hazzard leaned into the door with his bulk, closing it on my arm even tighter.

"Tell him to stop," he shouted.

I tried to speak but the pain in my arm took my breath away. I looked back at Harrison moving toward me with his gun raised and shook my head.

"Don't come any closer," I managed to say.

Harrison stopped, his weapon trained on the door that had me trapped and helpless.

"I'm not going to jail," Hazzard said. "Do you understand?"

I could only manage a nod as the music in the far room fell silent.

"Why the hell didn't you just walk away?" Hazzard said as he yanked the Glock out of my pinned hand and threw it across the room.

"Where's Cross?" I said.

Hazzard made a sound that could have been

a laugh. "What is it you think you've done, Lieutenant?" he said.

I glanced over to Harrison as he took a careful step forward, trying to place his foot between pieces of glass so it wouldn't give away his movement.

"Dazzle me with your detective skills," Hazzard said.

I began to put images together in a new way, as if I were looking at a photo album that had fallen off a table and spread across the floor. Two young black men falling to the ground while another stands defiantly. An out-of-control cop picks him up in a chokehold until the last breath of life is squeezed from his lungs. Victoria Fisher hiding a piece of paper in a file. My brother running down a street in his socks. A glowing yellow sign—PUBLIC FAX—and now a clean sheet of plastic spread across the floor in Cross's house.

Through the narrow opening in the doorway I could just see the edge of Hazzard's face as he leaned against the door pinning my arm.

"It wasn't you," I said.

I saw a flash of recognition in Hazzard's eyes.

"You haven't killed anyone—not twenty years ago, not today. That's why you brought Fleming here, why you saved her at Cross's house."

"Go on, Lieutenant," Hazzard said.

I looked back at Harrison as he took another step toward me, a piece of glass snapping under his foot.

"It was Cross who picked up that kid and choked him to death," I said. "It wasn't you."

Hazzard's eyes appeared to drift for just a moment.

"He was just standing there, wouldn't get down on the ground with the others," Hazzard said. "Cross killed him before I knew what he was doing."

"You were the senior officer about to make the leap to Homicide. You took responsibility because you knew there would be no questions asked of one of the force's rising young stars. You might even get a citation for bravely subduing a dangerous criminal with your bare hands. The investigation would go nowhere."

"And didn't," Hazzard said.

"Until Victoria Fisher."

"I didn't know about that," Hazzard said.

"Cross killed her when he discovered she knew the truth about the kid's death."

Harrison took a step toward me, pushing glass out of the way with the toe of his shoe.

"Did you help Cross make her death appear to be part of the River Killer's work, or did he do that by himself?" I said.

"It was done by the time I knew," Hazzard said.

"But you did nothing because it could have ruined you," I said.

"She was dead. I couldn't bring her back."

"She was murdered."

"I couldn't change that," Hazzard said.

Another piece of glass cracked under Harrison's foot as he inched closer.

"You could have stopped it from going any further," I said.

"It was stopped. I spent eighteen years making sure Cross was never in a position to do any more harm."

"Tell that to my brother."

"I told Gavin to let it go," Hazzard said.

Harrison took another step and was now nearly within reach of me.

"Cross killed three more people because of you," I said.

"I didn't know. I tried to stop it," Hazzard said.

"Dana Courson didn't even know why she died."

Hazzard leaned into the opening in the doorway and I saw tears in his eyes.

"It shouldn't have happened," he whispered.

"Detective Williams had his throat cut. And you let Hector Lopez get hunted down like an animal because you knew he could identify Cross as the cop at the Western Union office who took the security tape."

"I tried to stop that. I was there to stop it," Hazzard said.

"You didn't."

Harrison was now three feet from me, his gun raised toward the opening in the doorway.

"Cross killed my brother," I said.

Hazzard began to shake his head back and forth like a traumatized zoo animal in a cage.

"It's not my fault," Hazzard said.

"Then why are you burning your things?"

A piece of glass cracked under Harrison's foot and Hazzard pressed his weight against the door and raised the barrel of his gun into the opening a few inches from my face.

"Tell your partner to stop," Hazzard yelled.

Harrison froze.

"You're not a killer," I said. "You just watch people die so you can go on with your quiet life of collecting baseballs and hockey sticks."

I couldn't see Hazzard's face anymore, but I could hear his breathing on the other side of the door, each breath more labored than the last.

"Walk away, Lieutenant," he said softly.

"I can't."

Harrison started to move again toward the door.

"You used an innocent man to hide Fisher's murder. You used my father," I said. "You were Danny's dark angel, pointing him in the wrong direction."

"You don't want to know what I know," Hazzard said. "Turn around and walk away."

"What don't I want to know?" I said.

"Leave, Lieutenant," Hazzard said.

"I'm not moving," I said. "It all stops right here, right now."

"It's not going to stop," Hazzard said.

"What the hell do you know, Detective?" I yelled.

"Please," he whispered.

"What do you know?"

Hazzard exhaled heavily and cried out.

"Everything! . . . I know who he was in San Francisco, in Seattle, Portland. His name was Johnson in Minneapolis; Fisk in Philadelphia. He sold men's clothes in Cleveland. He acted in little theaters in Dallas, Chicago, and New York, and a dozen other cities where no one knew him except for me, because I never let it go. I spent years tracking credit cards and money orders, and driver's license applications. And before he ever touched another woman in any of those cities, I would make a phone call, and the next day a policeman would pay him a visit, and he would move on to find another shadow to hide in until I found him there, too."

A voice in my head began to say, *Don't, don't, don't*, as I felt myself being dragged back into a dark closet full of nightmares.

"My father," I said.

"Do you even remember the first two victims' names?" Hazzard said.

"Alice and Jenny."

He took a heavy breath.

"You should have walked away," Hazzard said.

I shook my head.

"You're not going to do this to me," I said.

"I didn't do this, he did."

"You can prove my father killed those women?"

"I don't have to prove it. I stopped him from killing again, that's all that matters," Hazzard said.

"Where's Cross?"

"Forget Cross. It's all here. I give you back your father. He's yours now. Never let him slip away, never let him go. Do you understand? Never."

"No, I don't understand. What do you mean?" I said.

In the distance I heard the sound of sirens approaching.

"I was a cop," Hazzard said.

"What the hell have you done?" I yelled.

I felt Hazzard's weight shift against the door as he looked around the edge of the door into my eyes.

"I was a great cop," Hazzard said.

"No," I started to yell as Hazzard lifted his gun toward his head.

43

Harrison was moving toward the door when I felt the heat of the concussion and Hazzard's blood hit the door frame. He dropped straight down, his bulk hitting the floor with such force it seemed to shake the entire house.

I staggered back from the doorway and Harrison caught me as I fell to the floor. For a moment the world seemed suspended in that moment of silence at a dinner when no one knows what to say next. My right ear was ringing from the sound of the gunshot as Harrison looked down at me, frantically saying something that I couldn't understand.

"Are you hit? Are you hit?"

I reached up and touched the moisture on the side of my face and saw my fingers covered in blood.

"No, it's not mine."

"You're sure?" Harrison asked, moving his hands

over my shoulder and down my arm that had been trapped in the door.

I nodded. "Do we need to call paramedics?"

Harrison rose and forced open the door and looked inside, then rushed across the hall to the bathroom and came back with a towel, knelt down, and began to wipe the blood off my face.

"He's gone," Harrison said.

The ringing in my right ear began to subside, replaced by a dull silence. I tried to run back through what Hazzard had said.

"He said, 'It's all here.' What did he mean by that?"

"I think he was talking about inside that room."

I got to my feet and stepped into the room. Hazzard lay facedown in a pool of blood that was slowly soaking into the carpet. A nickel-plated .38 revolver, the kind of old-school gun carried by older detectives, still rested in his hand.

I turned and looked around the room, then retrieved my gun from where Hazzard had thrown it. A large table with documents spread out across it was against the far wall. Next to that were several file cabinets. On the wall above the table was a large map of the United States, red pushpins spread across the entire country in no apparent pattern.

"Portland, Seattle, Dallas, Minneapolis, Cleveland."

I looked at Harrison.

"It's all here," I said.

"It's like the room used by a task force," Harrison

said, then he picked up a folder marked GAVIN.

He opened it and pulled out a sheet of paper and handed it to me. It was a surveillance report for the day my brother was killed. It was from a Hotmail account and listed the sender as Andi James, Sloan Investigations.

"He hired James to follow Gavin when he learned they had discovered something. He alerted Cross to the situation and Cross took matters into his own hands."

I ran through the details of my brother's movements on his last day, and just as James had told us, she lost contact with the subject at County USC.

"He was already way ahead of us when we met him that first time in this house," Harrison said.

"He was ahead of us long before that," I said, stepping over to the table.

Laid out in neat, straight rows were more than a dozen thin files, all labeled with a different name and a different city. I picked one up.

"Fisk, Philadelphia."

I opened the file. The top sheet was a copy of a driver's license.

"Edward Fisk, 1628 Fourteenth Street South. This is four years old."

The only other thing inside the file was a program from a theater company.

"*The Iceman Cometh*, by Eugene O'Neill."

I handed it to Harrison and he opened it, looked it over. "Edward Fisk as Harry Hope."

I looked at the names and cities and realized that my

father was all of them. More than a dozen different names, in a dozen cities. I started looking in the files one after the other, city after city. A year and two months in Portland. The same in Dallas. A year and four months in Minneapolis. And in each city the face on the driver's license grew a little more weary, the lines a little deeper.

"He's been hiding from Hazzard for eighteen years," I said.

Harrison stepped over and picked up one of the files.

"Andrew Keller, 3416 Puente Drive, Dallas. A Sam Shepard play."

Harrison stared at it for a moment, then looked over at Hazzard lying on the floor. "In each place he's there for a little over a year before Hazzard found him."

I looked over the table full of the people my father had lived as. On the wall were photographs of the first two victims of the River Killer, Jenny Roberts and Alice Lundholm. I stared at them for a moment, not wanting to believe what I was looking at, what I had feared from the moment this all began and the memories started crawling out of their dark hiding place.

"My father killed these two women. And Hazzard has spent the last eighteen years following him to make sure he never killed again."

I looked at Harrison. "My father was the River Killer."

For the first time since I had met him, Harrison appeared to be at a loss for words. I looked up at the map, trying to find my way back to the police work that would put all this madness back within the safe confines of the crime-scene tape that separates this job from the rest of the world. *Work it. Find something in this nightmare to hold on to.*

"There wasn't a file for Los Angeles, or a pin in the map," I said.

"He hadn't found him here yet. Why?"

"He was still using his last license from New York."

"Which would have made it even easier to track him. Why didn't Hazzard find him?"

Harrison worked it for a moment, his eyes going over the room, stopping on one of the file cabinets marked THEATER LISTING.

"He hasn't been in a play yet," Harrison said.

I looked across the table at the different faces of my father. How many secrets had he left behind with a different name? Was there another half sibling in one of these cities asking the same questions I had for thirty years about our father?

"Collect all these. I don't want to lose them to LAPD."

I took a breath but could not get air into my lungs. I realized the taste of spent gunpowder was on my lips, and the smell of blood was beginning to fill the room. I rushed past Hazzard's body on the floor as fast as I could and didn't stop until I stepped outside into the night air.

A moment later Harrison stepped outside carrying a stack of folders. The sirens we had heard before were now coming up the block. Candice Fleming was sitting in the front seat of my car staring out the window at me.

"When she's able to talk more, she should be able confirm Cross as the one who abducted her," I said.

"But where is he?" Harrison said.

Looking back through the house I could see that Hazzard's bonfire had burned down and was now little more than ashes.

"Cross is dead or is about to be."

"If Hazzard is right," Harrison said.

"Did you see anything in that room to suggest he was wrong?"

Harrison looked at me for a moment. "No."

The flashing lights of several squad cars came around the corner.

"Check every theater in southern California that has either opened a play in the last week or is going to this weekend. Match the cast list against the name Powell, and then every name in those files."

"I'll get it done," Harrison said.

The two squads slid to a stop and the doors flew open.

"LAPD," Harrison said.

We looked at each other for a moment as the officers took positions behind the doors with their weapons raised.

"I hope they're here to help," Harrison said.

44

"He was pulling me by the hair when I heard what sounded like a car accident," Candice Fleming said. She was sitting on the couch in my office, her son wrapped around her, sound asleep.

We had left Hazzard's in the hands of LAPD Devonshire division and the coroner and returned to Pasadena to reunite her with her son.

"Then I heard the sound of breaking glass and he let go of me," she said.

"Cross," I said.

Fleming nodded. "There was shouting after that, and someone picked me up and I was carried outside and put in a truck."

"That was Hazzard," I said.

"He was the one driving when I took the blindfold off. I don't know if he was the one who carried me. It could have been him."

"You saw no one else?" asked Chief Chavez, who

was sitting on the edge of my desk.

She shook her head. "No, but I'm certain it was more than one person who got me out of that house."

"But you saw no faces, heard no voices that you could identify?" I said.

She took a breath and looked down at her son. "No."

I looked at Chavez. He looked more tired than I had ever seen him. In his world, cops were the good guys, and he had spent a career making sure that it was the truth in Pasadena. That cops, even ones so historically prone to excess as LAPD, had gone so far over the line tore him apart inside.

"And you never saw Cross after that?" Chavez asked.

Fleming shook her head. "I don't know what happened to him."

Chavez stepped over from the desk and placed his big powerful hand on Fleming's sleeping son's head like it was a talisman that could lead him back to the world where right and wrong were separated by a cleanly discernible line.

"We'll keep you here until we're certain you're safe," he said.

Fleming smiled as if she had just been told a very old and familiar joke.

"How will you know that, exactly?" she asked.

We stepped out the door, leaving Fleming alone with her son.

"Five people are dead because Cross strangled a kid

twenty years ago, and then a law clerk in the DA's office discovered it," Chavez said.

I nodded.

"Hazzard sent letters to Danny about my father to throw him off the trail—his 'dark angel.' My father came back to town, Danny found him and tore his apartment to pieces. My father went to Gavin, and Gavin went to Hazzard thinking the cops were harassing his client. Hazzard hired Andi James to follow Gavin, and Cross followed them both. When Gavin and my brother found the witness deposition Fisher took, it all began to spin out of control."

"And Hazzard did nothing as Cross killed three people and was responsible for the deaths of two others," Chavez said.

"If he had, it would have exposed his involvement in the cover-up of the other murders."

"What about LAPD?" Chavez said. "How much did they know?"

"Enough to make an OID investigation into that kid's death vanish. Maybe enough to help Hazzard save Candice Fleming? Certainly enough to protect themselves."

Chavez looked at me for a moment in silence. "And your father?"

I reluctantly looked into Chavez's eyes. "My father took the lives of two young women."

"You're certain of this?" he asked, tears beginning to form in his eyes.

"I can't prove it," I said. "But for eighteen years

Hazzard believed every morning, every night, and every time he looked in the mirror that he had let a killer walk away."

Harrison stepped over from his desk in the squad room holding a phone. "I think you need to take this."

I glanced at my watch; it was nearly three-thirty in the morning

"Larson," Harrison said. "The IA officer who met us in Chinatown."

I took the phone and answered. "It's late, Detective, even for IA."

"A citizen reported that they saw a body fall into the river from the Glendale Avenue Bridge. The caller said they believed they saw an unmarked police car drive away from the scene. I thought that might interest you."

"Why would that interest me?" I said.

"Because all good things come to an end."

Before I could say another word the line went dead.

At four A.M. we pulled off the 2 freeway and stopped on the Fletcher Street Bridge over the L.A. River. The wind that had been a near constant presence since the morning I learned I had a brother had finally stopped. The sound of water rippling over the rocks and vegetation of the riverbed had replaced the din of wind and traffic. From the sidewalk we could see north nearly a mile to where the black ribbon of water began its turn around Griffith Park and the Los Feliz

Bridge—the section of river where my brother had died.

"There," Harrison said, pointing upstream several hundred yards.

Two white-and-green ranger units were parked at the top of the sloping concrete banks. Beyond them were several LAPD black-and-whites and a number of unmarked squads.

"Why here?" Harrison said.

An uneasiness in me seemed to make the ground shudder, and I looked over to the bank where my brother's life had ended.

"I don't know," I said.

We walked through the gate to the river where my brother's body had been discovered and walked the quarter mile upstream toward the vehicles. A ranger wearing waders was walking back to the bank of the river. The air held the strong scent of algae and the odd mix of every fluid that drains from L.A.'s streets into the river. A hundred yards from the scene a uniformed officer stopped us and checked our IDs. The detective from Robbery Homicide who had been at the shooting of Lopez and who had ever so subtly threatened us at the courthouse was on the phone at the bottom of the slope next to the water when we approached.

"Pearce," I said.

He looked at me for a moment, said something into the phone, and hung up. "Lieutenant, this has nothing to do with you."

"If that's Cross in the river, I think it does."

He looked at me for a moment, then shook his head. "Why would you think an investigator for the DA is laying out there?"

"The citizen who reported the body seemed to think a police car drove away afterward," I said.

Pearce stretched his neck to the side and I heard the crack of vertebrae realigning. "Nothing so unreliable as eyewitnesses, particularly unidentified ones."

I looked out into the dark water. Thirty feet out, a body was bent unnaturally around a small cluster of tall willows. The ranger wearing waders had secured a rope around the body to keep it from slipping downstream. He reached out and handed Pearce a plastic bag containing a waterlogged wallet that had belonged to the victim.

"Hazzard's dead," I said.

Pearce's jaw tightened, but he continued to stare out toward the body.

"He put a bullet in his head."

Pearce leaned back and looked at the row of trees flanking the fence at the top of the riverbank.

"Always seems to happen when the wind blows, people hurt themselves . . . others," Pearce said. "Sometimes they don't even know why."

"Hazzard knew why, Detective. Twenty years ago he helped cover up the murder of an unarmed suspect by his partner, and then the murder of a pretty young law student in the DA's office who stumbled on the truth."

Pearce turned and looked at me. "You sure about that?"

"Yes."

He took a deep breath. "It's been my experience that few people really know what they think they know."

He looked back out toward the body, then reached into the bag and removed the wallet and opened it. Cross's investigator's badge was on one side, his ID on the other.

"Looks like you're right, Detective," he said.

"I want to look at the body," I said.

He gestured with his hand toward the river. "You want to walk in that shit, be my guest. Don't touch anything. We haven't determined if this is a suicide or a homicide."

The ranger handed Harrison and me hip boots and we slipped them on and made our way across the dark water. With each step, thick clouds of mud rose around our feet, creating a slick that began to flow downstream. We reached the body, which was hung up and twisted around several thin willows.

His skin appeared unnaturally white against the dark water. Cross's face lay half submerged, one dull eye staring upstream. A great blue heron stood in the water on the opposite side of the river, staring at us as if we were the objects of mistrust.

I examined him as best I could in the water's flow. There was bruising and a number of cuts on his face and neck, a contact bullet wound in front of the left ear.

"I've never known a suicide to beat himself first," I said.

I turned and looked over to the riverbank.

"Cross put up a fight at his house," Harrison said.

I nodded.

"He lost," I said.

"This is why Hazzard told us to 'forget Cross,'" Harrison said. "LAPD dragged him kicking and fighting from his house after rescuing Fleming, put a bullet in his head, and dumped him off the bridge."

"None of which we can prove because Candice Fleming never saw anyone other than Hazzard."

"It still doesn't answer the question of why here of all places," Harrison said.

"No," I said, looking at Pearce on the riverbank. "But there is a reason, and I imagine he'll let us know."

I took one last look at the body, then turned and walked back to the riverbank, following the rope tied around Cross's waist; the slick of mud drifting downstream now glistened from the oil we had kicked up.

"You have an explanation for the bruising on his face and neck?" I asked.

Pearce stared at the river without making eye contact with me.

"The fall from the bridge did that," he said.

"You find the weapon?"

He shook his head. "Not yet, but I bet we do."

"This was no suicide, Pearce," I said.

"Well, if you're right, we have a strong suspect, with motive, and a long history with this river and the victim."

He motioned toward another detective, who reached

into his pocket and handed Pearce a sheet of paper. "I think you may even be familiar with him."

He handed Harrison the sheet. It was a copy of my father's New York driver's license.

"You can keep that, we have plenty," Pearce said. "I believe his real name is Manning, not Powell."

"I guess we know now why they put him here," Harrison said.

I turned to Pearce. "If you think this will keep me quiet, you're wrong."

"I'm just doing my job, Lieutenant."

"Old-fashioned police work."

He nodded. "That's exactly what it is."

"Candice Fleming knows there were other people at Cross's house. The district attorney might like to hear about that."

"Really? Because I was under the impression that she had been rescued by the lone work of a brave policeman's final act before tragically taking his own life. What happened before that doesn't really matter."

"It doesn't work that way," I said.

Pearce stared into the swirling eddies of black water drifting along the edge of the river. "Of course it does; it's always worked that way, Lieutenant. The guilty have been punished, Cross is dead, Hazzard's dead. What more can you ask from a system? Go back to Pasadena."

I looked out as Cross's twisted form half submerged in the water.

"This isn't the system," I said.

Pearce's phone beeped and he answered. After a few quick words he held it out to me. "The district attorney's office would like to speak with you."

I took the phone. "Delillo."

"This is Assistant Chief Deputy District Attorney Fuentes, Lieutenant. This is a courtesy call; the next one I make won't be. If you continue to interfere in any way with an an ongoing LAPD investigation, you will be charged with obstruction and I will proceed with whatever investigation, in whatever direction, is necessary to bring this mess to a close. Do we understand each other?"

"Perfectly."

"We didn't create this, Lieutenant, but we are putting an end to it."

I handed the phone back to Pearce.

"It *is* the system, Lieutenant," Pearce said.

"This isn't over," I said.

He glanced at the copy of my father's New York license in Harrison's hand, then back out at the body.

"It is for me," Pearce said. "The rest is up to you."

Harrison and I walked back along the river as the eastern sky above the San Gabriels began to show the hint of the coming dawn. Near the gate where my brother had died, we stopped and looked back upstream. Both my brother and his killer had been found in the one section of river that flows over actual rocks and sand as if it were a wild living thing, but it wasn't. And the more the river was made to look natural, the greater the sense of loss of what might have been, or once was.

If Pearce was right and it was over for him, then Hazzard was equally as right and it wasn't over for me.

"If I don't walk away, they'll pin this on my father," I said.

Harrison looked at me for a moment and nodded. "Then you walk away from this."

"The guilty have been punished," I said.

"Something like that."

I shook my head. "Do you remember what Hazzard said about my father?"

Harrison shook his head. "No."

"He's yours now. Never let him slip away . . . ever."

I looked out into the darkness at the last few spots of fire still burning in the distant mountains.

"Eighteen years ago my father strangled and raped two young women on the banks of this river. And now he's my responsibility. . . . How do I walk away from that?"

45

I laid out the files of my father's history that Hazzard had gathered in the same room where Danny's map still covered an entire wall. Fourteen different names in eighteen years. An equal number of cities. He had a beard and glasses in one place, he was gray-haired and clean-shaven in another. Each face slightly different from the one before. In each picture he stared straight into the camera as if testing its ability to see who he really was.

I had known only three different faces, flickering images on a TV screen, but I understood now that they were probably no closer to the real person than the faint memories of the Richard Widmark look-alike.

For a year in each place he would live quietly in the shadows, and then he would step out into the light, and Hazzard would find him, and it would start over. The pages on the table were the journal chronicling it all.

"Why did he come back here?" I said. "It wasn't just to walk in his granddaughter's room. Not after this many years. It couldn't have been to prove himself innocent of one of three murders. It wasn't to reach out to his son or me. Something brought him back here."

Harrison stared at the files laid out in a row, then looked up at Danny's map. "Maybe he had to."

I looked at Harrison and shook my head.

"Gravity," Harrison said. "He was pulled back."

"By what he did?"

Harrison nodded. "Or didn't do."

"A reckoning."

"Maybe."

I walked over to the window and looked out at the mountains. Toward the east a few wisps of smoke rose straight up like snuffed-out candles into the bright blue sky. We had spent the morning and now much of the afternoon going through websites and working the phones to the theaters in and around Los Angeles, looking for a match with any of the names my father had used in the past. We found nothing. We did the same with all the acting schools and came away with the same result. If he had stepped out of the shadows since returning to L.A., we had missed it, or were looking in the wrong places.

"What day of the week is it?" I asked.

Harrison had to think for a moment. "It's Sunday."

It had been a week since that call from the coroner's office. Tomorrow they would release the body to me and I would make plans to bury a brother I never knew.

"What if my father came back for another reason?" I said.

Harrison studied me for a moment, filling in the rest of what I was thinking. "To be Thomas Manning again?"

I nodded.

"Which one?"

"Maybe there is only one," I said.

"Hazzard never proved your father was guilty of killing those two young women."

"He couldn't. It would have implicated him in what Cross did to Victoria Fisher. But he was still a cop, so he did the next best thing—tracked him for eighteen years."

I looked at the line of different men my father had taken refuge in.

"There could be a thousand reasons for his return," Harrison said.

"But none of them is more compelling than his own history," I said.

"I'll run a search against all sexual-assault complaints since he returned," Harrison said. "If there's a match for a theater or an acting school, you have your answer."

I nodded. Harrison looked as if he was about to say something, but he didn't and started to leave the room.

"What?" I asked.

He hesitated for just an instant. "If we come up with nothing—no assaults, no complaints—are you sure you still want to find him?"

In the past week I had imagined standing in front him dozens of times, and each time when it came to the moment to confront him, I remained silent.

I nodded. "I'm sure."

"Why? You can't arrest him or charge him with anything . . . and you can't go back and fix the past just because it's broken." Harrison's eyes fixed on mine for a moment. "I have a little bit of experience with this."

"I want him to understand that I know who he is, that I know the names of Alice and Jenny and every one of those women who stepped on that stage with him thinking he was a teacher, someone they could trust."

We looked at each other in silence for a moment.

"It's more than that," Harrison said.

I nodded. "He has to know that I remember what the view is from inside a closet. And that I'm no longer afraid."

There was a knock on the door and Traver stepped in, holding a notepad.

"Maybe I got something," Traver said.

"Go on."

He walked over to the table and looked at the papers. "When we didn't get a match on any of these names I started trying to match actors' bios and places where they had performed in the past against all these different cities."

"You found something?"

"There are a dozen actors who match a few of the cities. Two performed in four, another in five, all three women. But one of them performed in eight of the fourteen cities your father was in. Those seemed like good odds."

"You have a name?"

Traver nodded. "The name he used is Brooks."

"Where's the theater?"

"Venice."

Both Harrison and I started moving toward the door.

"There's more," Traver said, and we stopped.

"According to the theater director, a little over two weeks ago Brooks lost his belongings in a fire."

"That would be about when Danny found him and tore the apartment to pieces," Harrison said.

"An assistant stage manager apparently put him up in an extra room in her house."

I felt the same flush of blood I had felt when I first stepped back into my childhood home.

"She's a woman," I said.

Traver nodded, and my heart began to beat faster.

"Did he describe her?" I asked.

"Mid-thirties, with long blond hair, pretty. According to the director, she's missed the last two performances."

"Why?"

"She left a message about not feeling well, but they haven't heard from her since. That was over two days ago."

"What's her name?"

Traver tore a sheet from the notepad and held it out to me. "That's her address. She lives down by the beach."

I looked at the name and then looked at Harrison. "Her first name is Jenny."

46

"It could be nothing more than a coincidence," Harrison said as we drove west on the 10 toward the beach. He didn't believe it any more than I did, but I wanted to.

Eighteen years ago a young woman named Jenny Roberts stayed late after an acting class to work on a scene with my father. He ripped open her shirt and dragged her across the stage. A month later she was dead.

In the world that exists within the confines of crime-scene tape, coincidence doesn't exist.

Passing over the 405, the thick gray clouds of a marine layer returned for the first time since the fires had begun to burn. The temperature dropped ten degrees and with each mile we drove the light failed just a little more until it seemed we had driven straight into a late winter afternoon instead of the height of fire season.

We exited on Fourth and headed south on Main.

Harrison knew the area. It was the one section of Venice where the old canals had been restored. One side of each house fronts the street, the other the canal.

As we drove into the neighborhood the fresh smell of the ocean that filled the rest of the beach communities became heavier, carrying the scent of the decaying sea life that dies from lack of oxygen in the water.

"The tide can't flush it," Harrison said. "It always reminds me of opening the door to a shuttered house."

We stopped on Howland in front of a small bungalow that was almost entirely hidden by lush tropical vegetation. A small picket fence painted bright yellow wrapped around the back of the property. The front door was bright blue, though even from the street I could see the paint had faded and chipped.

We stepped through the front gate and started toward the door. Two copies of the *Times* lay on the front walk. Half a dozen flyers for takeout were spread across the front step.

Behind the thick banana plants the front windows all appeared to have the shades drawn. Harrison rang the bell, and when there was no response he knocked heavily on the door.

"Miss Lowe, this is the police," Harrison said, but there was still no response.

"See if we can find an open window," I said, and started around the side.

The windows on the east were closed as tight as those at the front. On the canal side a tall row of bird-of-paradise obscured the house from the waterway. The back door was painted the same yellow as the picket fence, but it, too, seemed dulled. A small arched window in the door appeared to offer the only view inside.

I looked in the window. A thin blade of faint light cut across the room from one of the windows on the west side of the house, but the rest of the interior was nearly black with darkness.

"There's something on the floor in the center of the room," I said.

My eyes began to adjust and I saw the thin line of what looked like a snake coiled on the floor.

"Force the door," I said.

On Harrison's second kick the lock gave way and the door swung in. In the center of the room, light from the open door revealed several long coils of rope lying on the hardwood floor.

"Miss Lowe . . . Jenny, this is the police," I called out, but there was no response.

Harrison pulled out his weapon and flicked on the light.

"Look at the windows," he said.

An attempt had been made to secure them shut by tying one end of a length of rope to the window's handle and the other to a heavy piece of furniture pushed up against the wall.

"She's trying to keep something or someone from getting in," Harrison said. "It doesn't make any sense. All you have to do is break the glass and cut the rope."

I looked around the room and could feel fear as if it were still present.

"It makes sense if you're panicking," I said.

I stepped across the room to the entrance to the kitchen. A half-eaten meal sat on the table.

"This is days old," I said.

A shattered wineglass lay on the floor, the dried wine spread out in a pattern as if it had been thrown.

"One broken wineglass. Nothing else is out of place."

I walked over to the windows by the table, which had been secured like the others, only this time tied to the heating grate in the floor. My eyes drifted over the rest of the room, trying to find something that might reveal what had happened. The dead bolt on the inside of the door required a key to lock and unlock it. On the kitchen counter a butcher-block knife holder sat empty.

"We're missing something," I said.

I stared at it for a moment, then began opening the kitchen drawers one at a time, going through the silverware, plastics, teas, spices, towels, everything just as you would expect in a kitchen.

"There're no knives here. Nothing sharper than a butter knife," I said.

The creak of a floorboard somewhere in the house drew our attention. I slipped my Glock out of the holster and stepped into the hallway. The sound was coming from behind the door at the far end.

We eased along the wall to the door and took positions on either side and listened. It wasn't a floor-board that was creaking, it was a mechanical sound that seemed familiar but I couldn't place it.

I tested the doorknob and it moved, and then I pushed it open. It was a small bedroom. On a chest by the window a hamster was on a treadmill going round and round. Harrison held his weapon on it for a second and then smiled.

"Bed's been slept in."

Harrison walked over and opened the closet door.

"Nothing here," he said. "I'll clear the other bed-room."

I took one last look around the room and noticed something under the bed.

"What's that?" I said.

Harrison stopped, knelt down, and lifted the bedspread to get a better view. He looked for a moment, then reached under and pulled out a large kitchen knife.

"There're at least half a dozen under here."

He handed the first one to me, a large carving knife with a long thin blade. I walked over to the window, which was tied shut like the others.

"Windows tied shut, knives under a bed. What does this look like to you?" I asked.

"Fear."

"Of what?"

"Everything, or everyone."

We looked at each other for a moment, playing it out in our heads.

"Someone who spends every waking hour looking over his shoulder—my father."

From the back of the house we heard what sounded like a gasp and then a voice.

"What the hell . . ."

We stepped out of the bedroom and down the hall to the living room. Standing by the forced door was a blond woman in her mid-thirties, holding a bag of groceries.

I motioned Harrison to stay out of sight and I stepped out so she could see me.

"I'm a police officer," I said.

Startled, she dropped the groceries and started inching back out the door.

"Show me your ID," she said.

I held it up. "We're looking for someone who is staying here."

"What happened to my door?"

"Are you Jenny Lowe?

She nodded.

"I'm looking for a man named Brooks."

She started to answer, then turned and sprinted out the door. Before I could say anything Harrison was out the front door and cutting her off. I followed them around the corner, where Harrison had her down on the ground and was about to cuff her.

"You can let her up," I said.

He helped her up; her face was flushed from adrenaline.

"Are you all right?" I asked.

She nodded.

"I didn't think you were really police," she said. "He thought he was being followed."

"Brooks?"

She nodded.

"Tell me about him," I said.

"He told me if I saw anyone suspicious I should run. I wasn't sure I believed him, and then you were inside my house."

"Did he say who was following him or why?"

She shook her head. "He just seemed consumed with personal security issues. I guess I thought something bad must have happened to him once. What's going on here?"

Some neighbors walking by were beginning to take notice.

"Can we talk inside?"

She nodded and we went back into the house.

We began picking up the groceries that had spilled out of the bag. Then she saw the ropes securing the windows shut.

"What the hell's been going on?"

"You haven't been staying here?"

She shook her head. "I was here for a few nights when he came. I've been with a friend since. I told him he could stay until the show closed, then he had another gig in Denver, I think. He lost everything in the fire."

"There was no fire," I said.

"Of course there was a . . ." As the words sank in, an

entirely new reality appeared in her eyes. "What aren't you telling me?"

"Has he threatened you in any way?" I asked.

"Threatened me . . . This is crazy."

"Has he touched you, or made inappropriate advances?" Harrison asked.

She looked at me in surprise, and I saw there wasn't a hint of a lie in her words, but something in the question gave her pause.

"No. Why would you ask me if he touched me?"

I showed her the copy of my father's driver's license.

"Is this the man you know as Brooks?"

She looked at the picture for a moment and as she began to nod, she realized there was another name on the license.

"Powell . . . That's not his name."

"Why have you missed the last two performances?"

"I got pissed off with the director. It has nothing to do with . . . What has he done?"

"We just want to talk to him."

"You always break down doors when you want to just talk with someone?" She looked down at the lengths of rope on the floor. "One of the actresses said he touched her during a rehearsal. . . . He apologized, said it was an accident, and that was the end of it."

"When was the last time you saw him?" Harrison asked.

"Two nights ago at the theater."

She started shaking her head. "This doesn't make

sense. The man you watch on stage isn't someone who would do what you're suggesting. Everyone at the theater can't figure out why he isn't a big star."

"His voice was just a little too high," I said. "And he looked a little too much like Richard Widmark."

"You know him," she said.

I nodded.

"We met once a long time ago," I said.

She sighed heavily, then sat down on the couch.

"I suddenly don't feel very good," she said.

I sat down next to her.

"I was here two nights with him in the extra bedroom."

She looked down the hallway, retrieving or replaying something in her mind. "The second night I woke up and he was standing at my door, watching me. I just pretended to be asleep and rolled over."

Lowe turned and looked at me. "I thought I heard footsteps walk toward my bed, but nothing happened, and when I finally rolled back over and opened my eyes he was gone. I told myself it was just a dream."

"You moved to your friend's the next day."

She nodded. "I was going to anyway. I didn't want rumors to start at the theater."

"It may be too late for that."

"That's how you found me?"

I nodded.

"I wondered why I got that call."

"What call?"

"An agent looking for an actor named Powell. They described him to a T. I thought it was a mistake."

Harrison looked at me. "Could have been Hazzard."

I looked back at Lowe. "Do you know where we can find him?"

She glanced at her watch. "The theater. It's the last performance this afternoon."

"The show closes today?" I asked.

"Yes. We always end runs with matinees."

"You said something about him going to Denver next."

Lowe nodded.

My heart began to race, pressing against my cracked ribs, which I had almost forgotten about.

"Did he tell you when he was leaving town?" I asked.

"Right after the curtain. That's why I came home."

"He's not coming back here?" Harrison asked.

Lowe shook her head. I looked at my watch. It was a few minutes before six.

"How much time do we have before the show ends?"

"Almost none."

47

It was only a few miles to the theater as the crow flies. What should have been a five-minute drive stretched to six and then seven minutes. With each passing second I could feel him slipping away, as if he were stepping back into the grainy black-and-white image on the TV screen.

We turned the corner onto Venice. Two cars had collided in the center lane, and traffic was stopped in both directions. At the end of the block I could see the theater, which had been built out of an old warehouse. The sidewalk in front was empty. The play had either already ended and I had missed him or he was still inside.

"We won't get there like this," Harrison said.

He pulled over and I began running past storefronts and taco stands, silently telling myself I hadn't let him slip away. Halfway there the pain began to spread across my rib cage. As we reached the theater I took a breath and doubled over.

"You knocked a rib loose," Harrison said.

I eased a breath into my lungs, then straightened and walked over to the glass doors of the theater. The sound of applause began to drift out from inside.

"He's still here," I said, staring into the lobby.

My father was certainly guilty of the rape of Candice Fleming, and possibly the two River Killer murders, but Hazzard's cover-up had all but destroyed any chance of prosecution. Whatever I had to do inside, it was no longer just police work. Whatever I said, or didn't say, to him would be between father and daughter, as if that relationship even applied to the history between the man inside this theater and myself.

I looked at Harrison for a moment.

"Would you see if there's a stage door in the back and watch it?" I said.

Harrison looked into my eyes as if making certain of my resolve, then nodded and started around the side of the building. I watched him walk away, wanting to tell him to stop, but instead I turned and stared through the doors into the lobby.

Go, just go . . . he's waiting.

I stepped through the doors as the applause from the auditorium rose in pitch and fever. The lobby curved around in a U shape from left to right. Swinging doors led into the auditorium. I pushed them open and started up a dark ramp that led to the seats and the faint glow of the stage lights. I stepped into the theater itself and stopped to let my eyes adjust to the darkness. The stage was a thrust, surrounded by seats on three sides. I was standing in the center section; a dozen rows of seats were between me and the stage; the rest rose behind me in a long slope. Every seat appeared to be occupied.

A young man and woman were standing on the stage hand in hand acknowledging applause. The set looked like a living room from a 1960s ranch house like the one I grew up in.

The actors blew kisses to the audience and walked off, leaving the stage empty for a moment. I stared into the darkness of the wings, then another figure stepped out onto the set and walked to center stage, thirty feet from me. I didn't recognize him as any of the men in the driver's license pictures from around the country that Hazzard had collected. He could have been any man in those pictures, an ordinary man. But I knew the man in front of me was not just any man. His eyes were as black as coal. He commanded the space around him on the stage, and every eye in the theater was on him.

He bowed deeply, then rose, his face catching the light of a spot as the audience began to rise to their feet and clap. My father's eyes moved across the audience, and a faint smile appeared on his lips. He looked left and bowed, and as he swung to the right he hesitated and looked in my direction. I couldn't have been more than a dull shape in the darkness, but his eyes held on me longer than anywhere else in the auditorium, and the smile on his lips vanished.

My knees buckled ever so slightly and I heard my mother's voice in my head, *Don't make a sound*.

The applause rose as more of the audience stood. My knees held and I stepped into the center of the aisle leading to the stage where he stood.

It's our secret, she whispered again.

I stepped down a row and then another toward the stage.

Be a good girl.

The voice in my head fell silent. He finished his bow and stood absolutely still, staring into the darkness where I was standing, then turned and walked briskly off the stage into the wings.

I took a breath as the applause died and the auditorium lights came up. It felt like the aftermath of a storm. Before I could move, the rows of patrons began to empty into the aisle heading for the lobby. Behind me someone said, "Brooks," and then I heard his name again and again from the crowd in different directions. People were nodding their heads, taking deep breaths as if they hadn't breathed for the last ninety minutes. A few had tears in their eyes. Someone said very softly, "He had me."

An usher passed me and I reached out and touched his arm.

"Where are the dressing rooms?" I asked.

"Back into the lobby and to the left."

I looked at the crush of people heading for the exits.

"Can I reach them from the stage?"

He started to shake his head and I showed him my badge.

"Back of stage left." He pointed.

I waited for people to pass, then rushed down the aisle and up the steps to the stage. As I started to cross the make-believe world of the living room, I heard my father's voice jump from the past.

Where is she? Where'd you put her?

I tried to push it away but the memories came regardless of how much I tried to stop them.

Bitch, he yelled. *Where's my little girl?*

A lamp was smashed, a chair leg snapped and then the dull sound of my mother's small frame hitting the wall.

"Can I help you?"

A stage manager was standing a few feet from me, a headset around his neck. The lights ha'd dimmed so that the set appeared to be in twilight.

"Dressing rooms," I said.

He pointed toward the back and I rushed through the darkened wings into a bright, wide hallway that curved behind the stage. The sound of a heavy door opening somewhere was followed by laughter. I heard footsteps that sounded like someone running.

The two actors I had seen taking a curtain call came around the corner laughing and I passed them in a full run. Around the turn the scene and costume shops were on the left. Twenty feet farther on, two doors on the right were marked DRESSING ROOMS.

I stepped up to the first door and pulled it open. An

actress was standing in the center of the room buttoning her blouse. She turned and looked at me, holding a hand over her chest.

I stepped back out and over to the second door. As I reached for it, a stagehand dropped a ladder at the end of the hallway by the exit, then walked out of sight. I looked back at the door for a moment, letting my hand slip down to the Glock. My fingers closed briefly on the handle, then I released it and pulled open the door and stepped inside.

The scent of makeup, sweat, and cigarettes hung in the air. A row of dressing tables ran along the right side of the room. The clothes I'd seen my father wearing on stage were draped over a chair. From the back of the room came the sound of a shower. I crossed the room to a closed door that led to the sound of the shower.

I pulled open the door but didn't go in. The room was L-shaped. The sound of the shower was coming from around the corner in the back.

"Step out," I said.

The water continued to flow.

"Thomas Manning."

There was no change. I listened for the sound of the water's flow being interrupted by a hand or arm passing across it, but it was steady. I stepped onto the tile floor and walked past the sinks and stalls to the far corner. The shower was empty, just a stream of water pouring onto the white tiles and swirling down the drain.

"No," I whispered, rushing back out. I couldn't have missed him; it had only been a matter of minutes.

As I passed the dressing table where my father's costume was draped over the back of a chair, I stopped. On the table next to a makeup kit was my father's driver's license from New York and a small envelope with my name written on it in graceful, old-fashioned penmanship. I picked it up and opened it. A thick gold wedding ring slipped out into the palm of my hand. I remembered it. I knew the cool feel of it as his hand closed around my thin, five-year-old wrist or touched the side of my face. I remembered the small crescent bruise it left on my mother's skin again and again. My hand began to tremble and I set the ring down.

Also in the envelope was a small folded note card like you would use if sending flowers. I pulled it out and opened it.

I'm sorry, my father had written.

I put the driver's license, ring, and note into my pocket and rushed out of the dressing room and into the hallway. A light had been turned off at the far end. A small red exit sign glowed in the darkness.

I took a cautious step, listening for any sound that might reveal where he had gone. Nothing. I crossed the darkness at the end of the hallway at a run. The latch of the door hit my hip heavily, but the door gave way and I tumbled out into the dull gray coastal light. Before I could turn, I saw movement on my left. I tried to swing toward it, but a hand caught my arm, and another came toward my face, and I tried to spin away from the blow.

"Don't—" I started to say.

The hand gently touched my neck. "Alex."

I stared into his face for a moment before I fully realized it was Harrison.

"He didn't come this way?" I asked.

Harrison shook his head.

"He's going out the front door with the crowd," I said, already moving back toward the exit I had just come out.

Harrison raced down the alley to the theater's entrance as I stepped back into the hallway and ran past the dressing rooms and the stage, all the way to the far end. At the entrance to the lobby I flung open the door and stepped in.

Several hundred people filled the space from wall to wall, wineglasses in their hands, their voices engaged in as many different conversations. I tried to work through the crush of people but they were packed in tight. Some laughter erupted somewhere, then a short burst of applause. I scanned the faces closest to me, then across the lobby, and saw a figure moving and stopping, moving and stopping, as if he were shaking hands.

Someone in the crowd yelled "Brooks" and the figure turned and looked in my direction. For a moment all that was visible were pieces of a face, a flick of dark hair, a flash of a smile as he shook a hand. And then he stepped into view as if he'd known all along right where I was standing.

He reached up and removed the glasses he was wearing, looked at me, and for just an instant the hundreds of voices in the room seemed to fall silent. He reached up and rubbed his eyes, then slipped the glasses back on. The voices in the room returned and then he vanished into the crowd.

I pulled out my badge and held it out, shouting "Police" to try to clear a path, but only half the people in my way heard my voice. An elbow hit my rib and I stumbled to one knee, gasping for air as the pain gripped my chest.

A hand reached down and pulled me to my feet. It was Harrison.

"Did you see him?" I asked when I got enough air into my lungs to speak.

"No."

"He was moving toward the door," I shouted over the hundreds of voices.

Harrison looked at me and shook his head. "I just came from the door."

We looked at each other for a moment, then Harrison reached out and put his arm around my shoulder to protect my broken ribs. He began moving through the crowd, forcing people out of the way with his free hand until we stepped through the doors of the theater and were standing outside.

Forty or fifty people had spilled out onto the sidewalk with their glasses of wine. On the edge of the crowd near the street I saw movement and rushed toward it. The figure was moving toward a parked car, a baseball cap now covering his head. As he reached into his pocket for keys I took hold of his arm and spun him around. The man looked at me in surprise and took a step away.

"I'm sorr—" I started to say, then ran into the street and looked up and down the length of Venice Boulevard. The street had emptied of beach traffic, only a few cars were moving east or west. I studied the faces in the cars and followed the movement of each pedestrian on the sidewalk but all I saw were strangers.

"He's gone," Harrison said.

My father had vanished into a gray, colorless dusk.

48

We looked for my father in the fading light of Venice until darkness took hold. We searched through the crowd again, the theater itself, and all the surrounding streets, but found nothing. He had stepped back in and then out of my life, leaving behind a two-word note, a gold wedding band, and memories I could no longer hide from.

No physical evidence existed directly connecting my father to the River Killer murders. That Hazzard had spent eighteen years tracking him would be of little use in a justice system—even one as tarnished as this. But the cop inside me knew, just as the little girl in the blue dress did, that no other evidence was needed to know the truth of what my father had done on the banks of L.A.'s river of cement.

He was mine now. Every new name, new role, new city he adopted, every time he stepped out of his shadow existence, I would have to be there to shine a light on it. If I failed, whoever he touched or harmed, whoever he said "I'm sorry" to, was my responsibility. Until the day he dies, this would be how I would care for him. It's what children do for parents; it's part of the bargain that is struck every time a new life enters this world. The roles eventually reverse.

No actor named Brooks, or Powell, or Fisk, or even Manning appeared in Denver. In the weeks that followed I would search another city, and then another after that, and on and on because that's what you do for family. You never give up on them.

The following morning I signed the papers and legally became responsible for the remains of my half brother John Manning. In the days before the funeral I would go through his apartment and meet the man I never knew. The solitary life he led was a strange reflection of our father's isolation. His relationship with Dana Courson was only a little over a month old. If friends other than her existed in his life, he left no physical evidence of their presence. He had a library card, but I couldn't tell what he liked to read. If he had hobbies, he had either kept them secret or never had a chance to share them with anyone.

The few scraps of information I was able to piece together about his past suggested that he was seven years old when our father left his mother. If our father gave him the things I had longed for as a child but never received, no record exists. I don't know if they were a happy family. I don't know if our father was violent with him. I don't know what memories were held silently in his heart.

What I do know is that three months after my brother's seventh birthday, his father walked out of the house and never returned. Six months later the first River Killing took place.

How long John was aware that he had a half sister would also remain a secret. My phone number was written in his book, but his bills showed it had never been dialed. What I did know was that in a moment of fear, I was the person he thought of, and the last person he would ever reach out to.

On a sunny morning with a sky so blue it could have been drawn with a crayon, he was buried on the side of a hill in Forrest Lawn, just yards from the grave of the man who wrote *The Wizard of Oz*.

Lacy, Harrison, Chavez, and Traver stood with me as he was laid to rest. A priest spoke of the things he may have loved, and how he might have laughed, and as he did I thought that in the years to come, when asked if I had a brother, I would recite those imagined details as if I had known him.

As we walked away from the freshly turned earth, I paused and scanned the surrounding area for a lone figure. My father wasn't there. As I drove away I looked again, thinking I might have missed a place of concealment, but I hadn't. But it was what I did now. I would always be looking.

Both Cross's and Hazzard's deaths would be ruled

suicides by the county coroner. The SWAT officers who killed the Western Union clerk Hector Lopez were found to have acted in accordance with justifiable use of force. No record would ever officially list Cross as a suspect in the deaths of Victoria Fisher, Dana Courson, Detective Williams, and John Manning.

The record would show my brother's death was the result of a self-inflicted gunshot. The murders of Detective Williams, Victoria Fisher, Dana Courson, Jenny Roberts, and Alice Lundholm remained officially unsolved, the paperwork sinking deeper and deeper into the endless records in City Hall.

The drive back to my house after the funeral took a little over twenty minutes. I had nearly forgotten until I pulled back onto Mariposa that much of my neighborhood had been reduced to ashes. People I had known for twenty years were sifting through rubble for family treasures or the odd trinket that now took on the importance of lost memories.

At the end of the block a white sedan I recognized as a rental car was parked in front of my house. Turning up the driveway, I saw my mother sitting on the front steps. It had been nearly two years since I had seen her, the distance between us now equal to the years of silence. She was dressed in elegant slacks, a matching blouse, as if we still lived in a time when getting on a plane was stylish.

"My God," she whispered as I stepped up to her and gave her a hug. "What happened here? Are you all right?"

I sat down on the step and looked over what was left of the neighborhood.

"If you don't want to tell me, I'll understand," my mother said.

"I found . . ." I started to say, but let it go. "I remembered what our secret was," I said.

My mother stared at me, then shook her head.

"I can't imagine what you're talking—" she began to say, then stopped.

She closed her eyes for a moment, then looked out toward the blackened hills, tears beginning to form in her eyes.

"You found your father?" she whispered.

Overhead a pair of crows spun and dipped in the blue sky, playing a game of chance to see which one could fall farthest without touching the ground. I took hold of my mother's hand and tried to imagine an answer to such a question.

ACKNOWLEDGMENTS

This work would not have been possible without the assistance and support of David Highfill, Sarah Landis, and Elaine Koster.

NATIONAL BESTSELLER

RUN
THE RISK

"FROST DELIVERS
EVERYTHING A THRILLER
READER WOULD WANT."
—Rick Riordan

"A RIVETING THRILLER."
—Catherine Coulter

SCOTT
FROST

When a serial bomber kidnaps a
young girl and plans to unleash
his incendiary powers on live TV,
he ignites white-hot rage—and a
mother's revenge.

penguin.com

Don't miss the page-turning suspense, intriguing characters, and unstoppable action that keep readers coming back for more from these bestselling authors...

Tom Clancy
Robin Cook
Patricia Cornwell
Clive Cussler
Dean Koontz
J.D. Robb
John Sandford

Your favorite thrillers and suspense novels come from Berkley.

penguin.com

M14G0907